William Taylor Adams

Marrying a Beggar

Or the Angel in Disguise, and Other Tales

William Taylor Adams

Marrying a Beggar
Or the Angel in Disguise, and Other Tales

ISBN/EAN: 9783337026028

Printed in Europe, USA, Canada, Australia, Japan

Cover: Foto ©Andreas Hilbeck / pixelio.de

More available books at **www.hansebooks.com**

MARRYING A BEGGAR;

OR

THE ANGEL IN DISGUISE,

AND

Other Tales.

BY

WILLIAM T. ADAMS.

BOSTON:
THAYER AND ELDRIDGE,
114 & 116 WASHINGTON STREET.
1860.

CHARLES KIMBALL, ESQ.,

This Volume

IS RESPECTFULLY DEDICATED,

BY HIS FRIEND,

WILLIAM T. ADAMS.

PREFACE.

SOME of the sketches contained in this volume have appeared in the Boston True Flag, the American Union, and, one of them, — " The New Minister " — in Gleason's Pictorial; the remainder have not been published before.

A great variety of sketches has been introduced, nearly all of them practical in their application, and illustrative of the social and domestic duties of life. No attempt at " fine writing " has been made in them; they are simply *home* thrusts at the follies of the parlor and the kitchen; of the shop and the counting-room, in short, of life " in doors and out."

The author is encouraged to collect these simple stories in a volume by the advice of partial friends, and by a desire to redeem them from a kind of literary

1*   (5)

orphanage to which the unscrupulousness of some reckless man of paste and scissors has reduced them. Many
of them are now travelling over the country, like a
dog without a collar; but unlike that highly respectable
puppy which isn't any body's dog, they have an anxious
friend at home, who takes this method of calling them
back to the fold again.

W. T. A.

DORCHESTER.

CONTENTS.

(7)

MARRYING A BEGGAR.

MARRYING A BEGGAR.

CHAPTER I.

"So much for bringing poor relations into the house! I really believe that Charles has fallen in love with the girl!" exclaimed Mrs. Mason to her husband, a merchant in moderate circumstances in the city of Boston.

"Well, suppose he has; she is a good girl, is she not?" quickly responded the merchant.

"I don't know but that she is good enough; but she is a pauper!"

"Not exactly a pauper, Mrs. Mason."

"Didn't we take her into the family to keep her from starving?"

"I did not so understand it. You needed a young woman to assist you in sewing, and employed her at half the usual wages."

"Yes, and isn't she a pauper for all that?"

"Gently, Mrs. Mason; you forget that she is my sister's daughter," said the merchant, a little sternly.

"What if she is? She is a penniless girl for all that. A pretty match for *our* son!"

"And why not for our son? I am not a *millionnaire*. If the times don't come easier than they have been, I shall fail before the year is out."

"So much the more reason why Charles should look out for himself."

"If he loves my niece, I sincerely hope he will marry her, for I believe she is one of the best girls in the world; certainly she is vastly superior to the silly, affected, mincing, novel-reading misses of fashionable society. I commend his taste and his judgment."

"Well, Mr. Mason, I *am* surprised!"

"Not the least occasion to be surprised."

"Let me tell you, Mr. Mason, that I never will consent to see Charles throw himself away on a pauper. If you haven't the spirit to prevent so disgraceful a match, I shall send the girl away."

"Don't you do it, madam," said Mr. Mason, in a firm, decided tone.

"I *shall* do it!" replied the lady, waxing warm at the obstinacy of her husband, who, in trivial matters, was in the habit of letting her have her own way.

"Better not," quietly responded the gentleman.

"The minx put on such airs and smirked so, that I really believe she meant to catch him."

"What, Grace? Impossible! She is a little gentle, quiet thing, and I am sure the idea of a flirtation never entered her simple head."

"Humph!" sneered the lady. "I know better. And now that he is really making love to her, the provoking jade seems to look upon it as a matter of course; thinks it just as much a proper thing that she should be the wife of our Charles, as though she had been born a princess!"

"Poor thing! I suppose she is human, and actually loves the boy!"

"Loves him or not, I'll make an end of it."

"Don't be rash, Mrs. Mason," replied the husband, twirling in his fingers a buff envelope, marked "Telegraph."

"What have you got there?"

"I had almost forgot to mention that brother Joseph had arrived in New York, and telegraphs that he shall be here to-night by the New Haven train."

"Just like you! Never tell of a thing till the last moment!" said the lady, petulantly.

"I received the despatch only two hours ago."

"Here is another kettle of fish," continued the lady, musing. "That everlasting niece of yours is in the way again."

"I hope the poor girl has no more sins to answer for."

"Where do you suppose your brother Joseph will leave his property?"

"I have not the remotest idea."

"Don't you suppose that angelic niece of yours will wheedle him out of a part of it?"

"I hope so."

"You don't want he should leave it all in your family, then?" sneered the lady.

"No, I hope he will do justly."

"I wish I could get her out of the way before he comes."

"Don't attempt it, Mrs. Mason," said the merchant, with very decided emphasis.

"If she were only out of the way, Henrietta would come in for the whole," added the lady, as she hurried out of the room to make arrangements for the reception of uncle Joseph.

2

CHAPTER II.

UNCLE JOSEPH was a Calcutta merchant, in which capacity he had accumulated an immense fortune. Being a bachelor, the probable disposition of his property became a question of considerable interest among his relations.

The family of Mr. Mason, the merchant introduced in the last chapter, included but two children, a son and a daughter. Grace was the only daughter of a sister, recently deceased, who had been for many years a widow.

It was supposed that uncle Joseph would make one of his nieces his heiress. This was the old fellow's whim, and no one could gainsay the whim of a bachelor. From some indications of preference which he had bestowed upon Henrietta in her childhood, it was generally believed that she would prove to be the fortunate one.

Henrietta had been educated to be a lady. Her delicate fingers were never soiled by rude collision with pots and kettles, and she had been taught to believe that it was delicate sensibility to be afraid of a spider or a bullfrog. She played the piano with passable skill, and lingered away half her time at full length on the sofa, poring over the contents of a novel.

Such was the prospective heiress of uncle Joseph's large fortune. Her father was far from approving the education she had received, and had used all the influence he possessed, short of quarrelling, to have these defects remedied.

Uncle Joseph came, and was welcomed as became the dignity of one who had a fortune to bestow.

Henrietta thought he was a "dear love" of a man, and she wondered that the ladies ever let him remain a bachelor.

Grace, by the contrivance of Mrs. Mason, was not present when her uncle arrived; but Mr. Mason, understanding the trick, sought her in person, and introduced her to the man of money.

The poor girl was too modest and retiring to force herself upon the notice of uncle Joseph, who was too deeply absorbed by the unremitting attentions of Henrietta to perceive her situation, or discover the menial capacity in which she acted.

At tea, uncle Joseph complained of being ill, and said that he had not been well since he landed on the previous day .

Mrs. Mason and her daughter were all sympathy. The ailing bachelor was conducted to his apartment, and herb teas and jugs of hot water were put in requisition. Henrietta volunteered to sit all night by his bedside and minister to his wants; but the sick man did not deem it necessary.

During all this confusion Grace was not to be seen. She was not permitted to assist in the preparations for the sick man's comfort; every thing must be done by Henrietta's own hand.

Notwithstanding the kind attentions lavished upon uncle Joseph, there was no improvement in his condition; but, on the contrary, he rapidly grew worse, and at midnight the physician was sent for. Henrietta had not left the bedside for a moment. She was the most devoted creature in the world, and the bachelor could not but contrast her devotion with the utter neglect of Grace, who had not once entered his room, even to inquire how he did.   Henrietta's prospects were decidedly brilliant.

The physician came, and after feeling the pulse of the sufferer, inquired where he resided when at home.

Uncle Joseph replied that he had no home — had just come from Calcutta.

" I see," said the physician.   " Was there any sickness on board the ship ? "

" There was.   I came by the overland route to Liverpool, thence by a New York liner.   There was a steerage full of emigrants on board, among whom the fever raged fearfully."

" Just so," returned the physician, " and you have got the ship fever."

" The ship fever ! " exclaimed Henrietta, rushing out of the room.

The sick man turned, and witnessed her abrupt departure. With a sigh, such as can only be wrung from a bachelor conscious of his loneliness, he drew the bedclothes closely around him, and apparently abandoned himself to the fate which the dreadful disease seemed to foreshadow.

The physician made up his prescription and retired.   No one was left with uncle Joseph but his brother.

" I am deserted, brother," said the sick man.

" No, brother, I am here."

" But there is no hand of woman here ; well, it is a dreadful disease," and the sufferer sighed again.

Mr. Mason went down to the sitting room, whither his wife and daughter had fled.

" How is this, wife ? Is Joseph to be abandoned now that he most needs attention ? " asked he of Mrs. Mason.

"You don't think we are going to stay in the same room with the ship fever?" replied Mrs. Mason.

"You may as well be in the room as in the house."

"We must leave the house immediately. Why did he not go to the hospital? It was not very considerate of him to bring the ship fever into the family. He might have known that he had it."

"Heaven forgive your heartlessness! But is my brother to die with no one to care for him?" exclaimed Mr. Mason, indignantly.

"You must hire a nurse."

"And you will desert him?"

"We can't stay where the ship fever is."

"No, papa, it would be suicidal," added Henrietta. "His fortune would do us no good if we caught the fever."

"Go, then! but there is still one in the house who has a heart," replied Mr. Mason, as he left the room to seek the apartment of Grace.

Grace was ready in a moment to attend her uncle to the sick room, where, regardless of the danger of contagion, she laved the burning brow of the sufferer, and did all that an angel hand could do to render him comfortable.

Early in the morning, Mrs. Mason and her daughter departed for the residence of a friend in the country.

CHAPTER III.

FOR several weeks Grace, with such assistance as Mr. Mason and Charles could give, nursed the invalid with the most untiring devotion. All her time was spent by his bed-

2 *

side. She was all gentleness and sympathy, bearing patiently with his petulance and ill humor, and never betraying the slightest appearance of anger when he scolded and even swore at her.

The fever turned, and he began to mend. He was now out of danger, and rapidly advancing to complete restoration.

The physician commended the skill and devotion of his nurse, assuring him that he owed his life to her.

But the devotion of the poor girl cost her dearly; for scarcely had uncle Joseph recovered before she was taken down with the fever, and for weeks languished on the very verge of the grave.

Yet there was no female hand to lave her brow save that of a hired nurse. Charles Mason loved her as he did his own existence, and day and night he watched over her with a constancy and a devotion worthy the loving heart of the gentler sex.

Uncle Joseph, too, was an anxious watcher round her bed. Though he was a bachelor, and had spent the greater part of his life in India, away from the gentle influences of female society, he showed an aptness in the sick room that would have done honor to a Benedict.

To the intense relief of her devoted friends, Grace recovered. The disease was now banished from the house, and Mrs. Mason and Henrietta ventured to return.

"I trust you have had a pleasant visit, madam," said uncle Joseph, coldly.

"Pleasant! nay, far from it. You do us injustice; we were perfectly miserable on account of your dangerous illness."

"Humph!" said uncle Joseph, with a sneer.

The love between Charles and Grace, strengthened by the scenes of suffering through which they had passed, was now an unalterable sentiment. Of course uncle Joseph had not witnessed their mutual devotion to him in his illness without suspecting the existence of some strong bond of union between them. And the young man's untiring attention to her in her own sickness had confirmed the opinion.

Seeking a favorable opportunity, he conversed with Charles upon the subject, who readily admitted his affection. The bachelor recommended an immediate marriage.

The step was not, of course, ungrateful to the feelings of the lover. And the desire to redeem Grace from the life of drudgery to which she was reduced by the heartlessness of his mother, seemed to demand their immediate union.

The young man's intentions were soon noised through the family. Mrs. Mason renewed the opposition she had before made, and even went so far as to threaten that, if she could not break up the match, she would imbitter the lives of the parties.

Uncle Joseph remonstrated.

" May I ask, madam, what objection you can possibly have to the marriage? " said he, with considerable sternness in his manner.

" What objection ! why, the girl is a beggar ; I have employed her in my family to keep her out of the almshouse, which, I think, is objection enough," replied Mrs. Mason, disliking the interference of uncle Joseph.

" Your son, I think, is not wealthy, so that he need not *demand* a rich wife."

" He need not marry a beggar, though."

" She is worthy a prince, beggar though she is."

"O, very likely," sneered the lady.

"I owe my life to her, and I can never cease to be grateful to her. When *others* forsook me, *she* was constant," replied uncle Joseph, pointedly.

"She knew you were rich," said Mrs. Mason, sarcastically.

"So did you and your amiable daughter. You were like angels round my pillow till the doctor said ' ship fever,' when you fled like two frightened sheep."

The lady looked as black as a thunder cloud.

"I trust you will withdraw your objections to this marriage, Mrs. Mason. You perceive that Charles is resolute, and will have his own way about it," continued uncle Joseph, in a more pliable tone.

"His *own* way! All this for bad advising! I cannot prevent it, perhaps; but I will never consent to it. No! a son of mine shall never have my consent to marry a beggar girl."

"Madam, she is no longer a beggar. She is the heiress of all my fortune," said uncle Joseph, with sudden energy.

Mrs. Mason's brow contracted.

"And Henrietta?" said she.

"Never touches a penny! She deserted me when I most needed a friend," replied the bachelor, vehemently. "If I had ten thousand fortunes, they would be but a poor return for all that Grace has done for me. I make over fifty thousand dollars to the newly-married couple as soon as the knot is tied; the residue at my decease."

The marriage took place soon after. The ceremony was performed at the house of Mr. Mason, in spite of the opposition of his wife; for when the merchant said it should be so, he had the firmness to carry his point.

The newly-married couple took up their residence in a beautiful house, purchased for them by uncle Joseph, who consented to make his home with them.

Henrietta is now five-and-thirty years of age, and an " old maid." Mrs. Mason still continues to be a termagant, though her husband maintains his integrity with firmness and decision. She has never forgiven uncle Joseph for making Grace the heiress, and probably never will. But the worthy bachelor never ceases to rejoice over the disposition he has made of his property, and probably *he* never will.

"GOOD FOR NOTHINGS."

CHAPTER I.

"Your girl is a prize, Mrs. Bagley," said Mrs. Veazie, a lady whose physiognomy was rather indicative of a sour temper.

"Bridget is a good girl," responded the lady addressed; "and she has been with me over a year now."

"Indeed! Over a year! Well, I am astonished! For my part, if I *get* a good girl, I can't keep her."

"I have been very fortunate in that respect."

"You have indeed. O dear! it is really terrible to think how much one is dependent upon these Irish servant girls. They are such lazy, impudent, good-for-nothing creatures, that it is enough to weary out one's life."

"Some of them are. If I had been so unfortunate as to get such a one as you describe, I should instantly discharge her. But very few are of that description."

"Very few! Let me tell you that your girl is one in a thousand, Mrs. Bagley. Where you find one who is honest, faithful, and respectful, you will find nine hundred and ninety-nine who are just the reverse."

"I can hardly believe it," replied the good-natured Mrs. Bagley, with a smile of incredulity upon her pleasant features.

" It is as true as the gospel! Why, I have had no less than ten different girls within a year."

" Ten! Is it possible?"

" And my family is no larger and the work is no harder than yours. Isn't it singular?"

Politeness compelled Mrs. Bagley to answer that it was singular; but, at the same time, she knew that it was not so very singular, after all. If she had felt at liberty to do so, she could have given her friend a solution of the mystery.

" And the girl I have now I shall be compelled to discharge. She is discontented, impudent, and overbearing."

" I am sorry for you."

" She is a capital girl in every other respect, and I am sorry to part with her. She is a good cook, and — what you don't find in many girls — understands pastry, cake, and puddings."

" Too bad to lose her, isn't it?" said Mrs. Bagley, with a greater appearance of sympathy in her speech than found a place in her heart.

" It is; but one cannot put up with impudence, you know. I would send off the best girl in the world before I would submit to it."

" Certainly; impudence cannot be tolerated. Can't you teach her better?"

" No; she won't hear to any thing. It was only the other day, when I saw her washing the potatoes in the wash-hands basin, that I merely called her a nasty, good-for-nothing hussy; and, don't you think, the impudent jade told me to mind my own business, and not to be sticking my nose into her affairs! Did any one ever hear the like?"

Mrs. Bagley only smiled. If she had lived in a less civilized era, perhaps she would have been blunt enough to say that the fault was partly with the mistress, and not wholly with the servant.

"And then she is so ugly," continued Mrs. Veazie, "that I dare not trust my children with her."

"I leave the baby with Bridget for half a day sometimes, and feel perfectly safe."

"My girl don't like children; I know she hates them. Why, only yesterday I told her she might leave the washing for an hour or so, and take Charley out in the little wagon; and, don't you think, she had the impudence to tell me that, if I wanted Charley taken out, I might take him out myself! I never was so provoked in my life."

Mrs. Bagley's good nature was all exhausted; and, at the risk of being deemed uncivil, she had the hardihood to say she never took Bridget away from her washing unless in a case of absolute necessity.

"Wasn't this a case of absolute necessity?" asked Mrs. Veazie, with a rather uncompromising look upon her sharp features.

Poor Mrs. Bagley! She was in for it, and must needs defend the policy at which she had incautiously hinted.

"I should say not," replied she, not a little fearful that she was about to "stir up strife."

"What would you do? Charley ought to have the fresh air every day."

"I should have taken him out myself; for it is very annoying to a girl to be called away from the wash tub. She has to change her dress, which is a great deal of trouble, and leave her clothes in the water or on the fire."

"Yes, girls are desperate 'fraid of a little trouble."

"If they feel any pride about their work, they like to have it done up in good season, you know."

"And she insists upon being absent every fourth Sunday."

"I let Bridget go every third Sunday."

"You do?"

"I think it very reasonable."

"Who gets your dinner Sundays?"

"What little we get I attend to myself. But we always have baked beans Sunday, so that I don't have to stay at home from meeting."

"And you wash the dishes yourself!" exclaimed Mrs. Veazie, in utter astonishment.

"Certainly. The fact is, these Irish girls are human beings, after all, and need a little recreation as well as the rest of us."

"But they take advantage.'

"If you give them no advantages, they will take them. I have found out that, the better you use *good* girls, the more faithfully they will serve you. I make it a point to treat my girl well; and, having secured her good will, I feel a reasonable assurance that she will do the best she can for me."

"You don't mean to say that *I* don't treat my girl well?" said Mrs. Veazie, her features coloring under the insinuation she believed was aimed at her.

"Certainly not. My remark was intended to be very general."

Mrs. Veazie went home; and, though she was a little angry with her neighbor, she "set to thinking" upon what she had heard.

CHAPTER II.

MRS. BAGLEY'S girl, Bridget, had a beau, and, in the course of events, was married. Her mistress, though exceedingly sorry to part with her, could of course make 'no objections to her working out her woman's destiny. She was a good-hearted person, and did all she could to see the faithful girl, who had been almost a mother to her children, comfortably situated in her new relation.

Her first attempt to procure another good girl proved to be unsuccessful; for the new servant was, beyond the hope of remedy, slovenly and dirty. She was compelled to discharge her.

About this time Mrs. Veazie's girl was discharged. The lady, profiting by the lesson she had received of her neighbor, had for a few months treated Margaret with kindness and consideration. The change was appreciated by the girl. She was ignorant and headstrong; but neither so ignorant nor headstrong as not to be able to understand the meaning of kind words and considerate actions.

Mrs. Veazie was astonished at the change in the temper of the girl; and, for a time, she persevered in maintaining the new order of things. But it is useless for any one to attempt to be gentle and kind in their speech and action when there is neither gentleness nor kindness in the heart. A "change of heart," in the language of the Scriptures, is as necessary to make an ill-tempered person amiable towards others as it is in the working out of the more technical "profession" of religion. A "profession" of good nature is the first step towards piety.

When Mrs. Veazie relapsed, Margaret relapsed, and there was strife again. No sooner did the servant observe the unreasonableness of the mistress than she was in open rebellion again, as saucy as ever.

"I am determined to send her off, Mrs. Bagley," said she, as she was seated with her neighbor one afternoon.

"Send her off! Why, I thought she was doing nicely now."

"So she was; but this morning a couple of tons of coal came, and, as I had no one to get it in, I told her she might do it. I am sure I spoke very pleasantly to her," said Mrs. Veazie, with an abundance of self-complacency.

Mrs. Bagley held up both hands in astonishment.

"What did she say?"

"She told me very coolly that she had rather not do it. But I was angry then; I thought it was about time to be angry, too, when a girl answered me in that way; so I told her she was a lazy, good-for-nothing minx."

"Did you?"

"Indeed I did."

"Well, what did she say then?"

"'The same to yourself, ma'am,' says she. She has not been saucy before for a good while."

"Didn't it occur to you that your request was slightly unreasonable?"

"I'm sure it didn't. Why, these girls are used to working in the fields in Ireland, digging turf and pounding stones. I don't see why they should be so stuck up when they come to America."

"Well, I suppose, when they come to a country where even the rights of the poor are respected, they think better of themselves — very naturally too, I think. But, Mrs. Veazie, if you are going to discharge Margaret, I should like to take her."

"You?"

"If you have no objection."

"Of course not; but she never will suit you, I know."

And Margaret went to live with Mrs. Bagley. She was an able, capable, and industrious girl, and her mistress immediately took a great liking to her. Margaret had her faults, the most prominent of which was a quick temper, that often prompted her to give a saucy or a spiteful answer before she was aware.

She had not been a week with Mrs. Bagley before, without a reasonable provocation, she gave her mistress a short and crusty answer. No notice was taken of it, though the point was insisted upon and carried. A few days after, when she got a little perplexed, she was saucy; but Mrs. Bagley was as firm as she was even in her temper, and calmly rebuked the uncivil words. Margaret was abashed by the gentleness and decision of the rebuke, and readily understood with what manner of person she had to deal. She was conquered, and made as good a girl as the most obdurate of servant hunters could possibly desire.

In the course of the year Bridget's husband was killed on the railroad, and the poor girl found herself again compelled to go out to service. Mrs. Bagley was well suited with Margaret, and did not feel at liberty to discharge her, especially as both parties were satisfied.

Mrs. Veazie had tried half a dozen girls since Margaret

had left her, and, as usual, had been unable to retain them. It was with a thrill of satisfaction she heard that Bridget, "the prize of a girl," wanted a place again, and she lost not a moment in making an engagement with her.

About a week after this important event, Mrs. Veazie came in hot haste over to Mrs. Bagley's.

"Don't you think," exclaimed she, out of breath, "that Bridget has given me notice of her intention to leave."

"To leave?"

"Yes; I don't believe she meant to stay when she came."

"I think she did. Bridget wouldn't do a mean action, if she is an Irish girl."

"I don't know about that."

"But how did it happen?"

"Why, she was as saucy as ever Margaret was in the world."

"Bridget? Impossible!"

"I asked her as politely as though she had been a lady if she wouldn't be so kind as to black Mr. Veazie's boots."

"And she refused?"

"No; she did it. She said she would do it this time but she had rather not have it as part of her work."

"You couldn't blame her, could you?"

"Of course I could; and I told her she was a lazy, good-for-nothing vixen, and that she'd have to do it every day, if she staid with me. Why, Irish girls at home have to black their masters' boots."

"But it is not the custom here."

"It ought to be; and I told her, up and down, that she was not what she used to be when she lived with you. Upon that she told me she would leave. Did you ever see such

3 *

luck as I have?" and Mrs. Veazie puffed with excitement. She really believed she was the most unfortunate woman in the world.

" To be plain with you, Mrs. Veazie, I don't think Bridget was in the least to blame."

" Not to blame?"

" No. When you set your girls to getting in coal and cleaning boots, you must expect them to be rebellious, especially when you follow it up with such hard words."

Mrs. Veazie went out, and slammed the door after her. She has never crossed the threshold of her friend's door since; but it was a small loss.

The moral of our sketch is sufficiently apparent. When we hear ladies complaining that they can't keep a servant, we are a little disposed to doubt whether the fault is not in part upon their side.

THE TWO DAGUERREOTYPES.

A TEMPERANCE TALE.

CHAPTER I.

JIM SCROGGINS, though in the main an honest, peaceable, quiet, harmless, fellow, had a beastly habit of getting drunk whenever a fit opportunity presented itself; and, unfortunately, because "where there is a will there is a way," the opportunities were both fit and frequent.

Jim owned a little farm in the country, which, by his own industry and economy, he had almost paid for. Mrs. Scroggins was a "real worker," and, no doubt, did her full part in buying the homestead. She was endowed with a great deal of energy and good judgment, and people were so malicious as to say that she was the smartest man of the twain. Be this as it may, Mrs Scroggins was an industrious woman, nd took a great deal of pride in the little place, which had been bought by their united industry and economy, and the thought of having it wrested from them by a cold-hearted creditor was in the highest degree disagreeable; but to such a calamity her husband's infirmity, as the good minister of the village called it, seemed to point.

The habit grew upon him, as it almost always does upon those who once get into the way of imbibing too freely.

The miseries of the drunkard's wife had been too often presented to the good woman's understanding to be regarded
as simply creations of the imagination, and she looked forward with alarm to the prospect of enduring them and losing
the little place.

But what could be done? She had exhausted all her eloquence upon the infatuated man, without producing any
thing more than a temporary effect. She pointed out to
him, kindly, the inevitable consequences of his indulgence,
and Jim promised to amend; but — alas, for the vanity of
human expectations! — he got tipsy the very next day.

Then she appealed to his love of money — to his sense of
satisfaction in being the owner of a cottage and ten acres of
land. She assured him that he would certainly lose it all,
and warming up with the importance of the subject, declared
that she would not slave herself any longer to buy the place,
and then have it taken from them to pay a rum bill.

Jim listened patiently and without speaking a word to the
indignant dame's eloquence, and, as usual, promised to do
better; but, also, as usual, he came into the house the next
day tight as a fiddlestring.

Mrs. Scroggins was in despair; "what to do she didn't
know," as she expressed it to Parson Allwise, who was a
sincere sympathizer with her in her distress. She had entreated, she had scolded, she had threatened, and all to no
purpose. "What could a body do?"

Parson Allwise himself, though he made it a point never
to interfere in the domestic affairs of his parishioners, was
at last moved to try his powers of persuasion on the poor
fellow. But Jim, unfortunately for the success of the appeal, had but a poor opinion of ministers in general, and of

Parson Allwise in particular, and as good as told the worthy pastor that he had better mind his own business.

Mrs. Scroggins was shocked at the boldness of her spouse in answering a minister of the gospel in such a pointed manner, and was led to believe that the case was now hopeless, indeed.

But woman's wits are equal to almost any emergency; and, though she had professedly given Jim over to the tender mercies of the devil, she could not help thinking it would be a good thing if he could only be saved from himself.

One day circumstances seemed to conspire in favor of an experiment, which had suggested itself to her fertile brain, and she immediately carried it into effect with the most happy success, as the sequel will show.

CHAPTER II.

Jim had been cleaning out the pig pen, and as the operation was a rather disagreeable one, he had fortified his olfactories by drinking an inordinate quantity of vile New England rum.

The filthy stuff happily did not take effect on his brains till the job was done. The pig pen was cleaned out, but Jim was in a condition which better fitted him to occupy it, than the neat, white-floored kitchen of his cottage. But Jim did not realize this unpleasant truth, and leaving his shovel and hoe in the sty, staggered into the house.

"He was a sight to behold," as Mrs. Scroggins told the minister. The job he had just completed was eminently a nasty one, and Jim, as we have before remarked, being a prudent man, had prepared himself to perform it, without any detriment to the neat garments he ordinarily wore.

He was dressed in a suit of ragged clothes, and on his head rested a "shocking bad hat," with the crown stove in, and the brim half torn off. As the liquor began to fuddle him, he had moved it over from its perpendicular position, so that it rested jantily on one side of his head.

Jim settled himself heavily in a chair by the cooking stove, looked silly, and seemed disposed to address himself to slumber, his usual resort when inebriated. .

Mrs. Scroggins was mad at first; for it was only the day before that Jim, for the hundred and first time, had promised never to drink another drop, not even in case of sickness.

But what was the use of being mad with such a poor, silly, imbecile being as he was at that moment? He was not in a condition to appreciate a regular matrimonial "blow up," and she wisely resolved to reserve the vials of her wrath to be poured out at a more convenient season.

She looked at him, and thought of losing the little place, of penury, degradation, misery, and the poorhouse. A lucky thought rose, like the phœnix from the flames, out of the contemplation of the dark picture; and after a few minutes deliberation, she put on her bonnet and cloak, and hurried over to the village, not half a mile distant.

During the previous week, a young daguerreotypist, with a portable saloon — a kind of overgrown omnibus — had been delighting the villagers by giving them the semblance of their faces at prices varying from nine shillings to three dollars a head, depending upon the value of the case.

All the people in town had been daguerreotyped, and the omnibus man was the most popular person in the village.

All the dames and maidens were taken, and every Jonathan and Jehiel who could boast of a Susan, a Ruth, or a Sally, was taken, with her by his side in the picture, his arm thrown lovingly round her neck, and both looking unutterably affectionate.

But Mrs. Scroggins was not sentimental; she had gotten over all that long before Jim took to drinking. She proposed to put the skill of the daguerreotypist to a more practical use than that of propitiating a lover.

She entered the saloon, and though her heart did beat a little at the degradation of exposing her domestic matters to an entire stranger, she demeaned herself with all the firmness necessary for the trying occasion.

Fortunately for her, all the people in town "had been taken," and it was a dry time with the artist. In as few words as possible, she stated the case to him, and the young man readily promised his coöperation.

Taking his apparatus under his arm, he accompanied Mrs. Scroggins to the cottage, where Jim was sleeping off the effects of the villanous "New England."

The inebriate sat in precisely the same position in which his wife had left him. He was asleep in a high back chair, which kept his head up so that every thing was favorable for the sitting.

In a trice Jim Scroggins, old hat, ragged clothes, long beard, dozy, drunken expression and all, were transferred to the plate.

But the picture did not suit the artist; he thought one taken when the sitter was awake would be a more correct representation. Mrs. Scroggins thought so too, and after the daguerreotypist had put in a new plate, she waked him up.

"What d'ye want?" growled Jim.

"Wake up!" and the lady gave him a smart pinch, which opened his eyes, thus completing the expression of the drunkard.

The artist was prompt, and in an instant the second edition of Jim Scroggins was on the plate.

The original, not being required for further use, was suffered to sink away and complete his nap.

The pictures were put in a frame, and Mrs. Scroggins produced her money.

"Nothing, ma'am; I shall not charge you any thing."

"But, sir, I am able to pay."

The artist shook his head, and resolutely refused to touch her money.

Of course Mrs. Scroggins was grateful, and gave the young artist an invitation to take tea with her, which he accepted. In the course of the meal — the table being laid in the little front room — the daguerreotypist told the story of his own life; how he had been brought up in the midst of intemperance, and knew all about it. His father had died a drunkard, leaving his mother penniless, and he supported her by the profits of his portable saloon. Mrs. Scroggins, of course, sympathized with the young man, and readily understood why he would not take pay for the pictures.

But what was better than all, the young artist took quite a fancy to Jim's only daughter, a pretty little girl of eighteen, and after tea insisted upon taking her daguerreotype. And the sly rogue pretended that the first was not a good one, and took another, which he carried away with him, professedly for a show specimen, though, to my certain knowledge, he never exhibited it.

The tea things were cleared away, and still the young gentleman lingered, and talked a great deal with the pretty little Susan. But when he did go, the poor girl's heart followed him, and half the night she lay awake to think of him.

CHAPTER III.

JIM SCROGGINS recovered from his debauch; but the first thing he saw when he came into the kitchen, in the morning, was the case containing the two daguerreotypes, which lay open on the table.

He picked it up, and started back in confusion, when he recognized his own distorted features in one of the pictures.

He examined the other. It was the counterpart of the first, with the eyes open, and looking ten times more hideous than the sleeping picture.

"Good gracious!" exclaimed he; "did I ever look so infarnal homely as that?" and he proceeded to scrutinize the pictures a second time.

"Hang me! if I thought I ever looked so cussed mean as that, I'd go down and jump into the river.

"'I've seen men though, that looked just like that 'ere," continued he; "but them was drunkards. Now, I an't a drunkard, though I sometimes git a little sizzled. I never lit my pipe at the pump, though. Howsomever, them was took for me, though when or where I've no kind o' notion. There's the old hat, and that's the old coat — no mistake."

The footsteps of his wife caused him to drop the pictures, and he hastened out of the house to avoid the tempest which he thought his wickedness would call down upon his head.

4

It is a notable fact that he omitted his morning dram on this occasion, and his wife took courage. Like a prudent woman, as she was, she did not say a word about the occurrences of yesterday, and permitted him to eat his breakfast in peace.

He got through that day without drinking a drop; but on the following day the old appetite clamored for the usual dram, and in the afternoon, while his wife was in the sitting room, he went to the closet where he kept the bottle.

But the first thing that met his gaze was the two daguerreotypes resting against the black bottle. There was Jim Scroggins drunk asleep, and Jim Scroggins drunk awake.

" Them cussed dogerytypes ! " muttered he, starting back in confusion at the miserable-looking object they so faithfully shadowed to him.

Jim stopped to think. He fully resolved never again to be the loathsome being they represented him to be. Taking the black bottle, he went to the door with it, and with right good will hurled it on the door stone, where it was smashed into a thousand fragments, and the delectable stuff irretrievably lost.

" Halloo ! what are you about ? " said a young man, entering the yard.

" Smashing my rum bottle," replied Jim with admirable coolness.

" Bravo ! I commend your resolution," replied the young man.

" You are the dogerytype man, an't you ? " said Jim.

" I am."

" Walk in, if you please ; " and Jim ushered Mr. Shadow into the sitting room, where his wife and daughter were,

"Wife," said he, "you had them picters taken?"

"I did, James."

"I've broke the bottle; and as to looking like them creturs, I never will again."

"Thank God, James; I hope you never will."

"Here is the pledge," said Mr. Shadow, who was a temperance man in theory as well as practice.

"I'll sign it, by mighty!" and Jim did sign it.

"Now, wife, will you rub them things out?"

"Certainly, James;" and Mrs. Scroggins went for the pictures.

"And now, Mr. Scroggins, if you will walk over to my saloon, I shall be happy to take the real man as God made him."

"I'll do it; and, Betsey, you shall come, too; and Susey."

Susey went with her father and mother, though her picture had been taken. On the way Mr. Shadow walked by her side, and said a great many silly things, with which I will not trouble the reader.

The daguerreotypes were taken, and Jim was surprised at the difference between the picture of a drunken man and that of a sober man.

He drank no more liquor; and though this incident happened three years ago, he is still a sober and reputable man in the village. The little place is all paid for, and Mrs. Scroggins is superlatively happy.

Susan, in less than a year, became the wife of Mr. Shadow, who, notwithstanding his name, is a man of substance, and loves his wife all the more because he was instrumental in saving her from the degradation of being a drunkard's daughter.

SIX HUNDRED A YEAR.

CHAPTER I.

"WELL, Dixon, what is it?" asked Mr. Phogie of his assistant bookkeeper, who had been patiently waiting for half an hour in the private counting room of the merchant for an opportunity to speak with his employer.

"My second year in your service will begin to-morrow, sir; and I have taken the liberty to request your attention to a matter which, though of little consequence to you, perhaps, is of considerable moment to me."

The young man paused as if to note the effect of his words upon his employer.

"Indeed!" ejaculated the merchant, not half liking the cool and dignified way the young gentleman had of introducing himself.

To his mind there was a lack of that cringing, subservient tone and manner which his old-fashioned notions had taught him to believe was a dangerous deficiency in a clerk.

"I refer to my salary, sir."

"Well?"

There was a gathering frown upon the brow of the merchant.

"I have endeavored to serve you faithfully," continued the clerk, rather discouraged by the coldness with which he was received.

There was an awkward pause. Mr. Phogie's philosophy did not permit him to speak; and the young man was too much embarrassed to proceed with his application.

"My salary for the past year has been five hundred dollars," stammered Dixon, when he found his employer was bent on holding his peace.

"Well?" said Mr. Phogie, who still provokingly refused to take a hint.

"The object of my present visit is respectfully to request you to raise it to six hundred," continued Dixon, more boldly, as he began to appreciate the humor of his employer.

Mr. Phogie stared, aghast with astonishment and horror, at the supplicant. Cruikshank or Johnston would have accounted the scene quite equal to that in the workhouse, where Oliver Twist, in a less important matter, had the unheard-of presumption and impudence to "ask for more."

Dixon lost all hope.

"I trust, sir, I am not unreasonable," said he, excusing his boldness.

"Forty years ago, Dixon, when I was of your age," began Mr. Phogie, with solemn deliberateness, "I should have been glad to have received one half of your present salary."

The merchant looked complacently at the clerk, to note the effect of this astounding declaration.

Dixon ventured to suggest that the times had changed.

Mr. Phogie admitted it, but was quite sure the change had been for the worse.

"That is a matter of opinion, sir."

"Humph!"

"It costs much more to live now than it did then."

4 *

"Young men didn't drive fast horses then, nor go to the opera, nor board at fashionable hotels," sneered Mr. Phogie.

"I am guilty of none of these follies, sir," replied Dixon, a little indignant at the coarseness of the implication.

"Perhaps not; but five hundred dollars a year is a good salary for a prudent, careful young man."

"For one who can do no better it is very well."

"Clerks are vain nowadays, and over-estimate themselves," said Mr. Phogie, rebuking the complacence of his servant.

"I do not ask an increase of salary, sir, because I cannot live on five hundred dollars, but because I wish to advance myself, and, if you will pardon my vanity, because I think my services are worth more."

"Very well, sir; when young men get above their business, there is no knowing where they will stop. I cannot accede to your demand;" and Mr. Phogie, to show his indifference, busied himself in arranging some papers on the desk before him.

"Then, sir, I shall be obliged to give you notice of my intention to leave your service," returned Dixon, evidently relieved by the fact that the interview was concluded, even in this unsatisfactory manner.

Mr. Phogie paused in his occupation, and looked with surprise upon the clerk. It was doubtful whether Dixon meant so.

"Got another situation?" asked he.

"No, sir."

"Nothing in view?"

"Nothing, sir. Of course I could not make an arrangement till I had consulted you."

Mr. Phogie was not pleased with the result of the interview. Dixon was an honest, faithful, and devoted clerk, and the idea of parting with him was not agreeable. But to retract what he had hastily said would be an indication of weakness ; besides, he knew that any quantity of clerks could be obtained for four, or even three hundred dollars a year ; and he reasoned with himself that he should be a fool to pay Dixon six when he could get one for three.

Accordingly Dixon gave formal notice of intention to "quit ; " but, having already earned a reputation for integrity and fidelity, he could easily obtain a situation at the salary he had demanded of Mr. Phogie.

CHAPTER II.

" Good morning, Mr. Phogie," said Mr. Wyman, a liberal-minded merchant, as he entered the counting room of the former.

" Good morning, sir. Any thing new stirring ? "

" No ; I called to see you about a young man who has been in your employ ; I mean Dixon."

Phogie was all attention.

" I want a bookkeeper, and he has applied for the situation. How is he ? "

Phogie did not very well like to say he was a competent man, honest, faithful, and zealous ; he did not dare say he was any thing else : so he was compelled to compromise the matter for the moment by saying nothing.

" I was very much surprised to hear from him that he had left your service. Any thing unpleasant ? "

" No."

" Blot the books ? "

" No."

" Inaccurate ? "

" No."

" Off too much ? "

" No ; nothing of the kind."

" But he was always considered one of the most promising young men on the street."

" Yes."

Wyman was perplexed by the taciturnity of the other.

" I don't ask from idle curiosity ; I want a bookkeeper."

Phogie was dumb.

" Has the young man any fault ? " and there were visible evidences of impatience in the tones and manner of the matter-of-fact merchant.

" Not that I know of."

" O, you didn't want him ? "

" No — that is — yes — but ——— "

" Exactly so ! " exclaimed Wyman, laughing.

Phogie laughed too ; he could not help laughing when he saw what a figure he was making ; besides, a laugh is scmetimes a great relief to a man in a quandary.

" If you must know, Wyman, I'll tell you. I gave him five hundred for the last year ; he wants six for the next. I won't give it."

" No ? "

" Yes ; that is the whole story."

" Wait a minute till I have secured him, and then I will talk with you ; " and Wyman moved towards the door.

" Give him six hundred ? " asked Phogie, not a little

astonished to find his neighbor so eager to complete the engagement.

"Yes; seven if he demands it."

"I can send you half a dozen in an hour who will engage for three."

"Will you give bonds for their integrity and fidelity?" asked Wyman, with a sneer.

"Pooh!"

"Pooh? The fact is, I have suffered enough from cheap clerks. Assure me that a young man is honest and true to my interest, and I never will let him leave me on account of any reasonable difference about salary. All that Solomon said about a virtuous woman I believe in with regard to an honest and faithful clerk."

"I can't afford to pay these big salaries; and a young man gets above his business when you pay him too much."

"Nonsense! He will respect himself, which every man must do in order to keep himself honest."

"You are a transcendentalist."

"I'm common sense. You say you cannot afford to pay high salaries. Can you afford to have a semiannual deficit in your cash account of three hundred dollars, botched up with false entries, lying balances, and the like?"

Mr. Phogie had never been troubled in this way, and there was no probability that he ever should be; he looked out for his business himself, and he should like to see the clerk that could "bamboozle" him.

Mr. Wyman thought otherwise, and took his leave, wondering at the stupidity of his friend. It occurred to him, as he left the counting room, that it was not so very strange, after all, that clerks on three hundred a year can drive 2 : 40 horses and go to the opera three nights in a week ; not very strange, either, that petty defalcations were discovered occasionally, and that young men on small salaries got ahead amazingly fast.

CHAPTER III.

WYMAN engaged Dixon, and Phogie procured the services of an ill-looking fellow for three hundred dollars. The next time he saw Wyman, he indulged in a little innocent raillery over the fact that he paid his new clerk but just half the salary Dixon received ; and Phogie thought he was even a better bookkeeper than Dixon, wrote a plainer hand, and could run up a column of figures rather quicker. As to the new clerk's honesty, he had a bundle of testimonials as big as the invoice book ; and his maternal uncle was president of the Soap and Candle Makers' Bank. Of course he was honest!

Things went on swimmingly for six months. The new assistant was a jewel ; and when Mr. Quilldriver, the head bookkeeper, was taken down with rheumatism, which proved to be chronic, Mr. Phogie had so much confidence in this notable nephew of a notable uncle that he gave him the entire charge of the books, and, in the liberality of his big heart, advanced his salary voluntarily to four hundred dollars a year.

On the first of January, however, when Mr. Phogie called for the balance sheet, it was not ready. The trial balance didn't come out right, and the profit and loss account looked "thundering strange," as Mr. Phogie classically expressed it. Three days were hopelessly used up in "taking stock;" but the thing couldn't be figured out.

Mr. Phogie began to be alarmed. The general — a noted expert in unsnarling complicated and difficult accounts — was called in to examine into affairs; but no sooner did the smart nephew of the president of the Soap and Candle Makers' Bank see the well-known gray locks of the expert bent over the obstinate folios than he stepped out to lunch, and, by some singular oversight, forgot to return.

The upshot of the whole matter was, that the general discovered an "absquatulation" of some fifteen hundred dollars — just enough to keep the dapper little bookkeeper in opera tickets and 2 : 40's during the past season.

Of course the thing went up and down the street; and the little ragged news boys in State Street bellowed it at the top of their lungs into the ears of the passer by.

"Why, Phogie, how's this?" said Mr. Wyman, meeting the supporter of the cheap clerk system.

Mr. Phogie used a very hard word, which only the ministers are permitted to use in stirring sermons.

"Pay 'em well, Phogie, and they won't steal; and when you get a faithful servant, don't part with him."

Phogie scowled and edged off.

"By the way, Dixon has brought every thing out as square as a brick. Trial balance, balance sheet, every thing foots up without the variation of a penny," continued Wyman, maliciously, as Phogie increased his speed.

Poor penny-wise, pound-foolish merchant! He learned better after that.

For the satisfaction of the reader, I may as well add, that Dixon got a thousand for his next year's service, and that he is now engaged to his employer's pretty daughter, with the prospect of immediately becoming a partner in the concern.

THE NEW MINISTER;

OR,

"CHARITY BEGINS AT HOME."

CHAPTER I.

"It is abominable hypocrisy for you to talk so, Susan; you don't care any more about the missionaries than you do about the fifth wheel of a coach," exclaimed Louise Percy, the village schoolmistress, to her friend, Susan Maylie, at whose father's house she boarded.

"Why, Louise, how rude you are! You wouldn't like it if I should talk so about you," replied Susan, an angry flush gathering upon her cheek.

"Perhaps I shouldn't; but if it were true, I don't know that I could blame you for it."

"It is not true, Louise."

"Why, it is only two months since you refused to put any thing into the contribution box for the missions. You said you thought the missionaries were a set of lazy vagabonds, who had a good deal rather preach than work for a living. Now, since the new minister has come, all of a sudden you are a strenuous friend of missions and missionaries."

"Can't a body change her opinions, when they are found to be wrong?" replied Susan, petulantly.

"Certainly you can; but is your opinion really changed?"

5 (49)

"How strange you talk, Louise!"

"May be I do; truth is stranger than fiction."

"You must confess that our new minister's eloquence has been quite enough to convince any reasonable person that the propagation of the gospel among the heathen is a holy and beautiful work."

"Undoubtedly, it is a good work; and if you really feel called upon to labor so earnestly in the cause, I am sure I should be the last one to reprove you for it."

"You don't believe I am sincere, then?"

"I think you are very fond of the new minister. If an old man, with a wife and half a dozen children, had preached those missionary sermons, I hardly believe you would have felt so much interest in the work."

"Why, Louise, you astonish me! I really believe you hate the missionaries."

"On the contrary, I have the highest respect for them. I have always contributed my mite to sustain them. I think I was quite as strongly attached to the cause before this young and handsome Mr. Rogers made his appearance among us as I am now;" and Louise laughed merrily.

"He *is* handsome, isn't he?" said Susan, catching the playful spirit of her companion and confidant.

"I grant that with the greatest pleasure; but if you expect to catch him, you had better moderate your missionary ardor, and act yourself."

"Nay, Louise, I really feel an interest in the cause;" and Susan looked as sober as though she had been a missionary herself, just on the point of starting for the interior of Africa.

Louise laughed merrily again, as she looked doubtfully into the face of her friend.

A knock at the door started them from the revery into which both had fallen.

" Mr. Rogers, as I live!" exclaimed Louise, catching a glance at the new minister as he stood on the door stone.

" Pray, don't be rude, Louise," said Susan, as she adjusted her dress before the glass.

" Be rude! of course not; but I shall say just what I think."

" Don't, Louise. Be a friend of missions, for my sake."

Susan opened the door, and Mr. Rogers entered the house.

" I have called, Miss Maylie, to propose a plan for a tea party in aid of the missions," said he, after the common place introductories had been disposed of. " I look to you, who have been first and foremost in this good cause, for sympathy and coöperation."

" I shall be very glad, indeed, to do all I can to forward the good work," said Susan, demurely, " and so will Miss Percy."

" You must excuse me ; my time is so much occupied that I do not think I shall be able to render any essential aid," interposed Louise, scarcely able to restrain a laugh at the prompt tender Susan had made of her services.

" Perhaps you are not interested in the missions," suggested Mr. Rogers.

" To some extent, I am, sir."

" I trust, then, we shall be able to enlist your sympathies. Certainly the heathen, perishing in their sins, demand a noble effort on the part of the Christian world."

" I do not question the lofty character of the missionary enterprise, but I do think charity ought to begin at home."

" Why, Louise, how strange you talk!" exclaimed Susan.

"True, Miss Percy, but it ought not to end there. I see you favor the home missions."

"I do. I favor a mission nearer home than any society has been formed to advance, in our village at least — the mission to the poor and destitute."

"The gospel is preached for all," said the minister.

"*For* all, but not *to* all. There is poor Mrs. Weston, who cannot afford to buy clothes to send her children to meeting."

"Indeed!" ejaculated the minister.

"Her husband is a poor, miserable drunkard," added Susan. "You don't think her a worthier object of charity than the poor, suffering, dying heathen, who are perishing in their ignorance and sin?"

"Indeed, I do!" returned Louise.

"Her case ought to be attended to immediately," said Mr. Rogers.

"She ought to go to the poorhouse; the overseers offered to take her," continued Susan.

"The poorhouse! Mrs. Weston has seen better days, and, I doubt not, would rather die than be subjected to such a bitter humiliation."

"Her own fault, then; if she won't let the town help her, what more can be done?"

"She went to Deacon Hapgood, who owns the hovel in which she lives, to get him to take off ten dollars a year from her rent. But the deacon didn't see how he could afford it, and the poor woman left him, to continue alone her struggle with the demon of poverty as best she might. Yet the deacon can afford to give a hundred dollars a year to the missions, and says he never feels the sacrifice."

"I will see Deacon Hapgood," said the minister, musingly.

"I hope you will teach him that 'charity' begins at home.'"

"The hungry can be fed, the naked clothed, the houseless sheltered, and still there will be means left to carry on the missions. We are commanded to 'preach the gospel to all nations.'"

"And reminded that the poor are always with us. There is Farmer Jones; he can't afford to buy a spelling book for his daughter, but he gives large sums of money to the missionary society."

Mr. Rogers, who was an earnest seeker after truth, and who nobly endeavored to do his duty, began to feel that there was a great deal of practical wisdom in the remarks of the schoolmistress.

After a little more conversation, in relation to the proposed tea party, he took his leave.

CHAPTER II.

LOUISE PERCY, without being very beautiful or very bewitching, was a very sensible, earnest, straightforward girl. With a warm heart and a generous disposition, she was free, open, and sincere in her intercourse with the world.

Just the opposite was her friend and confidant, Susan Maylie, though, as the world goes, she passed for a good-hearted person. She lacked that transparency of motive which was so eminently the characteristic of Louise's temperament. Where no strong prejudice actuated her, she

5 *

was generally prompt in her choice of the good from the evil, though sometimes the most intimate friend was involuntarily led to suspect her motive.

Six months before we introduce them to the reader, the village in which they resided was thrown into commotion by the arrival of the new minister, who had been called to officiate in the parish church.

He was young, handsome, and, more than all, unmarried. Straightway, one half of the eligible maidens in town became interested in "serious things." The prayer meetings and the conference meetings were all at once found to be seasons of special interest. All the charitable societies connected with the church suddenly became prosperous. The missionary society, which was composed of ladies, who met once a month at the sewing circle, received a new impetus from the arrival of Mr. Rogers.

The young clergyman made it a point to attend these meetings, for he was particularly interested in the enterprise of sending the gospel to the heathen. He had preached several sermons on his favorite topic, and his exertions were rewarded by the creation of a strong and unusual feeling on the subject.

Susan, all at once, found her mind intently engaged in the engrossing subject. It is true she had learned from her father to ridicule and despise the missions; but then her heart was hard, and the ministrations of the handsome young clergyman had turned her mind from the vanities and vexations of life, to the lofty and substantial realities of "serious things."

Louise could not help noticing the sudden and remarkable change; but then Susan so constantly spoke of the minister's handsome face ; so often sneered at the thought of sundry village belles, whom she was malicious enough to accuse of attempting to "catch" him, that she readily fathomed the occasion of the singular transformation.

Louise got out of patience with her friend's duplicity, but suspecting that it might be involuntary, or the consequence of a want of consideration, she had plainly pointed out the inconsistency. Susan could hardly deny the fact, and feeling that Louise was a true friend, one who would not proclaim her infirmity to the world, she suffered the charge to pass unrefuted.

"I am going to set up an opposition to the missionary society," said Louise, after Mr. Rogers had gone.

"Pray, what mad scheme have you got in your brain now?" asked Susan.

"I am going to do something for the relief of Mrs. Weston."

"How foolish you are!"

"Am I?"

"You are, very foolish. It is the town's business to look out for paupers."

"It is my business, too, and yours, Susan."

"I am sure *I* shall not meddle with it."

"We have each of us reserved five dollars for charitable purposes, you know."

"Well?"

"I shall give mine to Mrs. Weston."

"And I shall give mine to the missions. I thought you were going to do the same."

"I have altered my mind. I cannot send my money across the ocean, when there is an abundance of heathen growing up in ignorance around us. Now, if you will put your five dollars with mine, it will just make up the amount the poor woman asked the deacon to abate her rent."

"I shall do no such thing, I assure you. I am too much interested in the missions to throw my money away upon the town's paupers."

"Very well; I will not urge you."

"What do you suppose Mr. Rogers would say if I should give nothing to the missions?"

"Are you beholden to him to render an account of your stewardship? For my part, I shouldn't care what he thought. Do your duty, Susan, let folks think as they may. If I had money enough, I would contribute handsomely towards having the gospel preached to such heathen as Deacon Hapgood, Farmer Jones, and some others who support missions, while they starve their own souls and those of their families."

Susan, knowing how obstinate Louise was when excited, refrained from opposing the purpose she had announced, and Louise retired to her room.

"Five dollars," said she, musingly; "it is more than a week's pay; but she shall have it; yes, and more too. Since Susan has refused to join me in this work of charity, I will give another five dollars; and then how happy the poor creature will be!"

The face of the gentle-hearted girl lighted up with an involuntary smile, as she opened her drawer and took therefrom the ten dollars. It was a large sum for her; but she cheerfully resigned the pleasures it would purchase, and looked forward to the joy she was about to carry to the cottage of the drunkard's wife.

With a light heart she tripped down the road to execute

her charitable mission. As she entered the hovel, she shrank back at the scene of wretchedness presented to her view. The poor woman, pale and haggard with care, apparently with one foot in the grave, was surrounded by half a dozen ragged children, whom her utmost exertions could hardly feed with the coarsest fare, and clothe even with the miserable garments that only half covered their nakedness.

Stating the object of her visit, Louise handed to her the ten dollars.

Mrs. Weston started back in amazement. Such unheard-of liberality overwhelmed her with confusion. If Deacon Hapgood could not afford to take off ten dollars from her rent, how could a poor girl afford to give her that sum outright? Before she could recover her self-possession sufficiently to express her gratitude, the young minister entered the house.

Mr. Rogers was almost as much astonished at the generosity of Louise as Mrs. Weston had been; and when he took his leave, he gladdened the poor creature's heart by adding another ten dollars to the gift.

CHAPTER III.

AFTER their departure from Mrs. Weston's, Mr. Rogers walked by the side of Louise towards her residence. The conversation was earnest, and at times warm, for Louise had opinions of her own, and was not diffident in maintaining them, even against the eloquence of the parson.

Mr. Rogers was not less pleased with the spirit and independence of his companion than he was with her warm heart and charitable disposition. And when he bade adieu to her at the door of Mr. Maylie's house, he could not banish her from his mind.

The following day was Sunday. Oddly enough for him, the minister had not a word to say about missions or the heathen. His text was, "The poor ye have always with you."

It was a noble sermon, showing that the poor, by being continually before the eye, came to be regarded with indifference and neglect, while objects of charity far removed by distance excited the liveliest sympathy and commiseration. He demonstrated that the first duty of all was to relieve distress in their midst; in fine, that " charity begins at home." It was shown, very much to the edification of Deacon Hapgood, who sat in the broad aisle, wondering " what the minister was driving at," that a rich man could not blind the eye of his Maker by giving large sums to the missions, while he oppressed the poor, and turned a deaf ear to their prayer for help.

Louise was deeply interested in the sermon, while a majority of the congregation arrived at the conclusion that Mr. Rogers had gone crazy. It was a reflection of her views, and a feeling of proud satisfaction pervaded her mind, as she reflected that she had been instrumental in calling the minister's attention to the subject.

The effect of the sermon was immediate and substantial. Every one of the " eligible young ladies " straightway emptied the contents of their purses into Mrs. Weston's lap. A society was proposed for ameliorating the condition of the poor, whom they always had with them. But Mr. Rogers cruelly vetoed the measure, not thinking an organized effort necessary to complete the work, especially as Mrs. Weston, who was, perhaps, the only destitute person in town, had money enough to pay a year's rent, and three months' provision in her cellar.

In the mean time, Mr. Rogers manifested a laudable interest in the welfare of the village school, and even preached a sermon on the duty of parents to their children. He visited the school three times in one week, besides conferring four distinct and separate times with the schoolmistress at her boarding-place in the evening.

Well, every body — except the eligible young ladies — said it was the minister's duty to look after the school, and see that the mistress did her duty ; so every body, with the exception mentioned, agreed that Mr. Rogers was particularly faithful in the discharge of *his* duty.

Susan was intensely astonished at the course of events, and more especially was she pained at the comparative neglect with which the missions had come to be regarded. Other charities, nearer home, shared the sympathies of the young and handsome pastor, and she suddenly realized that her extraordinary exertions in spreading the gospel among the heathen had failed to accomplish the purpose she had in view. But hope had not yet deserted her. Her eyes were not as wide open as they might have been, and she did not yet fully understand the "signs of the times."

"What a blessed field of usefulness is open to the teacher of the district school!" exclaimed she, one day, to her confidant, the schoolmistress.

Louise looked up from the book she was reading, astonished at the remark — not at the important truth involved in it, but that it should proceed from such a source.

"It is, indeed, an interesting field of labor to those who can appreciate it," replied she, a smile of intelligence crossing her good-natured countenance.

"I have been thinking, Louise, that *I* might be useful in that capacity."

"I do not doubt it."

"And I understand that the school in the south district will be vacant in a few weeks; don't you think I could procure the appointment?"

"Why, Susan, you do not really intend to become a teacher, do you?"

"I certainly do. I feel that I have suffered too many years of my life to pass away in idleness. I intend to redeem the time."

"You cannot mean it!"

"I am in earnest. Do you think I could get the appointment?"

"I can point you to a place nearer home, if you are really esirous of becoming a teacher."

"What place?"

"You may have mine in the course of a month or two."

"Yours, Louise!"

"I shall send in my resignation next week."

"Why, Louise, I had no idea that you intended to abandon teaching," said Susan, with undisguised astonishment; and, as she had regarded the attentions her friend received from the handsome young minister with a jealous eye, perhaps the announcement was received with some small degree of satisfaction.

"I had no such intention a few days ago. But if you

wish for my place, you can have the opportunity of making the first application."

" I shall be delighted to get it."

" I will mention the subject when I send in my resignation."

" But, Louise, you have never told us any thing about this. Pray, what is going to happen ? "

" I suppose I must tell you the secret. Of course you will not betray my confidence ? "

" Certainly not."

" I am going to be married this fall ; " and Louise blushed up to her eyes.

" Going to be married ! My goodness ! And we never even found out that you had a beau."

" It has been rather sudden."

" I should think it had. Who is the fortunate gentleman ? "

" Mr. Rogers."

" Mr. Rogers ! " exclaimed Susan, starting back in blank amazement, while the color deserted her cheeks, and her heart fluttered with emotion.

" Just so. From the time we met at Mrs. Weston's, when I gave the poor woman my money, he has been very attentive — and, in short, the matter is now settled."

" Well, I *am* astonished ! "

Susan *was* astonished.

" I cannot wonder ; I am astonished myself. But, Susan, I think I shall carry in my resignation to-morrow, and you had better have a written application ready."

Susan bit her lips with vexation, and even wondered tha

she had not been fool enough to give her money to Mrs. Weston, instead of the missionary society.

"I think, on the whole, Louise, that I shall not become a teacher at present," said she, as she turned, and abruptly left the room.

In the fall Mr. Rogers and Louise were married. The parsonage is the home of peace, love, and charity. Mrs. Rogers is a model minister's wife, and though the missionary cause receives an earnest support, she still believes, and acts upon the belief, that "CHARITY BEGINS AT HOME."

"OUT NIGHTS;"

OR,

BELONGING TO THE "SONS."

CHAPTER I.

"Don't go out to-night, Charles," said Mrs. Prescott, a pretty, sweet-smiling lady, who had been married just six months, to her husband.

"Really, Carrie, I am very sorry; but I do not see how I can be absent from the meeting to-night," replied the young husband, as he brought his great-coat from the entry.

"You always say so. I wish you did not belong to the 'Sons.' Can't you leave them?"

"I could, my dear, if I desired; I have no wish to do so."

"Wouldn't you do it to please me?" said the lady, smiling so sweetly that one could have found it in his heart to do almost any thing for her.

"You do not seriously wish me to do so."

"Nay, I do."

"Think, Carrie."

"I am jealous of that society."

"Fie!"

"You leave me here all alone, and you can't think how lonesome I am."

"I am very sorry to leave you; but, really, I feel it to be

(63)

my duty to sustain so good an association as the ' Sons of Temperance.' "

" There are enough without you."

" All might, with equal propriety, say so."

" They do not all leave a wife alone at home."

" Perhaps not."

" Can't you belong to them without going to the meetings every night ? "

"I should not wish to do that. To be a merely nominal member of the Order is to be nothing at all."

" You would be giving your name and influence to the cause of temperance just as much as you do by attending the meetings."

" What is the cause of temperance, Carrie? I fear you give it a very vague construction, like many others in the community."

" Why, preventing and curing intemperance."

" Preventing and curing it in whom ? "

" Every body, I suppose — all your friends and neighbors."

" But not yourself."

" There is no danger of you, Charles."

" But I joined the Sons quite as much for my own sake as for that of others."

" You don't think you are in any danger of becoming a drunkard, do you ? " asked Mrs. Prescott, with a smile of incredulity.

" Not while I am as strongly fortified against the vice of drinking as I am now."

" Pooh! I would risk you, even if you did not belong to the Sons."

" Suppose I should abandon them, and permit myself to

be influenced by the example of those around me — of your brother Frank, for example? Suppose I should shake off my allegiance to the principle of total abstinence, how long would it take me to get rid of all my scruples against drinking a glass of wine?"

"Can't you adhere to the principle without belonging to a society?"

"Association strengthens principle."

"You don't steal, Charles; on principle, you would not steal; but is it necessary that you should belong to an anti-thieving society?" and the pretty young wife's features wore an expression of triumph.

"Drinking is a fashionable vice; stealing is not. When the community regards the fashionable wine bibber as it does the thief, there will be no occasion for associated effort to restrain it. Popular opinion will do the work which the Sons are now doing."

"But I don't think there is any need of going so constantly," replied the wife. "*Do* stay with me to-night; I feel so lonesome."

"The Order acts upon some particular business to-night, and —— "

"Particular business again!" exclaimed Mrs. Prescott, with a good-natured laugh.

"It does indeed."

"Always so."

"Besides, I am W. P., you know."

"W. T., you mean."

"What's that?"

"Wife tormentor."

"Nay, Carrie —— "

"Go along; I will excuse you to-night; but don't stay late."

"No, dear."

"It was eleven o'clock before you got home last Saturday night."

"I will be home by ten to-night;" and Charles Prescott kissed his pretty, smiling wife — we beg the reader to remember that they had been married but six months — and left the house.

CHAPTER II.

MRS. PRESCOTT did not appear to be half so lonesome as she had pretended she was; for, as her little white hand delicately and daintily grasped the needle, the same involuntary smile played on her pretty lips that had been there while her husband was present.

Her thoughts must have been very pleasant, or she could not have worn that bewitching smile. Her soft, gazelle-like eye, too, beamed forth the language of a pure and beautiful soul — a soul at rest among the flowers of its own tender rearing.

She was thinking, and her thoughts were full of joy. What a happy wife she was! But perhaps her view of matrimony was mingled with something of sentiment — a few grains of that amiable moonshine which strews flowers and perfumes in the pathway of the young wife.

Alas that the blight of coldness should ever come to wither those flowers which the young and loving wife scatters in her pathway! Alas that the cares and trials of life should ever come and cast a great, broad shadow over that moon of her dreams.

Mrs. Prescott was happy, and she was *thinking* how happy she was. Charles was all love and devotion. He was industrious, frugal, and temperate; and, though they lived in a humble house and in a humble street, she sighed not for the fine things her neighbors had.

They lived comfortably; and, while her husband loved her, she cared not for tapestry carpets and velvet-covered lounges.

Charles had only one failing; and that was, an earnest devotion to the Order of the Sons of Temperance, which drew him away from her side every Saturday night. He never left the house any other evening without her; and undoubtedly he would have insisted on her joining the order, only that it was a *secret* society; consequently no women could be tolerated within its pale.

Mrs. Prescott could not see why her husband should be a "Son;" he was strictly temperate in his habits. Poor wife! She neglected to inquire into the reason of his being so.

She plied her needle, and smiled forth the joy that was in her heart. She was so happy and contented that there was only one thing left her to wish for — that her husband was with her.

About half an hour after Charles had gone, her brother Frank, who had been married nearly a year, called with his wife.

"I have got to go down to the store and post up the books, Carrie, and I have brought Lucy to stay with you; she was afraid to stay alone," said Frank Winslow, after the two wives had kissed each other, and said sundry pretty things about the weather and the walking.

"I am glad you did; I am all alone myself."

"Where's Charley?"

"Gone to the lodge."

"What lodge?"

"I don't mean the lodge — the meeting of the 'Sons.'"

"Bah!"

"He goes every Saturday night."

"What a pity! Charley is a good fellow, and it is a great shame that he should herd with those fanatics," said Frank Winslow.

"Don't you talk so about my husband, Frank," interposed the loving wife. "He is not half so much of a fanatic on temperance as you are on cognac and sherry."

"Fie, sis! I believe in all sorts of good things; and being a Son is, in my opinion, the next thing to being a fool."

"Why don't you tell him so?"

"I would if he were here. You don't think I am afraid of him, do you?"

"No; but the last time you argued the question with him ——".

"Bah!" exclaimed Frank, impatiently.

Promising to call for his wife by ten o'clock, he left the house.

"I hope our husbands won't quarrel over this temperance question," said Mrs. Winslow.

"I hope not."

"But this 'Sons' business does seem so silly to me that I cannot wonder Frank laughs at him."

"Well, I don't care any thing about it, only that Charles is out so late every night at the meetings."

"And leaves you all alone?" asked Mrs. Winslow.

"Yes."

"I wouldn't let him! It is a shame! Why, I should go into fits if my husband left me alone till eleven o'clock!" and Mrs. Winslow was horrified at the very thought.

"I have said a good deal about it."

"Said! Why, I would tip the house over before I would submit to it."

"He is so deeply interested in it."

"He ought to be deeply interested in his wife too."

"Nay, nay, Lucy, you wrong him. He loves me with all his soul."

"And leaves you alone till eleven o'clock?"

"I'm not afraid to stay alone."

"Why, it's almost as bad as having a drunken husband to sit up for."

"O, no, I'm sure it is not."

Charles Prescott was warmly condemned by the visitor, and warmly defended by the wife, who, poor thing, though she wished he would stay at home, could not bear to hear a word said against him.

CHAPTER III.

BEFORE ten o'clock, the two ladies had settled the question of Charles's defection, and passed naturally enough into mousse de laines, laces, and the newest fashions. Mrs. Winslow did not like to say that he was a monster in the hearing of his wife; but she fully believed it; and Mrs. Prescott, moved by the arguments of her friend, concluded that she was used much more hardly than she had ever suspected.

Punctual to his appointed hour, Charles came home. Mrs. Winslow playfully upbraided him for his want of constancy in leaving his wife to spend the evening alone; but the husband made a "moral question" of it, and proceeded to discuss the topic at length.

An hour was used up in the unprofitable argument, and the clock struck eleven.

Mrs. Winslow yawned, and wondered why Frank did not come — began to think the books must have gotten into a snarl to keep him so late.

It was half past eleven before he came.

"How are ye, old boy?" said he, grasping the hand of Prescott. "How are the Sons to-night?"

"As usual — thriving."

"What makes you so late, Frank?" asked Mrs. Winslow. "You promised to come at ten o'clock."

"The books got a little twisted. But sit down, Suke; I want to talk with Charley;" and Frank threw himself into a rocking chair before the fire.

"No, no, Frank; it is almost twelve o'clock."

"Never mind; sit down. They say there is more liquor drank since the Maine law was made than ever before," said Frank, turning to Charles Prescott.

"And there is more cheating, killing, and stealing since the ten commandments were made than ever before. What does that prove?"

"Bah!"

"You refer to the golden calf?"

"Seriously, Charley, in my opinion, the fanatics who made

that law ougat to be held responsible for half the drunkenness in the community."

" And Paul, Peter, and John for half the sin the gospel was intended to prevent."

" You talk like one of the fanatics," said Franк, nis cheek reddening with anger.

" I merely change the application of the principles which your remarks cover."

" You distort them. A fanatic can't argue the question fairly. Come, Suke, let's go home."

Frank Winslow rose from his chair, but instantly sank back again.

" What is the matter, Frank?" asked his wife.

" Nothing; don't you see?" and he attempted to rise again, but without success.

" What ails you? How strange you act!"

" Your Sons and your Maine laws are a humbug, Charley; there's no rubbing that out. Tell me about your — hic — Maine law!"

" O Heavens!" groaned the poor wife.

" What the deuse's the — hic — matter now?"

It was too plain to be longer concealed; Frank Winslow was drunk! The heat of the room was revealing the terrible truth to the poor wife, to the fond sister, that the husband and brother was helplessly intoxicated!

Charles Prescott was shocked; Carrie's cheek was pale, and her frame trembled; that smile was gone, for the loving brother was a drunkard!

It was an agonizing moment to the fond wife. Mountains of sombre clouds came rolling down before her bewildered senses, and the future was dark with poverty, woe, disgrace, and death. The drunkard's grave yawned like a cavern of hell in the path of her husband.

" O, Frank, Frank!" exclaimed she, throwing herself into his arms, and bathing his brow with her woman's tears.

" What in —— ails you all?" said Frank, gazing round him with a drunken leer.

Charles attempted to get him upon his feet; but he was utterly helpless.

"Let me — hic — alone. I am none of your cussed — hic — fanatics, that can't go alone;" and he fell at full length upon the floor.

Mrs. Winslow threw herself into a chair, and sobbed in bitterness of spirit. Carrie wept upon her bosom. It was a sad sight, that group of weepers over the drunken body of a noble-hearted, generous young man. Angels weep over such pitiable objects.

With much difficulty Charles Prescott succeeded in putting him to bed; but, to all save the besotted inebriate, it was a sleepless night. Tears stained the pillow of the wife and sister, and silent prayers rose to heaven for the preservation of the erring young man.

Morning came, and Frank had slept off his debauch. He was conscious of his position, and with shame and humiliation he presented himself in the breakfast room of his friend. The pale, anxious faces, the red and swollen eyes of his wife and sister, told him what they had suffered.

Like a true man, he acknowledged his fault, and promised to amend. Charles pointed out the necessity of making a principle of abstinence, to which he assented, and promised to connect himself with the Sons. He kept his promise, and in a few weeks was initiated.

Mrs. Prescott, after the impressive lesson she had received from the experience of her brother, was convinced that active membership in a temperance society, or at least a cherished *principle* of abstinence, was necessary in these degenerate days for the salvation of the young man.

Her husband had resisted temptation through the salutary influence of the "Sons;" and she could not but reflect how unreasonable she had been in attempting to lure him away from the fountain of his principle.

Even Mrs. Winslow has so far overcome her timidity as to be content to stay alone every Saturday night while her husband attends the meetings of the Order. It is a blessed thing for the wife to be assured that, while he is away from her in those hours which properly belong to her, he is fortifying his soul against the temptations that every where beset him.

7

BRING FLOWERS;

OR,

GOING INTO MOURNING.

CHAPTER I.

"I AM sure they cannot care much for their sister, for not one of them had even a black ribbon on her bonnet," said Mabel Grant to her invalid sister.

"Nay, Mabel, you must not judge them harshly."

"But only think of it! Even her mother did not so much as change her bonnet."

"Probably they have views and opinions of their own upon the subject," replied Mary Grant, feebly, for she was in the last stage of consumption, — that dreadful scourge of our northern clime, — and even the exertion of speaking a few words was exceedingly tiresome.

"And poor Ellen Lawson, our dear friend and schoolmate, one of the fairest and truest girls in the village — to think that she should go down to her early grave without even a show of mourning in her own family. It looks like sacrilege to me."

"Nay, Mabel, your respect for a mere custom causes you to disregard the plainest dictates of charity."

"I do not mean to be uncharitable."

"I know it, Mabel; but you must remember that the practice of putting on mourning is only a custom; and there is no sacrifice of love or principle in disregarding the custom."

"Well, I don't know; I cannot think they loved poor Ellen as she deserved to be loved."

"Why not?"

"Because, if they had, they would at least have shown a decent respect for her while they stood around her bier."

"Did they seem to be cold, indifferent?" asked the invalid, with a great deal of interest.

"No; Mrs. Lawson was very much affected while in the cemetery. She sobbed as though her heart would break."

"Indeed!"

"But it did not seem to be real, her dress was so inappropriate."

"You wrong her, Mabel."

"I hope I do."

"You cannot see into the heart."

"And her sisters, too, if they had not worn white bonnets, would have seemed like real mourners."

"The heart weeps, Mabel, not the dress, nor even the tearful eye. Many a one in sable weeds has felt no sorrow for the loss of a parent or a friend."

"That may be; but don't you think yourself that white bonnets and blue dresses are very improper at the funeral of a near friend?"

"It would not be my taste, Mabel," replied Mary, with a faint smile. "But I wish to accord to every one the privilege of doing as they please in a matter of this kind."

"So do I; of course they have the right to wear what they please."

"You censure them, though."

"Not censure them, Mary; I only say that it looks as though they did not care much for poor Ellen."

"You impugn their motives; you ought to be charitable to them, however strange they may seem to act."

"I will, sister; but if I had lost a friend, I should feel as though I was deficient in respect to the memory of that friend, if I did not put on mourning."

Mary sighed; she knew not how soon that dear sister would be called upon to put on mourning for her. Even another day of existence might not be permitted her. She was calmly waiting the hour that would bear her from the scenes of earth to that brighter realm beyond the dark grave. Already she heard the music of the angel's fluttering wing, and was ready to lay her head upon the lap of earth.

Mabel penetrated her sister's thoughts, and turned away to hide a tear, which sprung unbidden to her eye.

"There are many things to be considered, Mabel, in relation to the custom of wearing mourning. For my part I think it would be far better if the practice was entirely discontinued."

"Why, Mary! how strange you talk!"

"You can conceive how very disagreeable it must be for those who are waiting to consign the remains of a dear friend to the tomb, to be compelled to attend upon mantuamakers and milliners."

Mabel had never thought of that before.

"No sooner has the spirit taken its flight, than the house of death is made the scene of commotion and confusion by the preparations to appear in black. That holy sorrow, which craves solitude, is broken in upon by the cares of business — by the necessity of conforming to a mere fashion which requires the mourner to make a vain show."

"Perhaps you are right, Mary; pray, do not talk any more. You are quite exhausted."

Mary said no more. A shade of deep thought rested upon her pallid features. She was thinking how much more soothing it would be, when her redeemed spirit sped its flight, if her friends could only think of her while her lifeless clay remained with them, without the intrusion of milliners and dressmakers.

CHAPTER II.

It was spring time, and the joyous birds sung their cheerful notes upon the blossoming trees. The flowers were blooming upon the hill side, and Nature was assuming her verdant robes.

Under the influence of the mild, balmy air of the spring, Mary Grant seemed to revive. Her strength appeared to return with the opening buds, and her friends dared to hope that she might be spared to behold the profusion of another summer, the glories of another autumn. But the disease was deceptive. While hope smiles, the destroyer comes.

The physician, after giving the parents of Mary all the encouragement he could, directed his patient to ride out as often as the weather would permit.

The invalid was happy in the privilege of once more inhaling the balmy breezes, of once again visiting the cherished scenes, where, in the full vigor of health and joy, she had gayly and thoughtlessly roamed.

7 *

The village cemetery had always been a hallowed and beautiful spot to her, and she expressed a desire to visit it again, ere her inanimate form should be laid away to slumber beneath its peaceful bosom.

With Mabel for her companion, the carriage was slowly driven through the garden of graves. Mary was silent and thoughtful; and more than once a tear rose to the eye of Mabel, when she thought how soon she might be called upon to follow the cold form of the loved one to her resting-place.

The invalid was thoughtful, but not gloomy. Already the spirit had reached forward to the glories of that better world where there is no death, no sorrow. The grave had no terrors to her; it was a place of rest. Death was not a hideous, quaking skeleton to her imagination, but a white-winged angel, who would fold her upon his bosom, and bear her across the dark valley to the "house with many mansions, eternal in the heavens."

With introverted thoughts she gazed upon the memorials of the slumbering dead. The funereal fir, the pendent willow that swept over the green graves, diffused a heavenly calm in her heart, and she felt ready to join the great company that slept beneath them.

"There is a new-made grave," said she, as the carriage turned the angle of one of the avenues.

"It is the grave of poor Ellen Lawson," replied Mabel.

Mary requested the driver to stop.

On the grave, over which no marble had yet been reared, were several bouquets of fresh flowers. Some little white blossoms, which had been transplanted near the head, were opening their tiny buds.

"Still remembered, Mabel," said Mary, as she pointed to the flowers.

"They place fresh flowers upon her grave every day."

"And do you think they did not love her, Mabel?"

"O, sister, I know they did!"

"And wore no black at her funeral?"

"I was wrong, Mary."

"These are meet emblems of the heart's remembrance. When I go hence, may the flowers of spring blossom upon my grave. May some loving hand place flowers upon the sod that hides me from those I loved on earth."

"You are sad, sister; do not speak so gloomily."

"Nay, Mabel, I am not sad; I am happy."

Mabel shed a flood of tears upon the bosom of her sister.

"Do not weep, Mabel; we shall meet in heaven, and be happy there forever."

"You are better, dear sister; do not speak so hopelessly."

"Only a little while longer, and I shall rest beneath this sod. But do not be sad; I am happy: I am not afraid to die. I feel as though the angels were with me now, waiting to bear me to my home in the skies."

Mabel cast another glance at the flower-decked grave of Ellen Lawson, as the carriage drove on, and she felt that the heart could more eloquently express its remembrance of the loved and lost, than by a display of the sable weeds of the mourner.

CHAPTER III.

MARY GRANT went out of the house no more. In another week her waiting spirit bade farewell to earth, and winged its way to its native skies. Calmly and trustingly, while a heavenly smile played upon her irradiated features, she breathed her last in the arms of Mabel.

She was gone! Her wasted form, from which the undying soul had just taken its flight, lay in rigid silence before her. She was beautiful in death — so beautiful that Mabel could hardly believe she was dead; that those lips, parted in a placid smile, could no more speak gentle counsel to her; that those eyes, now motionless and sealed, could no more reflect the love of that affectionate heart upon her.

But a moment before, she had bidden her farewell. Could she be dead? Was it indeed true that those smiling lips were forever sealed; that another note of sisterly love could not proceed from them?

Kind friends were waiting to prepare the body for the sepulchre, and a gentle hand led her away from the inanimate form. Then, then she realized that her sister was indeed dead, and a torrent of woe swept wildly into her heart.

Flying to her chamber, she gave free vent to her grief.

" She is gone! She is gone!" sobbed she, as she buried her face beneath her hands, and trembled in the agony of her emotion.

Mary died as the sun was sinking behind the western hills. Her pure spirit had fled with the day; but the change bore her to an endless day, where there is no night and the sun never sets. ·

Mabel passed a sleepless night. Her pillow was wet with her tears. She rose in the morning, and hastened to gaze again upon the form of Mary. She was arrayed for the grave, and as Mabel bent over her, and printed a kiss upon the pallid, cold lips, the memories of the past rushed vividly into her heart. Her eyes rained tears upon the marble beauty of the corpse.

And there she stood for an hour communing with the days which were now no more; which could never be again, because the heart that made them glad was now still in death.

The formality of the morning meal was disposed of, — it was nothing more than a form to the weeping household, — and Mabel returned to the side of her departed sister. She kissed the cold lips again, and gave herself up to the flood of irresistible grief which faithful memory forced upon her.

"Excuse me, Miss Grant," said one of the neighbors, who had come in to assist the family, "but Miss Barnes, the dressmaker, is waiting to fit your dress."

Her dress! There was something heartless, cruelly repulsive in the word. Her dress at such a time as that! Must she leave the bier of her dead sister to converse upon the details of a garment? Must her mind abandon the thought of the dead to dwell upon the fashion of a dress?

Without a word she went to the sitting room. It was a busy scene for the house of mourning, and she learned that the mantuamaker had been there all night, for the weather was warm, and the funeral must take place on the following day.

The conversation of the apartment sounded loathsome to her. It was not of her dead sister, it was of the latest fashions, of the propriety of this and that; the fitness of one article and the unfitness of another.

They asked her how she would have her dress cut; but her thoughts were with Mary, and she answered not. As soon as she could be spared, she left the dressmakers, and returned to the chamber of the dead.

Again she wandered back with Mary to the scenes of their happy childhood. Again the tears flowed freely down her cheeks, and the spirit of the loved one seemed to_speak to her from the heaven to which she had ascended.

"The milliner has come, and wants to try on your bonnet," said the servant girl.

Mabel attended the summons and returned. Her grief was too deep to permit her to participate in the occupations of the sitting room, though her mother was compelled to be there, and had been there all night.

"Please ma'am, the shopkeeper has come over with some gloves, and they want you to pick out a pair," said the girl again.

She had scarcely disposed of this matter before another demanded her attention; and thus it was all day long. The house was full of bustle and confusion. The tailor, the hatter, the hosier, and a score of female artisans were constantly coming and going.

The solitude which her weeping heart craved was denied her. On the morrow that loved form was to be borne away and placed in the ground. They could never behold it again; but from the hour that Mary had breathed her last, to the arrival of the funeral guests, she heard more of business, of the repulsive details of dress and fashion, than of those more appropriate words which solace the mourner in the hour of trial.

The mourning garments were completed; but when Mabel was arrayed in them, they carried no comfort to the heart. She could not even feel that the wearing of them was a token of respect to her dead sister; for they had robbed her of the blessed privilege of weeping over her bier.

More than once she recalled the uncharitable judgment she had passed upon the Lawsons; but they had been privileged to mourn without interruption over their dead. The course they had chosen was reasonable ; and she could not but feel that if the heart alone were consulted, it would not weep in nodding plumes and sable weeds.

Around the grave of Mary the devoted sister planted the flowers she had loved so well, and every evening, as the sun sank away, she placed a fresh bouquet upon the green sod above her.

And close by, the hand of affection strewed. flowers upon the grave of Ellen Lawson ; and all summer long, and when the chill winds of autumn swept the cemetery, these floral offerings told the passer by that the dead were remembered every day.

Bring flowers ! Scatter them upon the graves of the dead ; for they are a far more grateful tribute to the memory of the departed than all the trappings of fashionable woe !

THE ACADEMY'S PRIZE.

CHAPTER I.

M. St. Pierre was the most noted artist in Paris, and his fame extended all over Europe. His studio was thronged with students from every country on the continent. To have been a student of M. St. Pierre was a passport to distinction.

Among the pupils of the noted master were two young Frenchmen, Jean and Paul Murot. They were cousins, and M. St. Pierre deemed them the most promising of all the students. They were about equally advanced in their art. An indifferent critic would hardly have been able to distinguish the works of one from those of the other.

But, equally endowed as they were in that genius which makes a painter, they were essentially different in disposition and character. Jean, the elder, was cold, dark, and revengeful, while Paul was gentle hearted, kind, and forgiving.

The ladies who frequented the studio of the great master were so impartial as to say that both the young artists were equally well endowed in the attributes of personal beauty. They were universal favorites. If the light blue eye of Paul seemed to exhale a profusion of smiles from his very heart, the dark, flashing eye of Jean spoke a soul full of manly energy, firmness, and decision.

M. St. Pierre had an only daughter, Emilie — a beautiful, simple-hearted maiden, upon whom her father lavished a world of endearments. The artist had a soul for beauty; and, if there had been no natural tie to bind him to the fair being, his soul would still have clung to her.

Emilie was a pupil of her father, and as earnestly devoted to her art as even the master himself. By the throng of students with whom she was associated she was almost worshipped as an angel of light.

Among those who bowed at her shrine were Jean and Paul Murot. They were both inspired by the genius of the art she loved, and, turning from the mediocrity of the mass, she dwelt with interest upon their lofty productions.

Both loved her; both had sought to win her heart, to make her choose between them; but Emilie was obstinate, and refused to smile more upon one than the other. Her heart had not yet been touched by any other love than that of the divine art.

The National Academy had offered a most magnificent premium for the best picture which should be submitted, before a given day, by the students of Paris. Jean and Paul were both competitors for the prize. For months they labored and studied with the most assiduous devotion; for he who should bear off the prize of the National Academy would already have won a fame which a lifetime might not accomplish.

M. St. Pierre was one of the umpires. From him Emilie learned, with an unspeakable satisfaction, that one of her favorites was sure of the premium. Her father's judgment to her was infallible, and she gloried in the laurels which were to be worn by Jean or Paul.

One day, she entered the apartment where the two pupils labored. Jean alone was there; but Paul's picture, sketched on the canvas, nestled on its easel.

"Jean," said she, smiling sweetly upon him, "you cannot both win the prize."

"Perhaps neither of us," responded Jean, with a sigh.

"Nay, one of you will; my father says so, and he knows the ability of every student in Paris."

"Said he so, Emilie?" said Jean, smiling.

"He did."

"But, Emilie — beautiful Emilie," said Jean, laying down his crayon, and fixing a tender glance upon her, "there is another prize we have both sought to win."

"Another prize!"

"One worth infinitely more than that the National Academy has offered."

"You speak in enigmas, Jean," said she, with a coquettish blush.

"Let me speak plain, then; I mean yourself, beautiful Emilie," continued Jean, throwing himself at the feet of the fair maiden.

"Ah, Monsieur Murot, you are losing your brains again; pray rise," answered Emilie, laughing.

"Nay, Emilie, I have not lost my brains, but my heart. I love you. Without you the prize of the Academy would be worthless to me. I would throw myself into the Seine, with the bawble in my hand."

"You are extravagant, Jean."

"Nay, I love you; bid me hope, and the prize is mine — the prize of art and the prize of beauty."

"And Paul, — he loves me too," pleaded Emilie, smiling.

" Choose between us ; choose him, and let *me* die."

" No, Monsieur Murot, you will not die."

" I swear to kill myself when you refuse me."

" And will Paul kill himself, too, if I refuse him ? " said Emilie, laughing gayly ; for she seemed not to regard seriously the ready hyperbole to which her countrymen are addicted.

" Nay, I know not, Emilie ; I will challenge him. One of us shall die, that your choice may be made."

" Fie, Monsieur Murot ; if you do, the survivor shall never see my face again."

" Cruel Emilie ! "

" But, Jean, I will decide ; I love you both. He who wins the prize of the Academy shall win my hand and heart with it."

" Hist ! Here is Paul."

" He shall know all."

The fair girl then related to Paul Murot the substance of the conversation that had just transpired. He, too, had declared his love to Emilie, and entered the lists with even more willingness than Jean had evinced.

" Bless you, Emilie," said he ; " we shall both strive to win the prize."

The brow of Jean darkened as he saw the mild, soft eye of Paul fixed lovingly upon the peerless maiden.

CHAPTER II.

THE period allotted for the completion of the pictures had passed away. Jean and Paul were putting the finishing touches to their productions, and the heart of each beat high with hope. The laurel wreath of fame was almost within their grasp, and the heart and hand of the most beautiful maiden in Paris was also to be the guerdon of the victor.

Paul was sad — sad because both could not be equally fortunate. The most lively friendship had always subsisted between them; at least, the heart of Paul was sincere, and that of Jean appeared to be so. But the gentle-hearted student grieved to think that his own success might be the herald of Jean's discomfiture — that it would, perhaps, mar his prospects for life, and forever imbitter his existence.

As he gazed with affectionate interest upon the canvas from which his genius spoke like the tongue of an angel, he could not help thinking of poor Jean, if his own picture should be the successful one. Forgetful of self, the thought of marring some of the fine effects of his painting occurred to him, that he might win the happiness of seeing his friend the victor in the lists.

A single stroke of the pencil across that gorgeous tint of summer sky, one dash over that striking contrast of light and shade, one touch over the reflected light on the trunk of that English oak, would utterly disqualify it to compete with the glowing wealth of Jean's production.

With an impulsive energy, he grasped the pencil, and moistened it with color from the palette. It seemed like a sacrilege to mar the beautiful work; but the happiness of Jean was in his hand, and he raised the pencil to impart the Vandal touch.

His hand dropped. Ah, Paul, know you not that you are sacrificing the fair Emilie? that you are shutting yourself out from the treasures of a paradise?

Paul could not do it. The love of Emilie could not be

given up — no, not even for Jean. Had the prize of the Academy been all there was at stake, Paul had had the courage to make him the victor.

Throwing down the pencil with an impatient gesture, as though he was ashamed of his own selfishness, he left the apartment just as Jean entered it.

The dark eye of the student kindled as he glanced first upon his own picture and then upon that of Paul. The trying hour of his lifetime had come. He should either be lifted to the pinnacle of distinction, and win the hand of Emilie, or be plunged into the abyss of disappointment. It was a vast chasm that yawned between success and failure, and he had no patience to look upon the darker side of the event.

If he failed, there was nothing in life worth living for, and again he glanced at the painting of Paul.

A single daub would ruin it — would insure him the hand of Emilie and the coveted prize. It was a thought born of the devil; but Jean's heart was black enough to harbor it.

It was nearly dark, and to-morrow would decide his fate. He took up the pencil.

Black-souled Jean! Couldst thou have read all that passed through the heart of thy friend an hour before, the devils within thee had grappled with thy soul!

He advanced to Paul's picture; but the entrance of two artisans, who had come to prepare the pictures for transportation, defeated his purpose — nay, only delayed it. Bidding the artisans defer their task till morning, he left the room.

He had scarcely gone before M. St. Pierre and Em-

8 *

ilie entered the studio to see the paintings of the students.

"Ah, my father, Jean has won the prize," said the fair maiden.

"Nay, Emilie, the evening light falls unfavorably upon Paul's. Let us change them, and you will see the effect."

The master changed the position of the two paintings, placing Paul's before the window where Jean's had stood. The pictures, though not identical, were similar. A large tree occupied the foreground in each.

"You are right, my father, and poor Paul's hope is not yet blasted."

The master was silent for a while.

"Paul has been nervous," said he, at last, with a sigh.

Poor Emilie! How her heart grieved for the gentle-hearted student!

The shades of night had gathered when Jean reëntered the studio. It was too dark to distinguish objects; but the heart of Jean was also black, and he groped about for the pencil.

Standing opposite Paul's picture, he endeavored to distinguish its outlines. Only the great tree in the foreground could be dimly made out by the light of a back window, near which it stood.

With remorseless hand, he drew the brush across the trunk of the tree; and the beautiful light reflected from a golden cloud which was the crowning glory of the picture, —across that he drew the pencil, and the labor of Paul was ruined!

With a cloth he wiped down the canvas, so as to remove the evidences of an intentional daub, and left the room.

CHAPTER III.

THE board of umpires was still in session. It was whispered through the mansion of M. St. Pierre that a decision had been made, and that it lay between Jean and Paul Murot, as every body had expected ; but no one knew which was the fortunate artist.

"The picture of one has been thrown out because it is disfigured," continued the bearer of the news.

"Thrown out! Mon Dieu!" exclaimed Jean.

"Thrown out!" repeated Paul, bewildered with astonishment.

Perfidious Jean! How his black heart leaped at the prospect of the victory! The stern judges had not troubled themselves to inquire into the origin of the defacement of Paul's picture, and he was safe. Already he congratulated himself on folding the beautiful Emilie to his heart, and calling her all his own.

Poor Paul! The tears trickled down his cheek as he thought of the disappointment that awaited one of them. Treading down the selfishness which he had combated unsuccessfully on the previous night, he even hoped that it might be his own which had been rejected.

But ah, there stood Emilie, beautiful as an angel. She was silent, for she, too, felt that the present was an eventful moment.

How could the painting have been disfigured? Poor, gentle-hearted thing! She dreamed not of the villany that had been perpetrated. She knew not that the heart of one of her .overs was as black as a demon's. If Jean was the winner, she knew not to what wicked arms she would be consigned.

But Jean felt that the victory was his. He only knew that it was Paul's picture that was rejected, and he could hardly refrain from revealing the abundant joy that filled his mind.

The arrival of M. St. Pierre awakened the silent group from their lethargy.

"Ah, my father, who has won the prize?" exclaimed Emilie, breathless with anxiety; while a crimson blush suffused her beautiful features.

"It lay between Jean and Paul," replied the master.

"But which, my father?"

"Nay, Emilie, I hardly dare say."

"Speak, M. St. Pierre," said Paul. "I can bear disappointment."

"So can I, my master," added Jean.

"One of the pictures was sadly disfigured."

"Mon Dieu! how could it happen!" exclaimed Jean.

"Indeed, I know not; but the majority of the umpires decided that it was done by carelessness, and, against my earnest remonstrance, threw the picture out of the competition."

"How unfortunate!" said Emilie, deeply grieved.

"It was, since I am confident it would otherwise have won the prize."

Jean's heart leaped when he thought how prudent he had been in wantonly ruining Paul's picture. If his conscience had been less scrupulous, Paul had been the victor!

"Here is the award, Emilie; you shall read it," continued M. St. Pierre, giving her a roll of parchment, and leaving the room.

Emilie, with trembling hand, unrolled the parchment.

Jean stood firm, while Paul trembled with emotion.

" *Award to Paul Murot*," continued she, reading.

" To *Paul* Murot!" shouted Jean, staggering forward with amazement, and clutching the parchment.

With quivering lip, he gazed at the fatal words.

" Hell and furies!" exclaimed he, while his dark eye flashed with anger, " this is wrong."

Emilie and Paul started back, shrinking from the fury of the disappointed student.

" Jean is right; there is some mistake," said Paul.

" There is no mistake," replied M. St. Pierre, reëntering the room. " Jean's was thrown out for being carelessly daubed."

" Was it *mine* that was thrown out?" said Jean, wildly.

" It was; your name was upon it. How was it defaced?"

" I know not."

" Last night it was in perfect condition when Emilie and myself visited the studio. I was sure then that you would be the victor; but, to form a better judgment, I changed the position of the pictures, so as to get a different light upon Paul's."

" You changed them!" gasped Jean, staggering to a chair.

" I did. Are you ill, Jean?"

Jean had daubed his own picture!

He was ill; a fever laid him at death's door, and remorse extorted a confession of his villany.

Emilie became the bride of Paul Murot. His painting that won the Academy's prize and the beautiful wife he still adores hangs in the Louvre.

THE DOMESTIC ELEMENT.

CHAPTER I.

"Julia has been to the public schools long enough," said Mrs. Mason to her husband. "She is fifteen years old, and I am sure she can learn nothing more till she is sent to a boarding school."

"Nonsense!"

"Besides, Mrs. Benson's daughter has left, and Julia don't want to go any longer."

"Let her stay at home then."

"Stay at home! Don't you mean she shall have any polish?"

"Can't you polish her, my dear?" asked the easy husband, with a good-natured smile.

"How absurdly you talk!"

"Why, my dear, you have got quite polish enough for the wife of a small merchant. I would not give a copper to have you any more of a lady than you are."

"But Julia may be the wife of a rich man; what would she be then without music, French, and painting?"

"And she may be the wife of a poor mechanic, and these accomplishments be useless and burdensome."

"She never shall be the wife of a mechanic if I can help t," retorted Mrs. Mason, smartly.

"Fie, Mary; you are unreasonable. Why should she look higher than a mechanic, especially as some of our best and most reputable men are mechanics?"

"She shall not be the wife of a mechanic if I can help it," repeated the lady.

"Why not?"

"She shall do better, and that is the reason why I want her better educated."

"She may do worse. What are we, my dear, that we need look among the nabobs for a husband for our daughter?"

"Are you not a merchant?"

"Only a small shopkeeper."

"Well, that's a merchant; and I mean Julia shall marry a merchant."

Mr. Mason yielded the point, and agreed that Julia should marry whomsoever she and her mother might choose.

"But she must be educated for her future station."

"True, she must."

"She must go to a boarding school, and learn French, music, painting, and German."

"And Chinese," interposed Mr. Mason.

"She must learn all the fashionable things."

"I believe English grammar, writing, and arithmetic are not in fashion."

"Pooh! she knows all about these things."

"I asked her to tell me how many bushels of potatoes a wagon seven feet long by four wide and three high would contain, and she could not make the first figure towards it."

"I suppose there was no such question in her book."

"Perhaps not; and she could not tell me where Sevastopol was — whether it was in China or the Sandwich Islands."

" How foolish you are! I think likely she never happened to see the place on the map."

" And that letter she wrote to her uncle was such horrible grammar that I was ashamed to send it."

" No matter for that; she understands grammar very well."

" May be she does; but she has an awkward way of showing it. I suppose washing, cooking, and baking are not fashionable either."

" There it is again."

" I think you would do better by her if you took her into the kitchen, and taught her these things. If she happens to marry a poor man, they will be of some service to her."

" Time enough for these things."

" Well, well, do as you please; but I am opposed to boarding schools; I think they do more harm than good."

" That's just like you! Opposed to boarding schools! Who ever heard of such a thing?"

" They spoil more young ladies than they ever benefit."

" How in the world can it spoil them?"

" Home is the place for girls. The first thing they should be taught to love is the fireside; they ought never to be weaned from it by sending them away to undergo monastic discipline in a boarding school."

" How foolish!"

" It gives them bad habits — makes them romantic — fills their silly heads with moonshine; and if you send Julia, ten to one she will run away with some bearded puppy.'

But it was no kind of use for Mr. Mason to argue with his wife on such a topic as this; she was bent on sending Julia to the boarding school. He was a man of peace, and, rather than make a tempest, he withdrew from the combat.

CHAPTER II.

JULIA MASON did not possess a very brilliant intellect. Nature had never intended her for a "blue stocking," and, live as long as she might, there was no probability that she would ever become even a "strong-minded woman." She had for many years attended one of the public schools, but had never risen above the second class, and the master did not believe she ever would.

Yet, for all this, Julia was a good-hearted, generous, whole-souled girl. What Nature had neglected to place in her head, she had beneficently put in her heart. She had a nice, womanly, domestic temperament, was quiet and unobtrusive in her manners, and without doubt, if no pains had been taken to spoil her, would have made somebody a very loving if not a very brilliant wife.

She was a little disposed to be romantic and sentimental — would have fed well and thriven on moonshine — a temperament which requires a great deal of prudent management on the part of the parent or guardian.

Julia went to the boarding school; but she had not been there three weeks before she wrote to her mother, begging her to take her away, or she declared she should certainly die.

The poor girl was homesick. Monastic discipline was an

9

outrage upon her affectionate, domestic nature. She had been accustomed to spend her evenings by the fireside at home, with her parents and younger brother and sisters; and it was a sad deprivation to her to be driven, at the stroke of a bell, into her chamber at seven o'clock, there to sit in painful silence with her roommate, and study her lesson. She was not a genius, and she hated study; it was uncongenial in the highest degree.

At nine o'clock, at the stroke of the bell, she must retire, and in fifteen minutes her light must be put out, or a black mark was made against her name on the following day; and so it was all day long, week in and week out. Her existence was odiously mechanical. Her life was regulated by that everlasting stroke of the bell. She was obliged to do every thing by rule — eat, drink, sleep, study, play, walk, by rule.

It was unnatural, and her soul cried out within her against such monstrous formality. She could not learn, her heart grieved so under the repulsive mechanism of her existence. Even the music lesson, which she had anticipated with the liveliest pleasure, was gloomy and distasteful. She was conscientious, and, though her companions laughed at her for it, she at first paid the most implicit obedience to the rules of the institution. Her roommate devised various happy expedients for relieving the tedium of their lives; but she refused to avail herself of them.

Her mother begged her to persevere for a time, assuring her that she was only homesick — a disease which a few weeks would effectually cure. She did persevere; but her "chum" finally succeeded in overcoming her conscientious scruples, and the evenings, instead of being passed in study, were devoted to a "good time generally." It is true, Julia got innumerable black marks for failures in her recitations; but the horrible bugbears soon became so familiar that they ceased to have any terrors. Before the first term had expired, she had so completely weaned herself from her domestic memories that home had lost all its charms.

She had learned a great many "new tricks." Indeed, the preceptor, in his report to her parents at the close of her first term, felt it his duty to say that her conduct had not been altogether satisfactory. She had gone to the boarding school the quietest person in the world; she returned a romp, her head full of strange notions about lovers, and her heart as washy as the moonshine in her head.

On the first evening after her return home she insisted on going to the opera; the second to a concert; the third to the theatre; the fourth to a lecture; the fifth to a party; the sixth to a conference meeting; and so on every evening.

"What in the world has got into you, Julia? You did not use to be fond of 'kiting' round in this manner," said the astonished Mrs. Mason.

"O mother, it is so insufferably dull at home! Besides, it is not fashionable to stay at home in the evening," drawled Julia.

"What has got into you?"

"Boarding schools," said Mr. Mason.

"I should die of *ennui* to stay at home an evening," continued the daughter, with a languishing sigh.

"You had better give her a lesson on the pots and kettles now," interrupted Mr. Mason.

"O papa, how cruel you are! Pray go to the opera with me."

Mr. Mason was an indulgent papa, and he was obliged to go; but he could not help wondering what Julia would finally come to if she was permitted to go on in this manner

CHAPTER III.

JULIA returned to the boarding school, and, in spite of the weak efforts of her father to avert the fashionable fate that awaited her, she continued there for nearly two years. In music and painting she made rapid progress; but in literature and science she failed to make even a decent proficiency.

She was an altered creature. She was vain, affected, romantic, and transcendental, cherishing all sorts of visionary notions about life, and especially about lovers and husbands, who filled a long space in her daily meditations. She had lost her domestic nature, and that was the saddest loss of all. Her heart was not actually corrupted; but it was so buried up in the weeds of vanity and folly that its gentle influence was almost entirely lost upon her life and character. If not unsexed, she had lost that hold upon woman's sphere which confers her chief charm in society. She was a creature for the ball room and the opera, and not for the quiet shades of home.

Perhaps a boarding school does not always make such sad havoc in the mind and heart of the young female; but such is the tendency of its artificial manner of existence. Monastic discipline spoils woman; it removes her from, and unfits her for, her social, domestic position.

When the two years had nearly expired, Mr. Mason one

day received a letter from the principal of the seminary, containing the astounding intelligence that Julia had eloped with a young gentleman who had come from the city on a visit in the neighborhood.

"The grand *finale* of the drama," said Mr. Mason, throwing the letter to his wife.

"Good Heaven! who is this Mr. Winchel?" exclaimed Mrs. Mason, when she had read the letter.

"A son of Winchel, the merchant in —— Street."

"Rich?"

"Yes."

"Thank God it is no worse!" replied Mrs. Mason, so far relieved that a pleasant smile played upon her lips.

A few days after, Julia and her husband presented themselves at the home of her father. They were received with open arms. Mrs. Mason was too much pleased with the match to make a fuss about it, and Mr. Mason followed his wife's "lead."

A few weeks after, they were comfortably settled in a pleasant house; for Mr. Winchel, who had some very clearly defined aspirations for the quiet joys of a fireside of his own, insisted upon going to housekeeping instead of boarding.

This kind of life was novel to Julia, and for the first six months, while her husband consented to take her every evening to the opera, a ball, party, or concert, she was tolerably contented.

But Mr. Winchel got sick of such an incessant round of amusement, and sighed for that paradise of home which his imagination had years ago painted. He reasoned with his giddy wife; but she hated home, and reproached him for

9 *

attempting to imprison her in the house, and thus make her life miserable.

Mr. Winchel was firm, and positively refused to go to any more operas, balls, parties, or concerts.

Julia was forced to accede to his reasonable desires; but home, even in the presence of her husband, had become an intolerable place. Indeed, the romance of a husband had worn itself away. He had fallen in love with her in the most natural way in the world, and had proposed to wait upon her father, and arrange the preliminaries for their marriage; but Julia was not content to be united to him in such a tame manner as that, and insisted upon an elopement. Her lover gratified her — to his sorrow, he now discovered.

Julia was unhappy. Her husband, disgusted at her folly, returned to the club he had abandoned when he married her, leaving her to comfort or amuse herself as best she might. And she found comfort and amusement in the society of a gay and dashing Lothario, who consoled her for her husband's absence by making love to her. It was not long before the world was again astonished by the publication of an elopement — not a harmless, sentimental affair, but a criminal elopement.

Julia was too romantic to consider the moral turpitude of the act. The pious preaching and praying of the boarding school had been lost upon her in the variety of more congenial topics that were there presented to her. The elopement was romance; she thought not of the crime.

Mr. Mason and his wife were in the deepest distress. Mr. Winchel called at her father's store, and stated the particulars of their domestic experience. It was plain to both that the distaste for home was traceable to the loss of the domestic element of the misguided wife.

Julia and her seducer — we wrong him — both were guilty — were heard from in New Orleans; but the villain soon became tired of her whims, and left her, and she died a few years later, a ruined, abandoned, off-cast creature, the victim of a false education.

Mr. Mason's remaining daughters were not sent to the boarding school. They received the best education to be had in the city, and there are noted institutions of learning there. They were thus kept constantly under the watchful care of their parents, and the domestic element in their natures was not unsettled by absence from home while the plastic mind was being moulded into its shape for life.

"BANG UP!"

OR,

THE RESULTS OF ADVERTISING.

CHAPTER I.

" Any thing over, Ben ? "

" Not a dollar ; I just paid the Journal's bill for advertising, which has pretty much cleaned me out."

" How much ? "

" Forty-two dollars and twenty-five cents."

" Ben, I don't like to tell you that you are the biggest
fool on the street ; but you are."

" Wait, Joe, and see," returned the other, with a confident smile.

" Forty-two dollars for advertising ! "

" Just so, and for three months' advertising."

The applicant for " any thing over " gave a peculiar whistle to define the length, breadth, and depth of his astonishment.

This conversation occurred in the store of Benjamin Weston, a young and enterprising merchant, who had just commenced business on his own account. The other person,
who, to use his own classic expression, was " bang up," and

wanted to borrow fifty dollars to make up the amount of a
note due that day, was Joseph Weston, a cousin of the other.
They had been playmates in youth and stanch friends in
maturity. Though there was a great diversity of opinion on
many topics, a strong sympathy existed between them.

They had commenced business at about the same time,
and under nearly the same circumstances, both being obliged
for the want of sufficient capital to mortgage the stock in
their respective stores.

Thus far they had done well, and the prospect was, that
both would become wealthy and distinguished merchants.

They had married sisters, and occupied tenements in the
same block. Their houses were furnished in substantially
the same style, and with no material difference of expenditure. Both had been brought up to business habits, and
educated into the principles of a rigid economy.

"Forty-two dollars for advertising," repeated Joe.

"And if I had the money to spare, I would spend double
that sum," replied Benjamin.

"What benefit do you expect to realize from it?"

"You are behind the times, Joe. Benefit! What a question! I expect to make my fortune by it."

"Humbug!"

"Look at Brandreth and Swaim."

"Both humbugs."

"No matter for that; if these fellows have been able to
make princely fortunes by advertising humbugs, how much
more so will he who deals in substantial realities!"

"All gammon!"

"We differ; time will tell who is in the right."

"Seriously, Ben, you will ruin yourself if you go on in

this manner.   Forty-two dollars a quarter for advertising !"

"I shall spend a hundred the next quarter."

"Don't do it, Ben."

"How does it happen, Joe, that you are in the street borrowing money? I never did such a thing since I commenced
business."

"How does it happen, Ben, that you haven't got any
money to lend?" asked Joe, with a smile.

"Because I spent it in advertising."

"Better have spent it for opera and 2 : 40's."

"Wait, Joe, wait."

"I spent nothing for advertising; but I will bet you the
oysters my sales for the last quarter are as large as yours."

"I will take you up on the next quarter."

"Why not the last?"

"Advertising is somewhat like planting potatoes; you
must wait for the crops."

"Don't believe in it, Ben.   When I have a fifty spot that
I don't know what to do with, I shall put it into my family.
Buy a library, a new sofa, or something of that sort.   I
should rather go to the White Mountains with it, than
throw it away upon newspapers."

"You don't know your own interest, Joe."

"Don't I?   Some kinds of business might thrive on advertising; but ours, never.   Do you believe the women look
in the newspapers before they go shopping?"

"Well, there was a lady in here just now, who said she
saw such and such goods advertised by me."

"Pshaw! and on the strength of that you intend to spend
fifty dollars more in advertising!   Ben, you are crazy;"

and Joseph Weston turned upon his heel and left the store, assured in his own mind that his friend was going to ruin.

In his estimation such loose principles would eventually bring him to bankruptcy. But Ben was his friend, and he deeply commiserated him because he clung to such weak and pernicious doctrines.

CHAPTER II.

BUSINESS prospered with the young men. By prudent and careful management, each had not only made a living, but had been able to pay a small portion of the mortgage on the stock, at the end of the first year.

Joseph had the advantage of his friend in possessing a better location, and though his rent was somewhat higher, the difference was more than compensated by the increased facilities it afforded him. The prospect was decidedly bright to him. If his business increased as it had done, he would be enabled to clear himself of debt in another year.

Under this encouraging aspect he ventured to expend a hundred dollars in additions to his furniture, which his wife insisted was absolutely necessary for their comfort and happiness. The house had been furnished altogether too plain for this progressive age, in her estimation. She was behind some of her friends, who, she was sure, were doing no better than her husband.

Joseph was a little obstinate at first; but then there was something so decidedly comfortable in a set of stuffed chairs and a lounge, that he did not hold out in his opposition.

He was doing well, and the expenditure would not seriously embarrass him.

With a nice new Brussels carpet and the new furniture, Mrs. Weston's little parlor looked exceedingly pleasant and comfortable. Besides, it looked as though her husband was prospering in his business.

It was so very nice that the young wife could not bear the idea of having the parlor shut up, so that no one should see it till the furniture had grown rusty; consequently she made up her mind that they must have a party.

Their friends had parties; why shouldn't they? It looked stingy not to have one. Mrs. Weston was an eloquent debater, and she gained the day in this matter. It is true the party was not a very extravagant affair; but it cost Joe some fifty dollars. In the mean time Benjamin had paid quite as much for advertising as his friend had for new furniture and the party. Joseph laughed at him, and finally came to believe that he was insane, and would certainly come to ruin within another year.

Mrs. Ben Weston, too, felt decidedly unpleasant about the improvements which had been going on in her sister's house.

"Why can't we have a rosewood table and a set of stuffed chairs, Benjamin?" asked she, pouting her pretty lips into a very unamiable position.

"Simply, my dear, because I cannot afford it," replied the philosophical merchant.

"How can Joe afford it?"

"I presume he knows his own business best."

"He has put over a hundred dollars into his house."

Ben whistled "T'other Side of Jordan," and made no reply.

" Do, Ben, buy some new chairs."

" Can't afford it."

" Yes, you can."

" No, I can't."

" *You* can afford it as well as Joe."

" Perhaps I can."

" Do buy some."

" I should be very glad to gratify you, but I cannot take the money from my business. A year hence, if business prospers with me, you shall have them."

" A year hence," pouted the wife.

" I must spend a hundred dollars in advertising the next quarter."

" How foolish ! "

" Very foolish, my dear ; but it must be done."

" That's the way you throw your money away. You don't catch Joe to do such a trick as that."

" True ; but though he has the advantage of having a corner store, I paid three hundred dollars more on my mortgage note than he did."

" Then you can afford the table and chairs."

" Nay, my dear, I will not spend a dollar for superfluities while I am in debt."

Mrs. Ben Weston felt very bad about it, but her husband was firm, and she was forced to content herself with the plain furniture.

Mrs. Joe Weston enjoyed her nice parlor till the novelty wore away, and then she discovered that there were a great many other articles wanted to make things look uniform. The two windows must have drapery curtains, a pier glass was needed, and some pictures were wanted to relieve the

10

walls. Her husband, who had once exceeded the limits of his means, found no great difficulty in doing so again, and the things were bought.

But Joe had some scruples about it. His notes began to be troublesome, and every day he was in the street borrowing money. His business, too, had not met his expectations. Instead of increasing in the ratio of his first year's experience, it hardly held its own, and the poor fellow began to have some serious misgivings about the future.

Before the year had half expired, he was obliged to introduce a rigid system of retrenchment into his family and business affairs, in order to keep his expenses within his means.

CHAPTER III.

ANOTHER year had passed away in the business experience of the young merchants. The books had been balanced, and the results stood in black and white before them.

Ben had followed up his system of advertising through the year. He had expended large sums, but had made the outlay with judgment and discretion.

The result exceeded his most sanguine expectations. His store was crowded with customers ; with genuine, *bona fide* customers, and with but a small proportion of gadders and fancy shoppers. The newspapers had borne to the best families in the city and country full descriptions of his stock. His name was as familiar as "household words" in the dwellings of the rich and poor, of the farmer, the mechanic, and the laborer.

Truly, the harvest was abundant, and Ben rubbed his

hands with delight as he cast his eyes over the figures which conveyed to him the pleasing results of his year's operations. He had the means, not only of clearing himself of debt, but also of gratifying his wife by giving her all the new furniture she required, besides a handsome surplus with which to increase his business.

The new furniture was bought and set up; every debt was discharged, and the importers and jobbers were eager to give him unlimited credit.

One day, while he was ruminating upon this pleasant state of things, Joe Weston entered the store. For some months past, the intercourse between the young merchants had not been as cordial as formerly. Joe's nice things had rather "set him up;" some of the upper ten had condescended to visit him; and he had attended the "Almack" parties with his wife.

He was getting ahead fast in his own estimation, and cherished a supreme contempt for the slow motion of his friend. But when, in the middle of the year, he found himself running down hill, and discovered that Ben's store was crowded with shoppers, while his own was empty, a feeling of envy took possession of him. Ben must be underselling, he concluded, and sooner or later the consequences would appear.

The prosperous merchant could not but notice the sad and dejected mien of his friend, as he entered the store.

"How are you, Joe? You are almost a stranger, lately. Where do you keep yourself?" said Ben.

"Business, Ben; business!" replied Joe, demurely.

"Good! Business before pleasure."

"Any thing over to-day?" asked Joe; but the query was

not put in that buoyant, elastic tone, which had distinguished him in former times.

"A trifle; how much do you want?" returned Ben, promptly.

"To tell the truth, I am 'bang up.' I have got a note of four hundred to pay, and I have not·yet raised the first dollar towards it."

"You are late; it is half past one now," replied Ben, consulting his watch.

"Ben, I am in a tight place," said Joe, in a low, solemn tone.

"Indeed! I am sorry to hear it," and Ben's face wore an expression of sincere sympathy. "Nothing serious, I hope?"

"I am afraid so."

"What can I do for you?" and the young merchant took down his check book, and examined the state of his bank account.

"I can give you a check for three hundred, if that will do you any good," continued he, taking up the pen to fill out the blank.

"Thank you, Ben; you are very kind; but I don't know as I ought to take it."

"Not take it! Why not?"

"If I should pay this note, there is hardly a possibility that I could get through the month."

"So bad as that? 'Pon my soul, I am sorry to hear it."

"Smith and Jones advise me to make an assignment."

"How does it happen? I thought you were doing well?"

"Business has been very dull for the last six months. Haven't you found it so?"

"Well, no; it has been driving with me."

Joe knew it had; indeed, his present visit was not to borrow money, but to prepare his friend for the "smash," which was now unavoidable.

"My sales have been light," continued he; "I can't account for it."

"I can; look here, Joe."

Ben took down his leger, and pointed to the account "Charges," where the sums paid for advertising had been entered. On a slip of paper he had footed them up.

"Five hundred and sixty-five dollars for advertising, Joe! That's what did the business."

Joe was astonished. It was quite as much as he had paid for fine things for his house, and for parties, and the opera; but the investment had been vastly more profitable, inasmuch as, taken in connection with his careful management of his business and his economical manner of living, it had laid the foundation of his future fortune. It had given him a good start in business, and a good beginning is half the battle.

Joe Weston failed, and paid only twenty cents on a dollar. His fine furniture was all sold, and he was obliged to board out. But in his extremity Ben was his true friend. He received him into his house, and when his business was settled up, took him into partnership.

The firm is now one of the most respectable and prosperous in the city. Joe, ever since he was "bang up," believes in advertising, and any one who opens the Journal, or, indeed, any of the daily papers, cannot fail to notice the conspicuous advertisement of "Weston & Co."

10 *

THE NEW CLOAK;

OR,

"MIND YOUR OWN BUSINESS."

CHAPTER I.

"THERE! I declare, if Mrs. Burton hasn't got a new cloak!" exclaimed Mrs. Waxwell to her intimate friend, Miss Vincy, as they came out of church one Sunday.

"I see she has," replied Miss Viney, very quietly.

"I know her husband can't afford it; she will be the ruin of him yet."

"I suppose they know their own business best. At any rate, it is a blessing that you and I are not accountable for her misdeeds," said Miss Viney, who, though what is technically termed an "old maid," was not of that class who have been slanderously styled gossips and busybodies; and we have purposely introduced her to refute the foul calumny that "old maids" are all meddlers, and we are sure that all spinsters will be grateful to us for the service.

"I don't know about that," returned Mrs. Waxwell, with a dubious shake of the head. "Mr. Burton owes my husband three hundred dollars, and I don't believe he will ever get his pay if things go on in this way. That cloak couldn't have cost less than thirty dollars."

"I presume they could afford it, or they would not have bought it. At any rate, they ought to know best."

"Mrs. Burton is a vain, conceited, proud woman, and pride will have a fall one of these days."

"I hope not."

"I hope she will have a fall; she would drop some of those airs then."

"I never thought she was what might be termed a vain woman."

"She is; she is an impudent minx, and the sooner she is brought down to a level with her circumstances, the better for her and the world."

"She has the reputation of being a very kind-hearted person and an excellent neighbor."

"I don't care if she has; she likes to 'lord' it through the village, and for one I won't be ruled by her."

"Really, I do not understand you; she is as amiable and humble as any one need be."

"Amiable and humble indeed! What did she buy that new cloak for except to excite the envy of half the town, and make them think she is somebody?"

"I hope there is no one so silly as to envy her;" and Miss Viney cast a significant glance full into the face of her companion.

"I don't, for one; but I should like to teach her that she is no better than the rest of the world."

"She don't profess to be; she visits the neighborhood; and I'm sure there is no better person in sickness than she is."

"All that may be."

"When you had the erysipelas, you remember she watched with you when no one else would."

"I know it; but is one to be tyrannized over forever because she watched a few nights with me?"

"How strange you talk!"

"Do I? Didn't she buy that cloak on purpose to cut a figure through the town, and make every body feel cheap?"

"No, I am sure she did not; she had no such motive," replied Miss Viney, smartly.

"I don't believe it, there!"

"She is not such a woman as that."

"Yes, she is, just such a woman as that."

"I have seen no one but you who feels bad about it."

"But me! Lor' sake! I wouldn't have you think *I* feel bad about it. She can wear what she's a mind to for all me; only I hope she can afford it — that's all."

"I think she can; she has the reputation of being a pretty careful woman."

"I don't care; but I feel it my duty to warn my husband to look out about his debt. When folks get to be so awful extravagant, there's no knowing what may happen."

"Mr. Burton is doing a very good business, people say."

"Nobody knows any thing about what he is doing. All I know is, that when Squire Smith sold him two cords of wood last week, and carried in the bill, he couldn't pay it. He actually put the squire off till next week. That looks as though they could afford thirty dollar cloaks, don't it?"

With these sage reflections, Mrs. Waxwell turned down the lane that led to her home, leaving Miss Viney to pursue her way and ponder the extravagance of " some folks."

CHAPTER II.

Mrs. Waxwell loved fine clothes quite as much as any other woman of the nineteenth century, and this is saying a great deal; but then her husband was parsimonious, and she was parsimonious; and, though she loved "nice things" very much, she loved money more, which, we take it, amounts to nothing more nor less than meanness.

Mr. Waxwell was a farmer, and well off in the world. The advent of the railroad into his native town had turned things topsy-turvy in general, and "put the devil into the women" in particular, to use Mr. Waxwell's classic language. Time was when they were content to wear a straw bonnet and a calico gown to meeting; but now they had to rig out in silks and satins, with flounces and furbelows, and all sorts of rigging hitched to 'em, for all the world just like a clown in the circus. Such were Mr. Waxwell's views of the social influence of the railroad.

Society began to be a little "select;" folks put on airs, and were so "stuck up" that you couldn't touch them with a ten foot pole.

Farmer Waxwell did not much like this state of things; it cost money on the one hand, and he did not like to be thrown into the shade on the other. He was about the richest man in the place; but ten dollar bonnets and thirty dollar cloaks were abominations that he could not tolerate. Mrs. Waxwell didn't like to be outdone in the matter of dress, and when she bought a new merino cloak the previous season, she had not a doubt but it would be unsurpassed for two seasons at least. When Mrs. Burton came out with the thirty dollar velvet, she found the wind was taken entirely out of her sail, and she was as indignant as the case demanded.

In the rise and progress of the village since the advent of the railroad, two new stores had gone into operation, one of which was conducted by Mr. Burton, an enterprising young man from the metropolis, who had brought a city wife and a great many city notions into the place with him.

As with a great many who go from the city to the country, he was exceedingly annoyed by that disinterested, charitable attention to other people's business which so extensively prevails in many rural districts. He kept his affairs to himself, and this bothered and perplexed the gossips. His wife had a way of attending to her own concerns; she had been brought up where people do not even know their next door neighbors. If she wanted a new dress or a new bonnet, she never deemed it necessary to consult the neighbors in regard to her ability to afford it, or about the style and material.

But, in spite of these peculiarities, she was a popular person in the village. She was amiable and kind to all, a friend and a comforter to the sick, and quite a useful person in the society of the place. She understood matters and things, had a larger experience of the world than those who had seen nothing of it; and the consequence was, that when a party was to be given, a picnic projected, or a ball got up, she was consulted, and her advice followed. She understood all these things, and was happy to explain the " fashion " in regard to them to all who asked her counsel.

Poor Mrs. Waxwell! Her star began to decline when

Mrs. Burton came to the village. She was no longer the leader of the *ton*, and her heart was bursting with envy. Though she had often received the kind offices of the store-keeper's wife, both in sickness and in health, she would willingly have crushed her. That new cloak was the cap-sheaf of the indignities which she fancied had been heaped upon her, and she determined that her unconscious rival should suffer the consequences of her temerity.

Her first demonstration was upon her husband, whom she found no difficulty in convincing that Mr. Burton must be ruined by the extravagance of his wife, and that, unless he immediately collected his debt, he would certainly lose it.

As soon as she had done her washing on Monday, she " made some calls," and embraced the opportunity of commenting freely upon that new cloak. The women told their husbands that Mr. Burton would certainly fail; and before three days had elapsed there was quite a ferment in the place.

Nobody knew any thing about Mr. Burton's affairs; he seemed to be doing a good business, though no one knew of his having any money. He did not even own the house in which he lived; he had no property, apparently, but his stock. The careful old farmers, to whom in the course of trade he had become indebted for produce which he sent to Boston, began to be alarmed by these rumors.

It was in the State of New Hampshire; and at the time of which I write, the "grab law" was in force, and is still, for aught I know.

One morning, as Mr. Burton returned from a journey to a neighboring town, he found his stock attached on the claim of Farmer Waxwell, and all on account of that new cloak which his wife had worn to meeting on the preceding Sunday.

He had not the means to pay the note at that moment, and while he was considering a plan to extricate himself from the dilemma, the news that his goods had been attached spread all over the place. All the creditors were in hot haste to follow the track of Farmer Waxwell; for it was "first come, first served," and in less than two hours a dozen had fastened upon the stock of his store.

This was a tremendous result to follow in the train of a thirty dollar cloak and a gossiping old woman.

CHAPTER III.

"WHAT do you think now, Miss Viney?" asked Mrs. Waxwell, as they met, soon after the storekeeper's disaster had been made public.

"I hope Mr. Burton will be able to pay his debts."

"But he won't — I know he won't."

"Probably, if they had given him any notice of their intention to demand the payment of their claims, he would have been prepared to meet them."

"I guess Mrs. Burton will not feel quite so stuck up after this."

"I hope *you* have done nothing to bring about this sad result."

"But I have; I made my husband sue his note, and when he put on, the others did. Thirty dollar cloak indeed!"

"I am sorry you have done this; you may ruin Mr. Burton by it."

"That's just what I mean to do!" and Mrs. Waxwell's malignant expression betrayed the jealousy she had so long harbored.

"You did? It was very unkind and ungrateful in you to do so," replied Miss Viney, indignantly.

"Humph!"

"Any trader would be likely to come out badly to have all his creditors pounce upon him without giving him a chance to collect his debts."

"I don't believe he has any to collect."

"Even your husband, as well off as he is, might be embarrassed if suddenly called upon to pay his debts;" and Miss Viney looked significantly at her angry companion.

"I doubt it."

"He may have a trial," said the maiden lady, as she moved towards the store.

"What can she mean by that?" thought Mrs. Waxwell.

Miss Viney had some property of her own, and it was all in the hands of Farmer Waxwell, who had, on his own account, invested the greater part of it in railroad stock.

This is what she meant. She would claim the three thousand dollars her husband owed her, and a cold chill passed through her veins as the thought struck her. Farmer Waxwell was rich in houses, lands, and stocks, all of which yielded him a good income; but he had not three thousand dollars in money, and it might cost him some trouble to raise it.

"Don't cry, my dear; I have enough due me in Boston to pay these debts ten times over," said Mr. Burton to his wife, who was much alarmed by the storm which threatened them.

"What will people think?"

"What will they think when I pay them all? The whole amount is not above nine hundred dollars."

Just then Miss Viney entered the house. In a few words, she explained the circumstances which had led to the sudden "strike" among the creditors.

Mrs. Burton, kind soul, shed a flood of tears when she heard how cruel Mrs. Waxwell had been — she whom she had nursed with all the tenderness of a mother when her frightened neighbors fled from the contagious disease.

"Never mind it, my dear. We may expect any thing from a meddler, a gossip, a slanderer," said Mr. Burton. "I must start for Boston in the noon train."

"Allow me, Mr. Burton, to offer you the money to discharge these liabilities. I have three thousand dollars in the hands of Mr. Waxwell."

"You are very kind, and I accept your offer," replied Mr. Burton, "and next week I shall have the means of repaying you. I assure you I am worth at least five thousand dollars."

In proof of his assertion, he showed her various notes, mortgages, and certificates of stock.

"I presume, if the people here knew that I was not a bankrupt, they would not have molested me. In spite of all my amiable neighbor, Mrs. Waxwell, may say, I think I am abundantly able to give my wife a thirty dollar cloak."

"I never doubted it," replied Miss Viney, as she hastened to the village lawyer to put her note in course of collection.

Farmer Waxwell was at dinner when the lawyer, who was a personal friend, called upon him.

"Sorry to trouble you, but I am instructed to collect this note," said he.

"The devil!" exclaimed Farmer Waxwell.

"The ugly hussy!" added Mrs. Waxwell, as she perceived that Miss Viney's prophetic words had been burdened with a meaning.

"I beg your pardon, madam," said the lawyer; "but if I understand it rightly, you have publicly boasted that you brought about all this difficulty."

"I?"

"Yes, madam; that new cloak did the business. You set your husband on, and all the rest followed him; so Miss Viney tells me."

"My gracious!"

"And now she wants the money to assist Mr. Burton out of the difficulty into which you have plunged him."

"That's plain speech, squire," said the farmer.

"But true."

"I can't raise the money."

"Then I must sue."

"Can't we compromise?"

"Burton is worth at least five thousand dollars, and, when he gets a remittance from Boston, will pay all."

"I will dissolve my attachment, and be bound for the payment of the others. Will that do it?"

"Yes, if Miss Viney will consent."

Miss Viney did consent, — she was a kind-hearted lady — and the matter was compromised.

"Now, wife," said Farmer Waxwell, on the following week, as he put the three hundred dollars in his pocket which Burton had paid, minus thirty which he held in his hand, " here's thirty dollars, and I think you'd better go and buy one of them 'ere cloaks. Your foolish envy like to have got me into the cu'sedest scrape I ever got into in my life."

She would not take it; she was too mean to dress well nerself, and too envious to permit others who were able to ao so in peace. But she gathered from the events of our story a healthy experience of the wisdom of that excellent maxim — "MIND YOUR OWN BUSINESS."

"EVERY THING COMFORTABLE."

CHAPTER I.

"You have every thing comfortable, Maria," said Mrs. Belladonna Buttercup, to her sister-in-law, Mrs. Sparrow, at whose house she was making a visit; "every thing *comfortable.*"

The speaker placed a very significant emphasis upon the last word, which, in connection with her peculiar tone of voice, and the half apparent sneer on her lips, was equivalent to saying, "You have all that is absolutely necessary to make your house habitable; you have beds, and chairs, and tables, but your furniture is of the most ordinary description — plain, cheap, and old-fashioned. It would not suit me."

Mrs. Belladonna Buttercup was a New York lady; that is to say, she had formerly been a shop girl in Boston, and, having considerable talent at diplomacy, had captivated the senses of a dry goods clerk on four hundred dollars salary, become Mrs. Buttercup, and moved to New York. She was an ambitious person, and though she had been brought up in a ten footer in an obscure street, she earnestly desired to become what is technically called a "lady." Fashion was her god. To dress well, to live in a fine house, furnished ·

11 *   (125)

à la mode, and to move in fashionable society constituted her highest ideal of human happiness.

Mr. Buttercup entertained similar views. It is true, he was only a poor clerk when he married, — he had married to redeem his wife from the drudgery of her occupation, — and when he went to New York he had a hard struggle to support her, even in a five dollar boarding house. At the end of a year, circumstances so favored him that he was enabled to go into business on his own account. In a small shop, which his former employer stocked for him, taking a mortgage with interest at the rate of twenty per cent. per annum, he rushed boldly into the stream, assured it would bear him to opulence and an influential position in society.

Fortune favored him, and the first year showed a gain of a thousand dollars. The young man was elated, and having lived within his means, he had a considerable surplus on his hands. Taking a larger store and employing two additional clerks, he commenced his second year. He was the biggest man on Broadway ; talked magnificently about his business operations, and innocently magnified his last year's profits to five thousand dollars. Things looked so promising with him that the importers and jobbers gave him all the credit he desired. Mr. Buttercup was perfectly satisfied that he was on the high road to fortune. As Richelieu says in the play, there was no such word as " fail " in his vocabulary.

Of course, a five dollar boarding house could no longer be tolerated, and to Mrs. Buttercup's inexpressible satisfaction, her husband engaged a room in a fashionable establishment "up town." It was only one room, and Mr. B. had contracted to pay twenty dollars a week for it, washing and

"sundries" extra. The ambitious lady went a shopping a
few days after, and contrived to get rid of a hundred dollars,
which the complacent shopkeeper in an impulsive moment
had placed in her hands. Milliners and dressmakers were
in demand for a time, and Mrs. Buttercup's present ambition
was fully satisfied. It is true, she could see in the distance
an establishment of her own, with imported carpets and
mirrors, with a train of liveried servants, a carriage with
the Buttercup arms blazoned on its panels; and a faint
whisper from the admiring crowd, "There goes the elegant Mrs. Buttercup!" reached her ears. The future was
full of glorious visions, full of royal splendors, full of every
thing that the heart of vanity could conceive. But for the
present, she was satisfied.

Things went on swimmingly at the new store, and when
Mrs. Buttercup proposed a tour to the east, her husband
readily assented. Our lady of magnificent aspirations had
considerable difficulty in deciding whether she should propose Saratoga or home for the summer excursion. On the
one hand, Saratoga was fashionable, and she would have
abundant opportunity to make the acquaintance of the ex-
clusives. But on the other hand, if she went home, she
could create a tremendous sensation among her own and her
husband's friends and relatives. She could carry the New
York fashions among them; could astonish them with a
display of her elegant silk, made by Madam Hippolyta Hy-
falutin, from Paris, and her splendid new bonnet from the
celebrated rooms of Madam Hesperiana Blomereaux, also
from Paris. These things would scarcely be noticed by the
fashionables of Saratoga — the absence of them alone would
make a noise there.

And then her husband's glorious prospects in the dry goods line, as well as the immense business he at present transacted — it would be so delightful to hear Tim tell them all about it! How his old father's eyes would stick out when he heard his son talk about a hundred thousand dollars so beautifully and so indifferently; how he would open his mouth with wonder, when Tim should tell him that the firm of Funk, Hunk, and Co. — the most extensive dry goods establishment in New York — had offered him three thousand dollars salary to superintend their retail department, and how indignantly he had rejected the offer. Tim had such a graceful way of telling these things; indeed, she knew that he could make the most out of a very small matter.

They could create a sensation at home, and the prospect of being the " bright particular star " of a circle of admiring and wondering friends enabled her to decide between Saratoga and the east. The preparations were completed, and in due time they reached the " village of Boston," as Tim facetiously termed it.

Father and mother were duly astonished when the magnificent Mr. Buttercup spread himself. The old gentleman's eyes stuck out, and his mouth was all agape with wonder. He " couldn't exactly see how Broadway, if 'twan't more'n a hund'ed foot wide, could hold all the carriages Tim telled on stoppin' afore his door."

· In the course of events, Tim and his accomplished lady called on his sister, Mrs. Sparrow, whose husband was the secretary of an insurance company. Mr. Sparrow lived in · his own house — a small, but neat and convenient structure. It was plainly furnished; but reasonable people said they were prettily situated, while those who knew them best were sure they were contented and happy.

Mrs. Belladonna Buttercup looked over the house, and turned up her nose at it. Tim's mother was with them, and the simple-minded old lady was so indiscreet as to ask her magnificent daughter-in-law how she would like just such an establishment. She should not like it; it would not suit her. When she went to housekeeping, not less than six thousand dollars would furnish her house. At present, she preferred boarding.

"Then you don't like my house, Belladonna?" asked Mrs. Swallow, with the slightest appearance of disappointment on her smiling face.

"Well, I can't say that I do, Maria," replied Mrs. Buttercup, languidly.

"It is as good as any body need have," added Mrs. Buttercup, Senior. "If I ever see Tim as comfortably settled as Charles is, I shall be perfectly satisfied."

"Dear me! Tim wouldn't look at such an establishment."

"He may be glad to yet."

"I am sure I always liked my house very much indeed," said Mrs. Swallow.

"You have every thing comfortable, Maria; every thing *comfortable*."

"It is as good as my husband can afford; and housekeeping is so much preferable to boarding."

"Do you think so? I would not go to housekeeping for all the world."

Mrs. Swallow shook her head.

"But then it depends, of course, upon whether you get a good boarding house," continued Mrs. Buttercup. "We are delightfully situated. Some of the first families in the city

board there. Besides, there is so much society in New York,
I really don't think I could find time to keep house. Why,
there is the Hon. Mr. Flunkey — he is a member of Congress, you know — invited us to go out to his country seat
on the Hudson and spend the summer. Mrs. Flunkey
pressed and insisted, and would not take 'no' for an
answer."

"Did you go?" asked Mrs. Buttercup, Senior.

"Why, no; we couldn't go. Tim's business drove him
so, that the poor fellow couldn't sleep nights. And there
are the Smallheads — they live next door to N. P. Willis,
out to Lazywild ——"

"Idlewild," suggested Mrs. Swallow.

"So it was; well, they would have us come and spend a
month with them. They are very fine folks. General
Smallhead was an aide-de-camp with General Washington
at Braddock's defeat, you remember."

"Indeed! then he must be a very old man," added Mrs.
Swallow.

"About fifty."

"Why, Braddock's defeat occurred a hundred years
ago!"

"O, no; you are mistaken," replied Mrs. Buttercup,
blushing a little. "But no matter; he insisted on a visit.
What could I do with a house?"

"Very true," answered Mrs. Swallow, politely.

"And then Tim has a season ticket at the opera. He
paid two hundred dollars for a choice of seats last season."

"Did he?" said the mother-in-law, with a frown.

"And it is so pleasant when you are away so much to be
rid of the responsibility of keeping house."

Mrs. Swallow did not think so. But Mrs. Buttercup had others in view whom it was her purpose to astonish, and she took her leave soon after.

CHAPTER II.

For the first time in her housekeeping experience, Mrs. Sparrow felt a little discontented, after her sister-in-law had gone. Her pleasant little house looked smaller than ever before; its plain, substantial furniture looked coarse and common. Why couldn't her husband have some of the fine things that other people had? Why couldn't she have a carved rosewood table, antique chairs, a tapestry carpet, and velvet draperies at the windows? Her husband owned the house in which they lived, and had over a thousand dollars in the bank. Mrs. Walbend, in the next house, had all these fine things, and her husband got but a thousand dollars a year, while Mr. Swallow got fifteen hundred.

"Charles," said she, when her husband came home to tea that evening, "I have been thinking of something."

"Have you, indeed! That is rather remarkable," replied Mr. Swallow, with a smile.

"You don't want to know what, I suppose."

"I do! I am 'dying with curiosity,' as the ladies say."

"Well, then, I will tell you; but don't be cross about it."

Mr. Swallow promised not to be cross about it.

"I have been thinking about having some new furniture."

The husband stuffed a tea roll into his mouth. Evidently the subject was not a very inviting one to him.

"I want you to entirely refurnish the house."

Mr. Swallow upset his tea.

"You can afford it, can't you?"

"I think not, my dear."

"Yes, you can, Charles."

"What has got into you, Maria?" asked her husband, very seriously.

"You promised not to be cross."

"I won't be; but I am very much surprised. I thought you were perfectly satisfied with your house and furniture."

"We have every thing comfortable, but ——" Mrs. Swallow paused.

"What more do you want?"

"Our furniture is not in fashion."

"The d—euse it isn't!"

"No; and I want some antique chairs, a carved centre table, a tapestry carpet, and velvet draperies, for the windows ——"

"What else?"

"And a mirror seven feet high to go between the windows."

"Call it twelve, my dear."

"If you could only hear Belladonna tell of the houses in New York. Why, she says the Hon. Mrs. Chopstick has a mirror in her parlor which is twenty feet high by fifteen wide."

"Did she tell you how big the doors of that house were?"

"And the carpet which General Smallhead bought last winter cost nineteen dollars and a half a yard."

"And a half?"

"Yes; they asked twenty, but the general bought so much that they took off half a dollar."

"Our rooms are so small that we should have to pay twenty, then," added Mr. Swallow, with a laugh.

"Other folks live so fine, why can't we?"

"Other folks have money."

"So have you."

"A little; but I mean to keep it in preference to buying this trumpery with it."

"Since Belladonna has been here, I feel quite discontented."

"Belladonna is a silly creature, and I thank my stars that my wife is not like her," replied Mr. Swallow, chucking the pretty little pouting wife under the chin.

"But she knows what the fashions are."

"And that is all she does know."

"She says we have 'every thing comfortable.'"

"Which is very true."

"But we are not in style."

"Pshaw!"

"Won't you buy some more stylish furniture, Charles?"

"No, my dear; I cannot afford it."

"If you could only hear Belladonna talk!"

"Probably she makes things appear full as bright as they are."

"Tim is doing a great business; making thousands and thousands of dollars."

"I *hope* he is."

"Why, Charles! he has taken a great store in Broadway, and keeps, I don't know how many clerks he said — fifty or a hundred."

Mr. Swallow's cough troubled him.

"Maria, you used to be very contented and happy. Don't

let this silly idea get possession of you. Our house is
furnished very well. If I had twenty thousand dollars, I
would not furnish it any better — that is, not to please myself. If Tim can afford to live in better shape than I do,
let him; it will not disturb me. Don't think any thing
more about it."

" I won't, Charles; but I felt so cheap when Belladonna
talked so familiarly of 'all those fine things, and of her acquaintances among the *élite ;* I felt as though I was nobody."

" Wait, my dear, wait a while. Time will show what all
these great pretensions amount to. I hope Tim will do
well; but with such loose ideas of economy as he appears
to have, and, more than all, with such a silly, extravagant
wife, there is much to fear."

Mrs. Swallow was satisfied. The words of her more experienced husband banished the feelings of chagrin and dis-
contentment she had permitted herself to harbor. A careful
reconsideration of Belladonna's extravagant stories convinced
her that some of them, if not made out of " whole cl
were greatly exaggerated, and she came to the co·
that her sister-in-law was no more of a lady in reality
she was herself.

CHAPTER III.

ABOUT six months after the events we have detailed, as
Mr. and Mrs. Swallow were sitting down to breakfast, they
were surprised by the abrupt appearance of Tim and his
wife.

" This is unexpected," said Mr. Swallow.

" Rather sudden," replied Tim, more seriously than he
was wont to speak.

"I am glad to see you.   Breakfast is all ready."

"We have left New York for good," interposed Belladonna, after she had kissed and hugged her sister-in-law
twenty times — an exhibition of affection which she had not
before manifested since she became Mrs. Buttercup.

"Indeed!" exclaimed Charles and Maria together.

"Fact!" said Tim, with a melancholy laugh.

"And I am so glad to get away from there! I always
hated New York!" added Belladonna.

"Why, I thought you liked New York.   Pray, how are
your friends the Smallheads, the Flunkeys, and the Chop-
sticks?"

"I hate them all!"

"Going into business in Boston, Tim?" asked Mr.
Swallow.

"Is it possible you have not heard of it?" said Tim, looking his brother-in-law hard in the face.

"Heard of what?"

"My misfortunes."

"What?"

"Bu'st up."

"I am sorry to hear it."

"Sad, but true;" and Tim essayed a stroke of humor.
"Yes, sir / bu'st up; not a sixpence left — poor as a church
mouse — borrowed the money to come on with."

"Tim makes the best of it, you see," added Belladonna,
with a laugh. "For my part, I was almost glad he failed,
I was so rejoiced to get away from New York.   But, Maria,
how have you been since I saw you?"

"Very well indeed."

"And how is little Charley? the dear little fellow!"

continued Mr. Buttercup, tenderly kissing the little boy, who sat in the high chair at the table, and who had contrived to daub his mouth pretty thoroughly with the molasses on his buckwheat cakes.

" How long since this affair happened ? " asked Mr. Swallow, when the party had seated themselves at the table.

" Three weeks," replied Tim. " Took every thing I had — tried to get a situation — couldn't find one."

" But where were Funks, Hunks, and Co.?   Didn't they want you ? " asked Maria.

Tim looked at her — looked queer.

" No ; they have a man now," replied he.

" What are you going to do ? " inquired Mr. Swallow.

" I happened to meet White in New York, and told him how I was situated — offered me five hundred a year to come on as salesman — accepted his offer."

Maria looked at Belladonna, and thought of furnishing a house at an expense of six thousand dollars.

After breakfast, when Tim and Charles had gone out, Mrs. Buttercup introduced another topic.

" How pleasant it would be if we could board with you ! " said she abruptly.

Mrs. Swallow did not think it would be so pleasant ; but of course she could not say so, and, being too honest to belie her own heart, she remarked that they did not live in very good style.

" Good enough for any body, Maria."

" But if your friends, the Smallheads or the Flunkeys, should happen to visit you —— "

" O, there is no fear of that ; if they did, I should not care."

"But we live so plainly compared with your fashionable boarding houses."

"You live well enough; and your house is so nice and convenient — O, I should be so happy!"

"We have every thing comfortable," added Maria, slyly.

Mrs. Belladonna Buttercup stopped to think. That remark sounded familiar to her ears.

"Very comfortable, and nice, and pretty! I wish Tim had just such a house!"

"You have altered your mind."

"And just such furniture — I should be so happy!"

At dinner time the matter was still further discussed. Though Mr. Swallow liked Tim very well, he did not like his wife; but in consideration of their unfortunate condition, he consented to receive them as boarders.

Mrs. Buttercup never says a word now about an establishment, and Tim has a more serious and respectful way of speaking of a hundred thousand dollars. The Smallheads are never mentioned, and Tim thinks he missed it when he moved into a larger store. Belladonna declares she never heard of such a thing as a mirror twenty feet long by fifteen high, and is quite sure the Smallhead carpet did not cost above three dollars a yard.

Mrs. Swallow is satisfied that fine furniture does not make a happy wife. She regards the New York experience of her brother and his wife as an excellent commentary on the vanity of magnificent pretensions. And though her husband has been elected cashier of the Bay State Bank, with a salary of twenty-five hundred dollars per annum, she is still content with hav'ng "EVERY THING COMFORTABLE."

12 *

FAMILY JARS.

A LESSON FOR WIVES.

CHAPTER I.

" HE's real ugly, there! He treats his wife shamefully!"
exclaimed Mrs. Benson, a pretty little woman, who had been
a wife just eleven months and twelve days.

" Perhaps not, my dear," replied the young husband,
quietly crossing his legs over the top of the fire frame, and
puffing out a long wreath of smoke from his mouth as he
removed the fragrant regalia.

" Perhaps not! Why, haven't I seen it myself? "

" You are not acquainted with all the circumstances."

" Pshaw! A man that can treat his wife so rudely is a
perfect brute ; I don't care what the circumstances are."

" Brown always was a good-hearted fellow, and if he is
changed at all, matrimony has done it."

" Thank you, Charles; you are very complimentary. I
wonder if matrimony has changed you."

" Why, Julia, we have not been married quite a year yet,"
replied the husband, smiling.

" Indeed ! "

" Brown has been married five years," replied Mr. Benson,
with admirable self-possession.

" Then you think *I* have not shown out what I am yet ? "

" Bah ! My dear, you are making quite a personal matter of it. We were speaking of Brown."

" Brown is a brute — a hog ! " said the lady, in a pet.

" What has Brown done ? "

" Done ? Why, good gracious ! he is enough to wear out a woman's patience."

" I dare say, my dear ; but what has he done ? "

" Every thing. He is wearing his poor, patient wife out ; she will die — poor, weak, sensitive thing — under such treatment."

" No doubt of it ; but you do not tell me what he has done."

" I don't mean to say that he beats her."

" No."

" Nor starves her."

" Does he scold at her ? "

" No ; if he would only scold, it would be a relief to her."

" Poor Mrs. Brown ! "

" He is so cold and distant ; I am sure he married her for her money."

" Quite likely ; but how is it with Mrs. Brown ? Is *she* an angel ? "

" I don't know as she is an angel ; but she bears her sorrows *like* an angel. The poor thing had been crying, I know, when I called there this afternoon."

" Did she tell you what the matter was ? "

" Yes ; you know we were children together, and never had any secrets," replied the young wife, with a troubled expression ; for she had some doubts as to the propriety of what she had done.

"Don't meddle with a quarrel between man and wife, Julia," said Mr. Benson, shaking his head.

"I could not bear to see her suffering; so I asked her what the matter was."

"I am sorry you did."

"I could not help it, Charles; I pitied her so, and I was pretty well satisfied as to the cause of her grief."

"And her husband illtreats her?"

"He does not love her. She says he has been two or three days without speaking to her."

"That is bad; but who is to blame?"

"Who is to blame? Why, *he*, of course;" and the pretty little Mrs. Benson looked up in astonishment from the little cap she was embroidering.

"Why '*of course*'?"

"He don't consult her tastes in regard to his dress. If she asks him to bring her home any thing from down town, ten chances to one he forgets it. He don't seem to care for her feelings. The poor thing says she has cried for an hour in his presence, and he has sat like a log, perfectly unmoved — so different from *you*, Charles."

"Perhaps Mrs. Brown is not in every respect like *you*, my dear."

The young wife looked up with a smile of gratified pride. She was yet young and beautiful, and, what was far better than youth and beauty, she was good tempered, kind, and reasonable. Mrs. Brown's case excited all her sympathies, and she proceeded to detail to her husband a list of the poor lady's trials. But, as the reader will be better able to appreciate them by being present during the scene described, we will introduce the injured lady and her unfeeling husband.

CHAPTER II.

MRS. BROWN sat by the fire in the parlor, turning over the pages of the last new novel. Occasionally she sighed, as though the world had used her badly, and she had not the means of paying off the world for its ill treatment.

Mr. Brown kept a dry goods store, and, being a prudent, industrious man, he substituted his own services for those of an extra clerk, which kept him busily occupied from an early hour in the morning till late in the evening.

He had been married five years, and, for some reason unknown beyond the pale of his own home, his matrimonial experience, without being decidedly stormy, was very far from being pleasant and profitable to either party. Brown was a good-hearted fellow, and always looked on the bright side of things. If the world would only move along smoothly, he was perfectly satisfied, and never felt disposed to quarrel with any body.

Mrs. Brown's disposition was not particularly objectionable; she was kindhearted, clever, and amiable, as the world goes; but some how nothing ever went right with her. It seemed as though every body took a malicious pride in tormenting her — Brown in particular. If Brown bought sausages for dinner, she was sure to want mutton, and if mutton, she was sure to want sausages.

Brown could not understand it. Whatever he did was sure to be exactly wrong. But Brown was a philosopher; and, though he sometimes got so disgusted that he held his

tongue for several days, he maintained a very tolerable degree of good nature.

Brown treated himself to a new overcoat. Being reasonably independent in such matters, he had assumed the
responsibility of purchasing the garment without consulting his wife.

Imprudent Brown, thus to expend the sum of eighteen
dollars without consulting Mrs. B.! Reckless Brown, thus
to buy that brown coat, when all the experience of the past
pointed to the appalling consequences! Did you not remember the last time you purchased a pair of pants, that
neither the hue nor the texture suited your amiable partner?
Did you not call to mind the last curtain lecture on this very
topic, when you audaciously ordered the tailor to make you
a coat off that piece? Knew you not that Mrs. B. likes not
black, drab, green, brown, olive, blue, nor any thing of the
fancy order?

But Brown recklessly ordered the coat, and when it was
done, he recklessly put it on. What made the offence a
hundred fold more horrible, he coolly marched, with the coat
on, into the parlor where Mrs. B. sat by the fire, turning
over the pages of the last new novel.

The lady was thunderstruck; but she was not one of your
spitfires, who make a tremendous tempest in your presence
when any thing does not suit them. She was meek, patient,
suffering, under any indignity, even one so pointed and
wicked as in the present case.

The lady looked up from her book, and bestowed a languid smile upon the partner of her joys, and, alas! of her
sorrows too.

Brown smiled in return; he could not do less than smile.

He even looked innocent, as though he had done nothing wrong — as though he had not aimed a blow at the peace of his amiable lady.

" What have you got on, Jonas? " asked she, mildly.

" An overcoat," replied Brown, sententiously.

" A new one?" sighed the lady.

" Just from the tailor's shop," answered Brown, screwing up his courage to meet the onslaught.

"You know I don't like brown, Jonas."

" *I* do," replied Brown, valorously.

"You know I *never* liked brown."

Brown had half a mind to construe the remark into a pun; but he was forbearing, thought no evil, and so kept silence.

" It's a sack too ; you know I *never* liked a sack."

" I always did."

" A surtout would become you much better."

" I like a sack."

" It is a horrid-looking coat," sighed Mrs. Brown.

"Muddle says it is the best looking coat I ever had on."

" Muddle! Of course *he* would say so."

" Temple said so too."

" Temple has no taste."

" I agree with Temple."

" You never *will* wear a coat that suits me."

Brown thought this was strictly true, but, being a prudent man, he held his peace.

" You still persist in letting Muddle make your clothes, though he charges you more than any one else would."

" His prices are reasonable."

" I wish you would let some other tailor make your coat; Muddle's clothes *never* set well."

" Fit me to a T."

" If it had only been black ! "

" But, my dear, you forget that my last coat was black, and you did not like that."

" It suits your figure better than brown."

Just at that moment the door bell rang, and the servant brought in a pair of pants.

" What is that ? " asked the lady.

" Pants."

Mrs. B. eagerly opened the bundle. The garment was black.

" Black pants ! " exclaimed the lady, holding them up before her ; " you *know* I don't like black pants."

" Indeed, my dear, you just now said you did like black."

" Not black *pants ;* you know I never *did* like them ; besides, they won't wear well."

" But, Mrs. B., I do not wish *you* to wear them."

The lady thought this was exceedingly cruel of Mr. Brown; for she, poor woman, had no more idea of " wearing the breeches " than she had of going to Congress.

" They suit me, my dear. *I* never interfere with your taste in regard to bonnets and dresses."

" I wish you would tell me what you like best; I am sure I desire to conform to your taste."

" Don't wish to. I cannot tell what is good taste in fur-belows and flounces any more than a woman can in coats and pants."

" But you might be a little more attentive to my wishes. You used to *once.*"

This was a hard hit, and Mr. Brown was silent.

" You don't seem to care whether I am suited or not now."

Brown still was silent; the story had been repeated so often that he knew precisely what to expect.

Mrs. Brown continued to rehearse her grievances, believing herself the most miserable woman in the world. Finally, the tears gathered in her eyes, and she sobbed bitterly. Brown was a monster; he never tried to please her, even in the slightest things; and the thought that her husband's affections were alienated was perfectly overwhelming.

Brown had picked up the last new novel, which had fallen from Mrs. B.'s lap, and sat turning over the leaves with the most stoical indifference. How could Brown sit and see his beloved wife, the partner of his joys and sorrows, weeping as though her heart would break, and not offer her a word of consolation? Brown was a philosopher.

CHAPTER III.

It was after such a scene as we have described that Mrs. Benson called upon the friend of her early years, and found her in tears. She believed that poor Mrs. Brown was cruelly treated by her hardhearted husband.

Several months elapsed, and the difficulty between Brown and his wife increased. The lady was an habitual grumbler; she grumbled for the sake of grumbling, because it seemed to be a "fixed fact" with her that grumbling was one of the essentials of her existence — one of the luxuries of life.

Though Brown *was* a philosopher, there is a point beyond which even philosophy cannot go to defend its votaries. The lady's unamiable peculiarity grew upon her, and Brown's disgust threatened to produce a fatal rupture.

Several times after the lady had given him a lesson on the duty of consulting a wife's taste, — after she had cried her eyes out with vexation because she could not grumble any more, — her unfeeling spouse had deserted the house, re- maining out till midnight. Some flying rumors were in cir- culation, too, that he had been seen "lingering long at the bowl," and even that he frequented gambling houses.

Then people felt sorry for poor Brown, an honest, hard- working, economical man as he was ; it was a great pity that he should go to destruction.

Mrs. Benson felt keenly for her friend. Brown was a monster; and the injured lady told her she should certainly die if a drunken husband were added to her other miseries. She even wished Mrs. Benson to request her husband to talk to Brown about his vicious propensities.

Mr. Benson had done so. Brown was a little "struck up" at first, but quietly informed the obliging remonstrant that, since home had become a hell to him, he had been obliged to seek comfort in a grog shop, and concluded his cold-blooded remark by suggesting that people had better mind their own business.

Benson thought so too, and fully resolved not to meddle with the matter again. But, although Brown had resisted his well-meaning neighbor's interference, it was not without its effect, and the injured lady had the satisfaction of inform- ing her sympathizing friend that he did much better, that his breath did not smell half so strong of rum, and that he was at home every evening by nine o'clock.

Mrs. Benson was encouraged, and a few days after ac- cepted an invitation to tea at the Browns'.

That day, the reckless, obstinate husband had worn

nome to dinner a new plaid vest — a pattern in fashion at that time.

The lady did not like plaid — she *never* liked plaid; and poor Brown went to the store leaving his wife in tears at his perverse taste. She had exhausted all her rhetoric in grumbling at the offending garment, and her hardhearted husband had maintained his usual indifference to sighs and tears. Brown was disgusted; and, though we heartily approve of husbands pleasing their wives in these matters, some how we cannot find it in our heart to blame him. She always grumbled at him, and, poor fellow, what could he do?

Mrs. Benson did not arrive in season to hear the lady's story about the vest before Brown himself came. He was in high glee, apparently, notwithstanding the recent tempest. The visitor thought him a " very nice man," and she sighed when she thought of his vicious propensities.

Brown was polite, very polite, and the pretty little Mrs. Benson felt no reserve in his presence.

" What a pretty vest you have got on, Mr. Brown!" said she, smiling sweetly upon the horrible husband.

" Do you think so?" exclaimed Brown, rubbing his hands with excitement.

"Certainly, I do; it's a perfect love of a vest. I shall persuade Charles to have one just like it."

" How strange you talk, Julia!" said Mrs. Brown.

" Strange! why?"

"To call *that* vest pretty."

" I'm sure it is."

" It's a perfect fright. My husband has no taste in his dress."

" Why, now, I think he dresses with admirable taste,"

replied Mrs. Benson, surveying the apparel of Brown, who stood like a show image in the middle of the room. "I admire his taste."

"It is not *my* taste," sighed Mrs. Brown.

The pretty little sympathizing woman was seized with a doubt whether Brown was such a monster, after all.

Just then Bridget popped her head in at the door to say that the baker had not sent the tea cakes.

"The tea cakes, Jonas," said Mrs. Brown.

"There! by all that is sweet and pleasant to the taste, I forgot all about them," exclaimed Brown, seizing his hat.

"Just the way always," groaned the suffering wife. "You never will do the little errands I ask you to."

"Why, my dear, I *intended* to do the errand, but I forgot it," pleaded Brown, with abundant good humor.

"You always forget what *I* want you to do."

"But, my love, I did not forget it on purpose."

"It's always the way;" and Mrs. Brown threw herself into a chair with an exhibition of despondency which would have answered very well for the concentrated miseries of a whole lifetime.

"There's no harm done; it is only half past five, and I will have the tea cakes here in ten minutes."

"You might just as well have brought them before."

Brown looked cross, threw down his hat in a pet, and settled himself upon the sofa.

Mrs. Benson was silent with astonishment. Brown rose fifty degrees in her estimation.

"Are you not going to get the tea cakes, Jonas?" asked Mrs. Brown, meekly, after the lapse of a few minutes.

Brown was silent.

"You will not get back in season if you don't go soon."

Brown picked up the evening paper, but said nothing.

"I must go myself then," said the suffering lady, rising from her chair.

Brown knew this was only a part of his wife's tactics; but the pretty little Mrs. Benson, for whose good opinion he entertained some anxiety, was present, and he concluded to go himself.

When he had gone, Mrs. Brown fixed a melancholy gaze upon her visitor.

"Now you have seen just how he behaves," said she, with a deep sigh.

"I have," replied Mrs. Benson, who for the first time perceived that poor Brown was not the greatest sinner in the world.

"And so he wears my life out."

"Perhaps your husband is not wholly to blame," suggested Mrs. Benson.

"Why, Julia!" exclaimed Mrs. Brown, with languid emphasis. "I am sure I bear and suffer every thing. I had nearly cried my eyes out once before to-day."

"Mr. Brown seems disposed to be very good natured."

"Good natured, Julia! Didn't you see how angry he got? He went out without speaking a word."

"But you do not reflect how cruelly you provoked him by needlessly finding fault with him. If I should say half as much to my husband as you said to Mr. Brown, he would turn me out of the house," answered Mrs. Benson, who, as she found herself implicated in the quarrel, was disposed to be very candid.

13 *

"I was not conscious of doing any thing to provoke him."

"You found fault with his vest."

"But such a horrid-looking vest!"

"There you and he differ; you say he never complains of your dress."

"No."

"He respects your tastes, then. You know how bad you feel when any person says any thing disparaging of your clothes; every body does."

"But he always dresses so shamefully out of taste."

"Other people do not think so; but even if he did, you should not find fault with him."

"I don't find fault," sighed Mrs. Brown; "I only mention what I like best."

"And the tea cakes,—you ought not to have said a word."

"Why, he is so careless——"

"All men are of things about the house; but you must consider that their minds are full of business. My husband is just so; but then he has so many things to think of, I wonder that he does not forget *every* little commission I give him."

"But your husband is different from mine. He *tries* to remember."

"Ah, Mary, I see now what has caused the rupture between you and Mr. Brown."

"Then you think *I* am altogether to blame?"

"Perhaps not entirely; but I am satisfied, from what I know of your husband, that, if you cease to find fault with him, he will be all that a husband should be."

Mrs. Brown bit her lip, and was silent. The truth had

forced itself home to her understanding. She was, as we have before remarked, an amiable, goodhearted body; but the fact that she had actually *grumbled* away the peace of her once happy fireside had never before occurred to her. Her eyes were opened, and she saw that even so little a thing as habitual fault finding can alienate the affections of man and wife, and transform home — the temple of love and peace — into a hell. Her resolution was formed, and fortified by all the strength of her nature.

Brown returned with the tea cakes. He was cold, sullen, and reserved; but a smile from his wife — albeit a boon seldom vouchsafed him — restored him to his former equanimity.

"Jonas, did you think to order some more coal to-day? Bridget says there is not enough to get breakfast with," observed Mrs. Brown, as she handed her husband his second cup of tea.

Brown confessed that he had forgotten it, and braced up his nerves to meet the storm.

"Never mind, Jonas; we will contrive to get along with wood."

Brown dropped his knife and fork in wonder, and looked aghast at his wife.

It was no illusion; his wife was as gentle in her thoughts as in her actions. She found no fault; and, for the first time in many months, Brown felt sorry that he had forgotten to execute her commission.

After tea, Mr. Benson came to spend the evening, and it was one of the happiest evenings ever known beneath the roof of the Browns. Nobody but the two ladies could tell why, but, some how, every thing went different from the ordinary course of events in the family circle. Brown was bewildered — didn't know what to make of it that his wife found no fault.

And she never found fault to any immoderate degree again. Peace was restored. Brown went no more to the drinking saloons, never staid out late at night, and never let his wife cry without wiping away her tears.

He never knew what had produced the wonderful change in his wife's temperament, but he always laid it to the visit of the pretty little woman who admired his plaid vest.

We never see a married man enter a drinking shop to spend an evening without thinking that, perhaps, he has been driven from his fireside by a snarling, petulant discontented, fault-finding wife.

LIFE INSURANCE;

OR,

THE POOR MAN'S LEGACY.

CHAPTER I.

" GOT his life insured! Then he will certainly die!" exclaimed Mrs. Jones, the mother of a family of three children,
to her intimate friend Mrs. Brown, also rejoicing in the ma-
ternity of a promising brood of little ones. " For my part,
I would no more let my husband get his life insured than I
would let him cut his head off. He will certainly die."

" That is the lot of all mortals, Mrs. Jones, and I presume
my husband does not consider himself exempt from the common lot," replied Mrs. Brown.

" You know what I mean; he will die before his time
comes."

" His time will have come when he dies."

" How captious you are ! "

" I do not understand you. The good book says that ' no
man knoweth the day nor the hour.' "

" But I never knew any man to get his life insured
without dying very soon after."

" Do you mean to say that getting a life insured is likely
to hasten the end of the assured ? " asked Mrs. Brown, with
a pleasant smile at the superstition of her friend.

"Well, no, not exactly that; only it is a bad sign."

"Pshaw! Do you think your husband's barn is any more likely to be burned down because he has taken the precaution to have it insured?"

"But that is not like getting one's life insured; it really seems to me just like trifling with serious things."

"How absurd!"

"But it does. Only think of attempting to thwart the will of God. Insuring a life!"

"You take the wrong view of it."

"Our minister takes the same view of it," returned Mrs. Jones, with triumphant assurance.

"He does not understand the subject then."

"Our minister don't?"

"I am sure he does not."

Mrs. Jones permitted a sneer to play upon her lips, as she paused in her sewing, and gazed at her friend.

"You don't mean to say that you know more than the Rev. Mr. Schism, a regularly educated minister of the gospel, in good and regular standing?" continued she, scarcely able to restrain her indignation within a reasonable limit.

"I presume the Rev. Mr. Schism has confined his attention mostly to the study of theology, and knows much more about that than he does about the practical affairs of everyday life," rejoined Mrs. Brown, somewhat warmly.

"He says that it is trifling with death to get one's life insured; and I am sure, if my husband got his life insured, I should certainly expect he would die the very next day after he did the sacrilegious thing."

"I think you told me the other day that Mr. Jones had put some money in the Savings Bank."

"Only twenty dollars — all he could spare."

"What did he put it there for?"

"What for? Why, to keep, of course."

"Why does he wish to keep it?"

"What a fool you pretend to be!"

"Pray answer me."

"Against a rainy day."

"Has he no definite purpose in laying up money?"

"To be sure he has. He means to have something for his family, in case he should be taken away."

"But isn't this trifling with serious things? What does your minister say about it?"

"How silly you are!"

"But you are providing against such a calamity as the death of your husband."

"It is not like life insurance."

"Just like it, only less efficient."

"I don't think so."

"Suppose your husband should die this year."

"Don't talk so."

"Nay, Mrs. Jones, it is well to look these things in the face, especially when you have used your influence to prevent your husband from making a provision for you in the event of his death."

"He is opposed to the whole thing himself."

"Only think, if he should die this year, what would become of you and your three children?"

"Well, I suppose we should get along just as a thousand others have done under the same circumstances."

"Think what a struggle you would have!"

"Sufficient unto the day is the evil thereof," replied Mrs. Jones, coldly. "But here is my husband; he can speak for himself."

CHAPTER II.

THE two ladies, with whose conversation we have prefaced our simple story, had been intimate friends for many years. About the same time they had married men in humble circumstances, and taken houses near each other.

Their husbands were journeymen mechanics, honest, industrious, and frugal men, fair specimens of the bone and sinew of New England. Their families had increased in about the same ratio, and though they received good wages, they found it required the most rigid system of domestic economy to enable them to keep along, and save a trifling sum against a "rainy day."

Brown was a thoughtful man, whose domestic and affectional nature was fully developed. He loved his wife and children with a devotion worthy a reasonable being. His happiest hours were spent by the cheerful fireside of home. He was a conscientious parent, and his care for his dependent loved ones reached beyond the day of their present prosperity.

In the future might be clouds and storms. The whirlwind of adversity might burst upon him, and then what would become of his wife — of Charley, and Joey, and Emma?

It was a question with which few would have troubled themselves; but it was a question of momentous importance. It was not borrowing trouble; it was prudent forethought. But Brown was strong in his bone and muscle, and while he had an arm, and there was bread in the land, he could procure it. All he could do was to save a scanty pittance from his wages to meet the hour of trial, if it should ever come.

Death is no respecter of persons. It takes not only those who leave houses, and lands, and money, and stocks behind them, but it snatches the poor man away from his dependent family. It robs the toiling wife and the helpless little ones of the protecting arm which had been bread, raiment, and shelter to them.

Brown hoped to live many years, to bring up his family, and when, by and by, business prospered with him, to be enabled to make a decent provision for them when he should go hence.

Every man hopes thus much; many more than hope — they feel sure of it.

Brown was reasonable. A falling timber, a fever, a thousand calamities, might carry him off before the year expired. And what would become of his family then? What more could his wife do, with three helpless children, than take care of them? He could leave them no legacy. He was a poor man.

The reflection was startling, The fear of death took possession of him — not the fear of passing through the dark valley, for Brown was an honest man, and trembled not in view of judgment and retribution, but the fear of leaving his wife and children to hunger for food, to tremble with cold, to starve for intellectual sustenance. For several weeks he was gloomy and sad, and more than once he questioned the wisdom of his getting married before he had the means to support his family in case of his decease.

While thus depressed in spirits, his eye was attracted by the advertisement of a Life Insurance Company. His coun-

14

tenance brightened up with a smile, as he read the notice.
The remedy was before him, and it seemed worse than folly
not to embrace it.

Before another week had passed away, he had thoroughly
investigated the whole subject, and insured his life in the
sum of three thousand dollars.

Like a true apostle of a good cause, he was not content to
enjoy the blessing alone; and more than once he had called
the attention of his fellow-workmen to the subject. Many
of them had followed his example; many of them were obstinate, and among them Jones was the most obstinate of all.

Brown was always pleased to discuss his favorite topic.
Life insurance had been a boon of happiness to him; it had
dispelled the dark clouds which lowered over the future; it
had done more to calm his mind in relation to that great
change which must come to all than the sermons of a hundred years could have done; and he was eager to confer
these blessings upon others.

Mrs. Brown was quite as enthusiastic as her husband; and
when Jones entered the room where we left the ladies, a
strong hope that she might yet convert him to her faith pervaded her mind.

But Jones was more than usually obstinate.

"It's all a humbug, Mrs. Brown, you may depend upon
it," said he. "These fellows mean to get your money, and
keep it. You never will catch them paying the policies."

Mrs. Brown pointed him to the recorded experience of the
past.

"I put my money in the bank, and feel that it is safe."

"How much can you save in a year?"

"Well, about a hundred dollars, as wages are now."

" Which is just my husband's estimate."

" But he pays nearly as much as that to keep insured."

" Very true. He is insured for three thousand dollars. If he should die to-day — which God forbid ! — his family would realize that sum."

" *Perhaps* they would."

" But, by putting one hundred dollars a year into the bank, even if you got six per cent., compound interest, your money would amount to only about six hundred dollars in five years."

" Call it twenty years — how then ? "

" If you could be sure of living twenty years, perhaps the money would amount to more than the policy. But only think of your family if you should die within one, or even five years ! "

" You are a shrewd one ! " said Jones, evasively.

" In twenty years your children will be able to take care of themselves."

" It's all a humbug, you may depend upon it, Mrs. Brown; got up to support lazy fellows in idleness — nothing more, I candidly believe," replied Jones ; and there the conversation ended, much to the regret of Mrs. Brown that she had been unable to win a convert to the faith.

CHAPTER III.

SOME six months after, while Jones was engaged in raising a house, he fell from the plate to the ground, striking upon a rock in his fall. He was conveyed to his home, and a council of physicians pronounced it a hopeless case. His spine was injured, and there was no possibility of recovery.

He lingered along for a month in the most excruciating agony, and then died. The expenses of his sickness and of the funeral absorbed all his little savings; and when his disconsolate wife, followed by her three fatherless children, returned from the grave of her husband, she realized that she was not only alone in the world, but that she was penniless — literally penniless.

It was a sad thought for the poor woman. Not even a short season of mourning, which her widowed heart craved, could be allowed her. Her children must not starve, and there was no bread in the house.

Her neighbors, suspecting her situation, were kind to her, and sent in provisions in abundance; but instinctively she shrunk from the mortifying alternative of accepting charity.

Poor woman! what could she do? How could she support her fatherless children? She had no wealthy relatives — she was from the house of poverty herself. But she could not live on charity.

The village in which she resided was a large place, and though she was too proud to accept a gift, she was not too proud to solicit work. With her eyes yet red with weeping over her husband's bier, she called upon several wealthy families to ask for their washing.

It was given her, and she began to feel a certain sense of independence again, as she returned with her bundles of clothes to her desolate home.

All she could do was given her; and with a severe struggle, she was able to support herself and children, and refused any overtures of aid which were made her by her neighbors. Mrs. Brown attempted to assist her friend, in a delicate way, but without success. Mrs. Jones toiled on with all her strength and energy, preferring independence to every other consideration.

But it soon became evident to her neighbors that her health was suffering severely from this unremitting toil. Remonstrances were in vain; and ere another six months had rolled away, Mrs. Brown was watching over the dying bed of her friend. Little children, not old enough to understand their lonely condition, were gathered around it to receive the parting kiss of a dying mother.

Poor orphans! God will take care of you, though all the world be cold and cruel! Ye shall not find another mother, but the Father of the fatherless shall watch over and protect you.

She died, and they placed her by the side of her husband, over whose grave the grass had not yet grown. The hard lot of poverty had hurried her into that early grave. The want of a few of those dollars which the gay and heartless thoughtlessly squander by the thousand, had carried her down to that bourn where there is no sorrow, and the weary are at rest.

The orphans were carried to the poorhouse. Life was a desert to them. Home was no more. Love was in the cold grave.

Was Jones right, or was he wrong? Would not that boon of our progressive age, life insurance, have averted some part of this long list of calamities? Would it not have saved a mother's life? Would it not have redeemed those lonely orphans from the degradation and neglect of the poorhouse?

It could not have saved Jones's life, but it could have been a blessing to his family — a blessing that would have reached down to distant generations. It might have saved a home, and more, far more than all beside, a devoted mother, to those fatherless little ones.

Brown, too, has gone to his rest. But his death entailed none of the miseries upon his family, which were the lot of Jones's. His widow is a frugal and industrious woman; but labor is her helpmate — her husband now; she is not the slave of toil. Brown left her the Poor Man's Legacy.

LAST DAY OF GRACE;

OR,

MR. LAWTON'S MOTHER-IN-LAW.

CHAPTER I.

"I can't stand it any longer, Lottie; I won't have her in the house!" exclaimed Samuel Lawton to his wife.

"But what are you going to do about it, Samuel? You surely wouldn't have me turn my own mother into the street."

"No, no — not exactly that; but can't you give her a hint that she has staid long enough?"

"I'm sure I can't, Samuel," replied the young wife, with a sad and troubled look on her pretty face. "I don't see why you should be so prejudiced against her."

"Don't you, my dear? Do you think it is pleasant for me to have one continually telling me I am extravagant, or something of that sort? She told me just now that I could not afford to buy turkeys for our Sunday dinner, when she saw me bring one home."

- "She meant right, Samuel."

"But it is none of her business, Lottie."

"She is older and more experienced in these matters than we are."

"Fudge! Do you believe, Lottie, that I don't know my own business a great deal better than she or any one else can teach me?" and the young husband put on a look of dignity which showed how deeply conscious he was of his own ability.

"I hope you do, Samuel," replied Lottie, who, as can easily be supposed, was sorely perplexed by the difficulties of her unfortunate position.

Poor thing! She was a gentle-hearted, kind, and tender woman, and loved her mother as truly as becomes a married daughter. She was conscious that her mother had her peculiarities, — as who has not? — and it was a source of continued regret to her that her husband could neither understand nor bear with them.

They had been married about a year and a half. Samuel Lawton was a merchant on a small scale. His employer had set him up in business about a year before his marriage, and he had done well; that is, above his expenses he had cleared some eight hundred or a thousand dollars, which was considered a very fair income for a young man.

The young merchant was elated with his success, and, like very many others in his situation, felt that he was an enterprising young man, and a thorough financier. The road to wealth was before him, and already he had formed a very clear idea of being at the head of a large importing house, with clerks and lumpers by the dozen at his command. His fancy also gilded the picture with a very costly mansion on Pemberton Hill, with a carriage and two sleek horses, a footman, and opera, concerts, and great parties to match.

Samuel Lawton formerly belonged to a "debating society," in which the question of "early marriages" had been thoroughly discussed. The chairman had appointed him to sustain the affirmative; and either on account of the skill and eloquence with which he argued the point, or because the members were in favor of matrimony at the earliest possible day, it was decided that early marriages *were* eminently conducive to the morality and happiness of mankind in general.

One of the strongest arguments which our hero could offer in support of his cause was, that matrimony would save the young man from early dissipation. He even went so far in his zeal as to declare that a young man, even if he had not a penny in the world, had better be married than wait till he had the means. I will not trouble the reader with the facts and statistics by which he made it appear that it was cheaper to support man and wife than to support man alone. But the best evidence he could give of his devotion to his philosophy was to get married himself; and accordingly, though he had not the means of furnishing his house, and though he was still deeply in debt for his stock, he took a wife in the person of the youngest and last remaining daughter of a widow lady, possessing a little property in her own right.

Of course the young man had to run in debt for all the appurtenances of housekeeping; but this was nothing; he was doing well. It made no difference how much a man owed, provided he had the means to pay. He was very sanguine of his future success. His profits would be at least a thousand dollars a year; but, reckless fellow, he had no more idea how far a thousand dollars would go than a baby. It seemed to him a very large sum, and he gauged his domestic expenditures on a pretty high scale.

When he married Mrs. Harding's last remaining daughter, the widow was left alone. Lottie said it would be so nice to have her "dear mother" with her, and accordingly Samuel had invited her to make his house her home.

The good lady was in the main a very clever sort of person, who probably talked quite as bad, possibly a little worse, than she meant. She saw that her son-in-law was going too fast, and, in her own way, she made such comments as she deemed it the duty of a faithful mother-in-law to make.

Mr. Lawton did not relish what he deemed her interference. He was very clear in his own way, and to have a woman dictate to him, and croak about the possible result of his lavish expenditure, was intolerable; and when his patience was thoroughly exhausted, he spoke to his wife upon the subject, as we have written.

Truth has been compared to a two-edged sword, though it is generally believed that one edge to the sinner is sufficiently uncomfortable. Samuel Lawton had listened to his mother-in-law's good advice, to her suggestions on the economy of the household, for more than a year, and Mrs. Lawton could not but wonder what it was that made her husband so "touchy" about it just now. He had always turned off the point of her rebuke with a jest; but now he looked sour, and actually wanted to get her mother out of the house.

The fact was, the young merchant had just begun to find out that a thousand dollars a year would not "keep house" like a nabob. Certain notes were about to fall due, and little debts without number had been contracted. The unpleasant truth began to dawn upon him that he was going faster than his means would permit.

In view of the consequences, he could already hear Mrs. Harding's triumphant "I told you so." He had resolved to reduce his expenses, to give over roast turkeys for his Sunday

dinner, and come down to plain, old-fashioned pork and
beans; but the idea of giving in that the odious mother-in-
law was in the right was not to be harbored. He had postponed the contemplated retrenchment till those said certain
notes began to cast ominous shadows in his pathway. It
must be done, and Mrs. Harding's presence became doubly
troublesome.

CHAPTER II.

THE poor, despised mother-in-law was so unfortunate as
to overhear some portion of the conversation which so nearly concerned her; and the consequence was, that in less than
a week after, she left the house, bag and baggage, for the
home of another daughter, who had repeatedly pressed her
to come and live with her.

Mrs. Harding might have been provoked with her son-in-
law, but she prudently held her tongue, and made no mention of the reason for her sudden departure.

Samuel felt quite a relief the very hour she left, and in the
evening, while they were seated in the little parlor, the baby
sleeping in the crib between them, he was so ungenerous
and unkind as to express himself to this effect.

"But, Samuel, you can't think how lonesome I shall be;
you are in town all day," said the poor wife.

"Well, perhaps you will be for a few days; but you will
get used to it."

Mrs. Lawton sighed.

"And then," continued Mr. Lawton, "you have the baby
to occupy the time."

Just then there came from the cradle a single rough, ring-

ing cough — that peculiar, metallic-sounding cough which is
like the knell of death to the ear of the loving mother.

"O mercy!" exclaimed Mrs. Lawton, in tremulous tones,
as she sprang to the side of the cradle.

"What's the matter, Lottie?" asked Samuel.

"Didn't you hear that cough?" and the poor mother's
frame trembled, and her teeth chattered with alarm.

"I suppose Sammy has got a little cold."

"It's the croup, Samuel! Do run for the doctor as quick
as you can."

"To-night?"

"O Samuel, he may be dead before morning!" and the
tears coursed freely down the cheek of the anxious mother.

"Nay, Lottie, you are nervous."

"I know it; but do go for the doctor."

"I will go if there is any need of it; but, really, I do not
see that there is;" and Samuel bent over the cradle to discover what had so alarmed his wife.

But the child still slept, and apparently breathed as freely
as ever.

"Nay, Samuel, go; you know what the croup is."

"Certainly, I will go if you wish;" and the young husband put on his overcoat and left the house.

The residence of the young merchant was in D——, a
town adjoining Boston, and the physician's house was full
half a mile distant. He could hardly restrain a smile at the
idea of going for a doctor when the baby had only coughed
once.

Dr. F—— was fortunately at home, and the two proceeded on their return together. The physician considered
the case much more serious than the inexperienced father had
deemed it.

On their arrival, they found the child awake. The little patient was breathing laboriously, and occasionally that brazen cough rang from his throat.

"Croup!" said the doctor, the moment he entered the room.

"O doctor, do you think he will die?" exclaimed the agonized mother.

"No, no, no!" replied Dr. F——, confidently.

The physician was a good-natured, good-hearted German, who was thoroughly master of his profession. He had been eminently successful in his practice, especially with children, and his words were like oil upon the troubled waters to the anxious mother.

"I am so frightened, doctor!"

"There is nothing to fear; we have the case in season, and there is no danger. Suppose you wait till to-morrow morning before you call me? I shrug my shoulders, and tell you the child must die."

"O Samuel!" exclaimed Lottie, looking at her husband.

Mr. Lawton was appalled by the significant words. His frame shook with terror. The child was his idol. He knew nothing of the symptoms of the insidious and terrible disease that menaced the life of his darling little one; he was nervous and uneasy. Death seemed to cast a broad shadow upon his home.

The doctor gave the child a little white powder, and placed some bandages wet in cold water upon its throat and chest. The effect was instantaneous; the child instantly breathed easier. Leaving the necessary medicines, Dr. F—— took his leave, assuring the anxious parents that the little one would be nearly well by morning.

15

But Mr. Lawton was uneasy, and Lottie was uneasy. An undefinable dread had taken possession of their hearts. Samuel was troubled. The child breathed with a sad, groaning sound, which shook every fibre in the nervous system of the father and mother. He was conscious of their inexperience; the child might relapse, and symptoms which they did not understand might appear.

"How I wish mother was here, Samuel!" said poor Lottie, awed by the fearful responsibility that rested upon her.

Mr. Lawton had wished so before, and thought if he once more had her in the house, he would give the world to keep her there — mothers-in-law are so exceedingly useful at times!

Samuel made no reply. Even in his terrible anxiety for the life of his child, pride had not entirely deserted him.

Lottie shed a flood of tears. For the first time in her life, her husband seemed cold and unfeeling, and it was cruel in him not to second her wish in such an hour of trial.

"If he should grow worse, Samuel!" continued the poor wife. "O, I am so fearful!"

"I will go for your mother if you wish," replied Mr. Lawton, the anguish of his wife getting the mastery of his feelings.

"She has got cold; I don't know as she would dare to come out in the night air."

"I will try, at least."

Mr. Lawton left the house. Mrs. Harding's new home was not far off. He succeeded in rousing her, and, in spite of her cold, she was ready in five minutes to accompany him.

His heart smote him as he thought how hard he had been upon her — how he had almost attempted to drive her from his roof; and in his soul he thanked God that she did not know how mean he had been.

Her advice had been good. She had spoken to him for his interest, not for her own ; and if she had not spoken it exactly as he wished, why, it was only because she was human, and had infirmities, like all the rest of mankind.

In the moment of peril and trial, he felt what a blessing it was to have a mother-in-law.

Mrs. Harding soon comforted Lottie. She understood the case, and perceived that the danger was past. Her presence was like that of an angel. It restored the drooping spirits of the devoted parents, and by midnight, worn out with anxiety, they went to sleep by the side of the child, whose slumbers, though troubled, were deep and sound.

The next morning, as Dr. F—— had predicted, Sammy was nearly well, and Mr. Lawton went to his business as usual; but there was trouble brewing around him. He spent nearly all the forenoon in vain attempts to raise the money to meet one of his notes which came due that day. He was unsuccessful, and, worn out and dispirited by his anxiety on the previous night, he gave up in despair, and went home, resolved to let the note be protested.

"You come home early, Samuel," said his wife.

The young merchant made no reply, but threw himself, with a heavy sigh, into a chair.

"Why, what's the matter, Samuel ? "

"I am ruined, Lottie ! " replied he, gloomily. " I must fail. This is the last day of grace, and I have left a note to be protested."

Lottie was appalled by this intelligence. Mrs. Harding, who sat by the fire, holding little Sammy, merely glanced at him. She did not use those awful words, "I knew it would be so."

"Mother, you were right; I have been too fast," said Mr. Lawton, gazing sheepishly at her. "I thought very hard of you for telling me I lived better than I could afford; but you were right; I may as well own it."

"I am sorry for you, Samuel. How much is the note?" said Mrs. Harding, with a gentle look — a look so kind and forgiving that it wrung his soul.

"Eight hundred dollars," replied Lawton.

"Will you take the baby a moment, Lottie?" continued Mrs. Harding, who, giving Sammy into the hands of his mother, went to the secretary, and wrote a check on her bank for the amount.

"Why, mother, you wrong yourself," exclaimed the astonished Lawton, as she handed him the check.

"Take it, Samuel; pay your note, and live and learn," replied she, with a benignant smile.

Lawton took the money, and hastened back to the city to pay his note. His credit was saved, and hope again smiled upon him.

In the course of conversation that evening, Lawton was so far humiliated as to make this remark, —

"Mother, you will come and live with us again, won't you?"

"What! after you have wished me out of the house?" replied Mrs. Harding, with a smile. "I heard your conversation the other day."

"Forgive me, mother."

"Perhaps, Samuel, I am not always just as I ought to be; but we all have our weaknesses. I mean to do right."

"I know you do; I understand you now. Last night and to-day have taught me your value; and if I had heeded your counsel, I need not have been pressed for money to-day. Forgive me, mother."

"Freely, Samuel. I live only to make my children happy."

Mrs. Harding resumed her residence at Lottie's, and from that time to this she has been appreciated. Mr. Lawton learned a lesson. The long proposed retrenchment was executed, and the prospect now is that he will die a rich man, if he don't die too soon.

We were provoked to write this sketch by that contemptible squib from Punch, to the effect that Adam was a happy man because he had no mother-in-law. If Cain or Abel, in their babyhood, had the croup, measles, whooping cough, or any thing of that sort, we warrant he sighed for that squib-ridden, conundrum-defamed commodity — a MOTHER-IN-LAW.

15 *

MONTAGUE AND LADY.

A LESSON FOR HUSBANDS.

CHAPTER I.

"ANOTHER new dress!" exclaimed Mr. Simeon Montague to his wife. "It does not seem to be more than three weeks since you had one."

"Just two months, Simeon."

"And you need another?"

"I should not ask for the money if I did not. And Franky must have a new jacket, and Nellie a new cloak."

Mr. Montague sighed.

"I gave you fifteen dollars only a few weeks ago."

"What is fifteen dollars? Do you think it will clothe me and the children a year?" replied Mrs. Montague indignantly.

"Money comes hard," suggested Mr. Montague.

"I suppose it does; but if you wish me and the children to go half clothed, why, only say so."

"Of course, I wish nothing of the kind; I only want you to be as prudent as possible."

"I intend to be so."

"These are dreadful tight times."

"I should think they were," replied the lady, with a palpable sneer on her lip. "They have been just so, though, ever since we have been married."

"Won't next week do?"

"I engaged a dressmaker for next Friday."

"I don't see how I can spare fifteen dollars to-day," said Mr. Montague, musing, apparently, upon his financial affairs. "I have a note to pay to-day."

"You have had a note to pay every time I have asked you for money since we were married."

"I will try and have it for you to-morrow."

"I wan't to go out shopping to-day; I can't go to-morrow."

"I cannot possibly spare it to-day. Won't ten dollars answer your purpose?"

"Perhaps I can make it do."

"If you can, I wish you would," replied the husband, as he took out his pocket book and handed her that amount.

"I can only get a calico for myself."

"Well, won't that answer?"

"Are you willing to go to church with me with a calico dress on?"

"Certainly, my dear. Why not?"

"I thought you had some pride."

"I have, but no foolish pride."

"A twenty-five dollar coat is hardly good enough for you to wear to church."

"But I don't have one every month."

"You have two every year."

Mr. Montague did not think it was prudent to say any more; and putting on his hat, which he had just been brushing with the most scrupulous care, he surveyed his person before the looking glass. His collar needed a little elevating, his cravat had to be readjusted, and he discovered a speck of dirt on his black coat, which was carefully removed. His lady looked at him with a smile as he stood before the glass.

"Calico dress, indeed!" thought she. "There is not a prouder man walks Washington Street than my husband."

Mr. Montague smoothed down his whiskers, and was leaving the room, when a gentleman wishing to see him was announced.

"Ah, Butler," said he, as the gentleman entered the room.

"I called at your store yesterday, but did not find you," said Butler, handing him a little paper.

"Just so," said he, opening it.

Mrs. Montague was impertinent enough to look over his shoulder as he read the paper. It ran as follows : —

"Mr. Simeon Montague

                    To Apollo Club Rooms, Dr.

To your Quarterly Assessment,	$25,00
" 1 Basket Heidsick Champagne,	16,00
" 100 Concha Cigars,	4,00
	$45,00

                Received Payment,

                        B. BUTLER, Steward."

"Just so," repeated Mr. Montague, throwing the bill on the table, and taking out his pocket book. Sorry to trouble you ; meant to have paid it last night."

"No trouble at all," replied Butler.

" Forty-five, is it ? " continued Montague, as he counted out the money.

" Forty-five."

The steward of the "Apollo Club Rooms " put the money in his pocket, and bade his liberal patron good morning.

" It was too bad to make him call twice for that money, wasn't it, Simeon ? " asked Mrs. Montague, when the steward had gone.

" Of course I was sorry to give him any unnecessary trouble," replied Mr. Montague.

" I thought you had a note to pay to-day ? "

" So I have."

" But can't you spare me the other five dollars for which I asked you ? "

" Can't, possibly."

" I think your family ought to receive as much considera-tion as the Club House, at least."

" I must go to the store, my dear ; I am in a great hurry."

" Sixteen dollars for champagne," said the wife, reading from the bill, which she had picked up from the table. " I only asked for fifteen."

" You would not have me niggardly at the Club Rooms, would you ? "

" I would not have you go there at all. I suppose it is nothing to be niggardly in your family ? "

" Am I niggardly ? " asked Mr. Montague, rather sternly. The lady was silent.

" One would think that I was made of money, by the way you ask me for it," continued Mr. Montague.

" One would think you were, to see you paying forty-five dollars a quarter at the Club House," replied Mrs. Montague, meekly. " A married man too."

" I wasn't born to be tied to a woman's apron string," added Mr. Montague, rushing from the house.

The lady looked at the door which had just closed upon him. Her heart was sad, and 'she burst into tears.

CHAPTER II.

MR. SIMEON MONTAGUE thought the money he bestowed upon his family was as good as wasted. He was not a domestic man. He had married his wife, with a reasonable show of affection, because her father was rich, and she was an only daughter. Of course, he would not even confess to his own heart that he was so selfish and cruel as to marry for sordid motives — that he had prostituted the holy altar of Hymen by sacrificing to Plutus upon it; but it was none the less true because he denied it to himself and every body else.

Mrs. Montague's father at her marriage was only about forty-five years of age; yet his health was so feeble that there was not one chance in ten of his living another year. But the old gentleman had revived, and now, after twelve years had expired, seemed to be completely rejuvenated. He was hale and hearty, and gave the promise of living twenty years more. Of course the sordid son-in-law was disappointed. He had thrown himself into the sea of matrimony with an unworthy motive, and if he had been drowned there it would have served him just right.

Poor Mrs. Montague! her bright hopes were all wrecked. Instead of the world of affection she had anticipated in the connubial relation, she found nothing but coldness and sordid selfishness. Her husband still frequented the Club House; and when at home, he seemed to have no sympathy with her. His business seemed to engross all his attention, and he had no time to think of his wife, none to devote to his children.

Yet Mr. Montague was not a morose or an ill-natured man. He loved the good opinion of the world, and would have made almost any sacrifice rather than have had an imputation cast upon his domestic character. He paid the most scrupulous attention to all the forms of life, walked to church every Sunday with his wife on his arm, always found the place in the hymn book for her, and never failed abroad to manifest the most lively interest in his family. He always called his wife " my dear," and spoke affectionately to the children in the presence of company.

The eye of affection could penetrate all this mass of conventionalism, and the poor wife, in less than a year after her marriage, realized that she had thrown herself away upon a hollow-hearted man — one who, without loving her, would keep the peace at almost any sacrifice — one who would compel the world to believe that he was the most tender and devoted husband, even while his heart was petrified and cold. His devotion was mere mechanism; it was a kind of habit, acquired by an active desire to secure the good will of all his friends.

Perhaps, even if there had been none to see him, Mr. Montague would not have been harsh; it was not his nature. He was a smooth-tongued, plausible man under all circumstances. He could appear to love when his heart was perfectly indifferent. He could avoid the most palpable of his domestic duties even while he professed the most earnest devotion to the welfare of his family.

Twelve years had in a measure reconciled the disappointed wife to her lot. She was contented with it because her maiden visions of connubial bliss had evaporated, and she knew no other existence than that to which she had been so long accustomed. Her air castles, reared in the sunny years of her girlhood, had long since tumbled to the ground, and left her in a world of reality, cold and repulsive at first, but rendered tolerable by long endurance.

Her husband was sordid and selfish. He never felt a hundred dollars expended in champagne suppers at the Club House; but half that sum given to his wife wrung his soul. Though he was in a good business, lived in good style, and always had money at his command, his brow always darkened when his wife asked him for any sum to be expended upon herself or her children. He was absolutely unwilling to give it, though he could not possibly have endured the mortification of seeing them shabbily dressed.   •

Mr. Montague is not an anomaly among men. There are thousands as sordid and inconsistent as he was — thousands who wish to have their wives and children appear well in the world, and at the same time deny them the means of doing so.

Mrs. Montague was in tears. She was both grieved and provoked at the conduct of her husband. The promptness with which he had paid his Club House bill, while he denied her the trifling sum she had asked, was a sad commentary on his devotion. For more than an hour she thought the matter over, and became fully assured that she was a much-injured wife. Her spirit was roused, and, putting on her bonnet, she left the house to do her shopping.

The calico dress her husband had professed to think was

good enough for her to wear to church was purchased, and before Sunday was made up.

The second bells were ringing for church. Mr. Montague, elegantly dressed, was all ready, and stood before the glass, contemplating his prepossessing appearance.

"Are you ready, Ellen?" said he, calling to his wife, who was up stairs.

"I shall be in a moment. Walk along slowly with Franky, and I will overtake you," replied she.

Mr. Montague took his son by the hand, and walked up the street. He looked like a model head of the family — so benignant and dignified on that Sabbath morning.

His wife did not overtake him till he had got half way to church.

"Why, my dear, what have you got on?" asked Mr. Montague, when, to his horror, he saw her clothed in a common calico dress.

"My new calico," replied she, coolly, as she took his arm.

"Are you mad, Ellen?"

"It was the best I could buy with the money you gave me."

"But you are not going to church in that shape?"

"Why, Simeon, didn't you say you were willing to go to church with me with a calico dress on?"

"Pshaw! Hadn't you sense enough to see that I was jesting?"

"Jesting! If you were, it was the first time I ever knew you to jest in your own house."

"Don't be foolish, Ellen."

"Come; we shall be late, and all the folks in the street are staring at us."

16

" Staring at you. What a ridiculous figure you make in that attire ! Your Irish girl is better dressed than you are."

" I can't help it."

" Pray, go home."

" I am going to church."

" Not with me, Ellen, in that plight."

" Then I leave you," said she, taking Franky by the hand, and continuing her walk.

Mr. Montague was bewildered. It was a very awkward position ; but the natural duplicity of his character came to his aid, and, placing his hand upon his forehead, as though suffering a severe headache, he retraced his steps homeward.

CHAPTER III.

Mr. Montague was greatly incensed at the conduct of his wife ; but an experience of a dozen years had fully convinced her that her husband could not be easily reformed. During that long period, while he was living in plenty, was throwing away hundreds, and she did not know but thousands, on his club, his champagne suppers, and other selfish gratifications, she had found it exceedingly difficult to wring from his hard grasp the money to clothe herself and children. To ask for it was a loathsome task, and nothing but the most urgent necessity could induce her to do so.

Much as her husband had resented her conduct on the occasion mentioned, he did not offer the means of supplying her wants. The lady had become so disgusted with his niggardly conduct that she had fully determined never to ask him for another dollar. Her father was rich, and very indulgent to her, his only child. To him she disclosed her grievances; and though it was repugnant to her sense of delicacy to speak ill of her husband, she gave her father a complete history of her financial experience. The old gentleman was exceedingly indignant, as a matter of course, and stormed like a madman at the sordid character of his son-in-law.

"But don't you say a word to him, pa, nor to any one else," pleaded the daughter.

"I will blow him sky high! He shall never darken my door again!"

"Nay, nay, pa, for my sake, do not mention it."

The old man stopped to think.

"You are right, Nellie; not a word," said he, rubbing his bald head.

"It would sound very bad abroad, pa."

"So it would; but, Nellie, hand me that book, and the pen and ink."

The daughter obeyed, and the old gentleman wrote a hasty note.

"Now ring the bell, Nellie."

Mrs. Montague did as she was requested, and a servant appeared.

"Here, John, take that to No. 10 Court Street," said the old gentleman, as he opened the book and wrote a check for five hundred dollars. "Now, Nellie, spend it as fast as you can, and when that is gone, come and get some more."

Mrs. Montague kissed her fond father, and left him to ruminate upon the astonishing fact which had been revealed to him.

"Not give her any money!" muttered he. "The scoundrel!"

His lips were frequently compressed, and occasionally he rose and strode with hasty step across the room. The arrival of the lawyer for whom he had sent seemed to relieve him.

Mrs. Montague appeared the next Sunday in an elegant brocade silk, a new bonnet, and a most magnificent mantilla. Her husband, who was an importer and jobber of dry goods, could readily perceive that she wore at least two hundred dollars upon her person. He was confounded. She had asked him for no money lately. He was uneasy. What could it mean? Mrs. Montague refused to answer any questions.

Six months passed by, and the lady still remained independent of her husband. She always had money in abundance, but she positively refused to converse upon the subject. Of course he could understand that her father furnished her with funds. He was perplexed to discover the circumstances under which he supplied her. Had his wife told him that she was refused by her husband? Had she been to her father with her grievances? He would not have had such a thing happen for all the world; his reputation, which he valued more highly than his integrity, would be sacrificed. He was sorely troubled.

One day, about this time, when he came home to dinner, he found that his father-in-law had been prostrated by an apoplectic fit, and that his wife had gone to attend him. Before he could finish his dinner, a messenger announced his death.

Mr. Montague was very much grieved, of course. He mourned in bitterness of spirit for more than a month after the funeral, his father-in-law was such a kindhearted, noble old gentleman; he thought there were few men like him in the world.

Every thing went on as usual in the Montague family. Not a word was said about the large property of the deceased. Mr. Montague felt some delicacy in mentioning the subject to his wife, and no one else appeared to know any thing about the business. He wondered that nothing had been said to him about being executor or administrator. Of course he was the only proper person to execute this trust.

He hinted at the matter as broadly as he dared; but his wife refused to take the hint. One morning, however, as he was looking over the paper, he noticed an advertisement concerning the probate of the will; he pointed it out to his wife.

"Then your father made a will?" said he.

"He did."

"I was not aware of it; but then I haven't devoted even a thought to his property.'

Mrs. Montague looked at him.

"Your father was one of the best of men," continued he, seriously.

"He was."

"Did you learn who had been named as executor?"

"My uncle John."

"Ah! a capital selection; your father was an excellent business man."

"And three of his personal friends were appointed trustees."

"Trustees!" exclaimed Mr. Montague, with a violent start.

"Yes; but you have not seen the will?"

"No."

16 *

"I have a copy here," said the wife, taking the document from a drawer.

With a beating heart, Mr. Montague opened the copy, and proceeded to read it.

His cheek blanched and his lip quivered as he read. The property was much greater than he had ever suspected, amounting to over a hundred thousand dollars. It was all secured to his wife, to the entire exclusion of her husband; and the instrument was so adroitly drawn up that he could not even touch the income of the estate without her permission.

He was thunderstruck; his matrimonial hopes were all blasted, and, what added to his chagrin, his own affairs, in the stringency of the time, had become hopelessly embarrassed.

"What does this mean, Ellen?" asked he, in a husky voice.

"You just remarked that my father was an excellent business man; don't you understand it?"

"If I had been a drunkard or a gambler, it would have been plain to me. As it is, it looks like an entire want of confidence in me on the part of your deceased father; not that I care about the property," whined Mr. Montague.

"Of course you don't care for *that*."

"I was not aware before that your father was prejudiced against me. Did he ever mention this matter?"

Mrs. Montague was silent, and the husband pressed her for an answer.

"There was something said."

"What, my dear?"

"When I went to him for money, of course that led to some explanations."

"You went to him for money?" gasped Mr. Montague.

"I could not get it from you."

Mr. Montague used an exceedingly hard word, which I dare not transfer to my page, and rushed out of the house.

In a month he failed, — made a bad failure, — and it took him a year to get out of the difficulty. The assignees had every thing; he could not put his hand upon a single dollar. His domestic affairs somehow got into the street, and nobody would trust him; every body despised him.

But Mrs. Montague was not so sordid as he had been, and when he had received a discharge from his debts, she furnished the means for him to commence business again. The club and champagne suppers are abandoned; matters are reversed. The lady is always "flush," the gentleman generally short; and, poor fellow, he is sometimes so hard pressed as to ask her for a few hundred dollars "to help him out."

TAKING THE NEWSPAPERS.

CHAPTER I.

"Talk to me about your newspapers! I tell you, neigh-bor Parker, they are a consarned humbug!" exclaimed Farmer Cheney.

"That's a great mistake of yours, neighbor. For my part, I would rather live on two meals a day than be with-out a good newspaper."

"Git out! I wonder what the world's a comin' to. There's my gals have teased me to take Harper's Magazine till I hadn't any peace o' my life. But I put my foot right down; you can't humbug me with sich trash;" and Farmer Cheney complacently wiped away the tobacco juice which was streaming down from the corners of his mouth.

"You are in the wrong, neighbor Cheney."

"No, I ain't, nuther. Then Tom wan't satisfied, and nothin' would do but I must take the American Union and the Practical Farmer. But it wan't no use; I wouldn't have the trash in the house, say nothin' o' wastin' money on it."

"Do you ever read the papers?"

"Me! no, not I; I've got a better use for my time."

"But the long winter evenings?"

"Well, we allers have corn to shell."

" Not all winter ? "

" No ; but when I can't find no work to do, I'd a nuff sight rather set in the corner, and go to sleep."

" But your son Reuben takes the papers."

" Yes ; but I never brought him up to do any sich thing. He takes the Union and the Farmer both, and stews his brains over 'em half the time. That ain't the wo'st on't, nuther."

" No evil effects have followed from it, I trust ? "

" Yes, there has ; there's my youngest boy, Tom, read sunthin' or nuther over to Reuben's t'other day about a ' chance for young men,' and nothin'll do but he must go right into it ; he's off to Boston next week. So much for havin' newspapers round."

" But perhaps he may improve the opportunity, and make money by it."

" No sich thing. He's got two hundred dollars, and when that's all gone, he'll be back again ; see if he don't."

" Perhaps not."

" Well, my mind's made up about it ; but between you and I and the side of that gate post, I wouldn't mind givin' Reuben the price of the papers if he only wouldn't take 'em."

" But Reuben has the reputation of being one of the best farmers in town."

" That's all true enough ; but he didn't learn how to farm it from his newspapers, let me tell you. He was brought up in the good old way, when there wan't no books round but the Bible and the almanac."

" You will grant that he does not follow all the old-fashioned methods ? "

" Well, pooty much all ; he's got some notions of his own, though."

"How was it about planting corn in rows, neighbor Cheney?"

"That's one of Reuben's notions, to plant in rows."

"And he got seventy bushels to the acre, you know."

"Yes; but the ashes did the business."

"The ashes, the rows, and the cultivator, between them."

"Well, there ain't no doubt but what that's the best way to raise corn.   At any rate, all the neighbors foller it now."

"It is not the old-fashioned way."

"No; it's Reuben's way."

"Where do you suppose Reuben got it?"

"I don't know; not from your darn newspapers, though."

"But he did."

"Git out!"

"It is a fact."

"Now, neighbor Parker, you don't mean to say that them fellers in Boston, that never saw a cornfield in their life, can tell me how to raise corn," said Farmer Cheney, a little warmly.

"They have correspondents all over the country, and the subscribers have the benefit of their united experience."

"Don't believe a word on't."

But it was no use arguing the matter, and the two farmers separated.   When Farmer Cheney got home, he found a visitor waiting him

CHAPTER II.

"I UNDERSTOOD you had a large quanity of corn for sale," said the stranger.

"Well, I've got consider'ble, but I don't care no great about sellin' it."

"I should like to buy."

"I can spare a couple o' hund'ed bushels for a fair price."

"What do you ask for it?"

"Well, I don't know, how is corn nowadays?"

"Last sales in Boston were sixty-eight to seventy cents."

"Rather low; I meant to git seventy-one for mine," returned Farmer Cheney, who was disposed to be shrewd.

"What will you take for the lot?"

"Seventy-one."

"Say seventy, and we won't stand about trifles."

"Can't do it; seventy-one is my lowest price," replied Farmer Cheney, finding that he had got an available customer.

"Split the difference, and it's a trade," said the stranger, nervously.

"Couldn't do it."

"I'll take it then. Give me a receipt for this cash to bind the bargain."

Farmer Cheney, congratulating himself on the good trade he had made, wrote the receipt after considerable labor, and put the money in his pocket book.

"Know of any one else who has got any corn to sell?"

"My neighbor Parker, I rather guess, has got some."

"You won't say a word that I paid you seventy-one for yours? It might spoil a trade."

"Not a word," replied Farmer Cheney.

Towards night our two farmers happened to meet again.

"Sold your corn to-day, neighbor Parker?" inquired Farmer Cheney.

"Every speck of it," replied Parker.

"Did you? What did you get?"

"Eighty-one."

"How much?"

"Eighty-one."

"You didn't, though, did ye?" exclaimed the man who would not take the newspaper.

"That is just what I got, and I think I could have got eighty-two if I had stuck a little longer."

"You don't, though!"

"The same man bought yours, I believe."

"Yes," replied Farmer Cheney, edging off.

"What did you get — eighty-two?"

"Well, I guess I didn't git quite that."

"O, eighty-one. Well, after all, that is a good price, and ten cents on a bushel more than I had any idea of getting."

"I did not get eighty-one," replied Farmer Cheney, rather crestfallen.

He did not like to deceive his neighbor; he had studied the Bible and the almanac enough to know better than that; but it came "dreadful hard" to own up the truth.

"How much did you get?"

"I dar'sent tell."

"Why not?"

"I've got took in if the feller gave you eighty-one."

"What did you get, though, neighbor — seventy-five?"

"Seventy-one."

"Well, you have been taken in, then; I guess you haven't heard the news."

"No — what?"

"Crops failed in the west."

"How you talk!"

"And the prospect of a war in Europe; so that our breadstuffs will be extensively exported, which run up the price of flour and grain."

"What war?"

"Between Russia and Turkey."

"Turkey! Well, I hope them cu'sed Turks will get licked!" exclaimed Farmer Cheney, whose ideas were somewhat antiquated.

"You differ from the world in general. The sympathies of all civilized nations go with Turkey in this quarrel."

"You don't say so! When I was a boy, the schoolmaster used to teach us to hate the Turks. They are a barbarous race."

"I think, neighbor Cheney, you will confess now that you had better take a paper."

"Confess no sich thing; I wouldn't have one round the house."

"If you had taken the papers, you would have known about this rise in grain."

"Perhaps I should; but Reuben generally tells me about these things."

"It was only in the paper that came to-day; I read it since I saw you this morning. But I should no more think of selling any thing of any consequence without seeing how the Boston markets were than I should think of cutting my own throat."

"Kind of a dog's life to be tied to a newspaper," sneered Farmer Cheney.

"But if you had taken a newspaper, neighbor, and read

17

it, you would have made twenty dollars by it in this one
trade; twenty dollars, neighbor — enough to pay for the
paper ten years."

"Git out! These things look well enough as you book
farmers figger 'em up; but, you see, when you come to the
scratch, they ain't nowhere."

" It looks to me like a plain case."

" Now, 'spose I could make twenty dollars by takin' the
paper; it would do me a darn sight more mischief than
that."

" How ? "

" Why, the newspaper puts the very devil in the gals'
heads. Now, they never use to have their cu'sed picnics
round here till the gals got to readin' on 'em in the papers.
And then the buryin' ground, they couldn't even let that
alone. Some feller put a piece in the paper about Mount
Auburn, Sorrel Hill, Greenbush, and some sich place, and
the fust thing we know the gravestones are all jumbled up in
a heap, gravel is carted in, and posies set out all over it.
Now they call it a ' symmetry,' I b'leve."

" A cemetery, neighbor; but we who read the newspapers
like these things. There is something pleasant in ornament-
ng with flowers the resting-place of our dead."

" It looks to me more like ' sacrelation.' "

" Sacrilege ! O, no ; far from it."

" Well, I think so ; and then we've got to have new
school housen, a new town house, and the roads must all be
' McDonalized.' "

" McAdamized."

" Well, no matter what it is; it all comes of these cu'sed
newspapers. My taxes are twenty dollars a year more than
they used to be."

" And you sell the produce of your farm for five hundred dollars more."

" Well, that's true; but there's no kind of need of makin' the taxes any more, all for newspapers."

" But you must think how much better and wiser your family would be with a newspaper to read."

" By mighty! I should think they would! Only look at Deacon Craig's folks. Them gals cost him a fortin every year in books and new gowns. The newspapers won't do; they must have books, and waste half their time readin' on 'em."

" But it is a very worthy and intelligent family, and the deacon's income, owing to his more enlightened method of conducting business, is at least ten times as great as it used to be, and he can well afford to spend all he does in educating his children."

" No use o' talkin' about it; give me the good old way; and when I'm dead, I ain't at all particular about havin' buttercups and whiteweed growin' on my grave;" and Farmer Cheney went off, " wondering what the world was coming to."

CHAPTER III

About a year after their conversations, Tom Cheney came home to visit his father. The ambitious youth, who had acquired half his education by reading the newspapers, had not written his father concerning his business prospects.

" Why, Tom, what have you been about all this time? " asked the old gentleman, as he surveyed Tom's spruce appearance.

"Making money, father," replied the hopeful son.

" Have you made any, Tom ? "

" A little."

" A little !   Guess you'd better staid at home, and worked on the farm.   You was doin' well here."

" Done pretty well as it is."

" How much you made, Tom ? "

" Five thousand."

" Git out !   You are jokin', Tom."

" True as preaching."

" How did you do it ? "

" Well, I went into that ' chance for young men ; ' but that wan't much ; so I looked into the newspapers for something better."

" Newspapers again," sneered Farmer Cheney.

" The first thing I saw was, that peaches were selling down south for ten cents a bushel, while they brought two dollars here.   You see, the risk of transporting them makes the difference.   Then I saw in the same paper that preserved peaches brought two shilling a pound north ; so I put that and that together, and hatched out a speculation.   I bought the sugar, and sent it down to Delaware, where the peaches were cheap, and went to making preserves there.   In this way I made money."

" You are a shrewd one, Tom."

" All owing to the newspapers, father."

" Git out ! "

" I see by the papers that the Chinese empire has been divided, and the rebels are in a fair way of making China a Christian country.   I have a great notion of going out there to establish a line of stages between Shanghae and Nankin. What do you think about it ? "

" Don't know what to think. I'm done thinkin' ; but,
Tom, when you go to Boston again, just drop in and tell 'em
to send me the American Union and the Practical Farmer
for one year.   Here's the three dollars."

" Bravo ! you are a brick, after all, pa ! "

17 *

"CIGARS FOR TWO;"

OR,

CURING A SMOKER.

CHAPTER I.

"SMOKES, does he? The abominable wretch!" exclaimed Mrs. Volant to her friend, Mrs. Washburn, a young wife who had just gone to housekeeping.

"He smokes, but he is not an abominable wretch — I am sure he is not," replied Mrs. Washburn, a little startled by the hard name applied to her husband, whom she both loved and esteemed.

"Not a wretch?"

"No, I'm sure he is not!"

"Yes, he is; any husband, especially one who has been married only a year, and won't leave off smoking when his wife desires it, must be a wretch."

"No, you overstate the case. He is every thing a husband ought to be — so kind, so devoted, so indulgent. But then, I do wish he would not smoke."

"You must break him of it — the cruel monster."

"Nay, do not call him such hard names; I love him with all my heart, though he does smoke."

"Well, I suppose you do; young wives are apt to be foolish."

" Foolish ! "

" Yes; he sees, I dare say, that you lore him, and so he takes the advantage of you."

" Why, Mrs. Volant, don't you love your husband ? "

" Well, suppose I do ; there is no need of telling him of it. I make him think I don't care any thing about him. Why, I can manage him as easily as I could a kitten."

" I don't like that ; I think there ought to be love and confidence between man and wife."

" Pooh ! "

" You cannot be happy with him."

" I should not be, if I became his slave."

" Not his slave ! "

" Don't you believe it ! When you have been married as long as I have, you will get rid of some of these sentimental notions, which answer very well for the first year or so, but become very inconvenient after that."

" For my part, I always mean to love my husband as much as I do now, even if it is sentimental."

" See if you do ! Husbands must be carefully managed, or they become tyrants. Now, my husband smoked the first year after marriage ; but then he was a little careful about bringing his cigar into the house, for I told him, up and down, I wouldn't have it."

" I should suppose he would have rebelled."

" He did, but not at first. One night, nearly a year after we were married, he brought home a whole bundle of cigars, and put them on the mantel-piece. Taking one, he very coolly lighted it, and proceeded to read the evening paper."

" That's just the way my husband does."

"1 was downright mad at his impudence; but I did not say a word. The next day I bought a monstrous great snuff-box, and filled it full of rappee. In the evening he lighted his cigar as before; but no sooner had he done so, than I seated myself opposite to him, and drawing out my snuff box, I took a generous pinch, snuffing the filthy stuff into my nostrils, at the risk of sneezing my head off."

"How funny!"

"My husband did not think so. He looked at me with astonishment. 'You take snuff?' said he. 'I do; at least, I mean to learn,' I replied. 'It is a filthy habit,' says he. 'No worse than smoking,' says I. We debated the matter for a long time, and at last he gave up the point, and promised to throw away his cigars if I would throw away my snuff. My point was gained, and of course I gave up my snuff."

"And he never smoked any more?" asked Mrs. Washburn, laughing.

"Yes, he began once after; but I took to the snuff again, and he gave it up."

"Are you sure he don't smoke now?".

"If he does, he never lets me see him. My sitting room is not all smoked up as yours is."

"It was a glorious trick!"

"That it was, and I advise you to try it upon Mr. Washburn."

"I! I couldn't take a pinch of snuff any more than I could swallow an elephant."

"Smoke, then. There are some nice little cigars sold at the apothecaries, made on purpose for ladies. They are so mild that they wouldn't make you sick; though, even if they did, you wouldn't mind, so they cure your husband of smoking."

" It seems too bad to play such a trick upon him — he is always so kind, and permits me to do just as I please," said the tender-hearted Mrs. Washburn.

" What else could he do ? "

" It looks kind of mean to me."

" Not a bit."

" I don't know as it would succeed."

" Nonsense ! I am sure it would. He never would let you smoke, for these husbands have an awful horror of any impropriety in their wives."

" Then, he says he has always smoked, and can't leave it off."

" Pshaw ! The old story ! "

" I am almost tempted to try it."

. " I would."

" It seems so unkind, though, that I have hardly the heart to do it."

" You are notional, my dear Mrs. Washburn. When you have been married —— "

The remark was broken off by the abrupt entrance of the "abominable wretch" himself. Mrs. Washburn rose as he entered, and in spite of the abominable odor that his breath must have exhaled, printed a kiss upon his tobacco-stained lips.

The lady " who had been married several years " was disgusted, and after a few words concerning the weather, took her leave.

CHAPTER II.

Mrs. Washburn was a pretty, affectionate, gentle-hearted wife. Her whole existence was bound up in her husband, as well it might be ; for never was husband more devoted to his wife than he was. To our mind she was a model wife ; none of your stormy vixens, that set their hearts upon attaining a point, and will pull the house down upon your head but they *will* attain it.

In her eye, Mr. Washburn had only one fault ; and that was the villanous habit of smoking, which all her eloquence nad been powerless to overcome. She didn't " put her foot down," as her friend, Mrs. Volant, had done ; for — poor, gentle-hearted creature — she couldn't think of provoking a quarrel with him, and had about concluded to make the best of it, and let him smoke in peace.

But there was something so irresistibly funny about Mrs. Volant's plan, that she determined to try it, and, accordingly, on the afternoon of the next day, she sent the Irish girl to the apothecary's shop for a bunch of " Bagdad cigars." Disposing a few of them in her work basket, ready for the momentous occasion, her mind pictured the scene that would ensue when she should light one of them. It was so funny that she laughed out loud at the idea. Wouldn't he be surprised to see her, who had teased him so much to leave off smoking, commence the practice herself! Wouldn't his eyes stick out, when he should see her puffing a cigar at her sewing, as he did when he read the evening paper !

She was so pleased with the plan, that she would have put

it in execution, even if it had been only for the sport it promised her, independently of any good result which might flow from it. Wouldn't he beg her to smoke no more! Wouldn't he be mortified, and wouldn't she win the day, and glory over his defeat! Wouldn't he be glad to promise her that he wouldn't smoke another cigar as long as he lived! She was so delighted that she could hardly contain herself.

Mr. Washburn came home to tea, and, as usual when he entered the house, he gave her a kiss, and a tender greeting. They were seated at the tea table; Mrs. Washburn was so full of mirth, that she came near scalding herself with the hot tea when she poured it out. Her merry, mischievous laugh rang pleasantly on her husband's ear, who, poor fellow, could have had no idea of the terrible ordeal through which he was doomed to pass.

When tea was over, the astral lamp transferred to the lightstand, and Mr. Washburn had stretched himself into a comfortable position in the large easy rocking chair, with his legs lazily reposing in another chair, the everlasting cigar was produced, lighted, and began to diffuse its fragrance through the room.

Mrs. Washburn could hardly control her inclination to burst into a laugh at the mere thought of what she was about to do. Seating herself at the side of the table opposite her husband, she took from the work basket, with an air as grave and solemn as a judge, one of the "Bagdads." Placing the filthy roll between her ruby lips, she glanced at her husband.

"Now, Mr. Smoker," thought she, — it would have spoiled the joke to have said it, — we "will see whether you don't abandon that nasty habit."

Mr. Washburn happened to glance at her; but, contrary to her expectation, he manifested no surprise, and went on reading the Transcript.

"So, so, Mr. Smoker," thought she again, "you think I am joking, do you? I will soon convince you;" and the lady took a taper, and applied a light to the cigar.

But Mrs. Washburn was rather inexperienced in the *modus operandi* of lighting a cigar, and she was unable to make it "go." She lit another taper, and puffed away with all her might; but the Bagdad was as resolute as the great caliph himself. She persevered, till her extraordinary exertions again attracted the attention of Mr. Washburn.

"You are lighting the wrong end, my dear," said he, with the utmost *nonchalance*.

"How provoking he is!" thought Mrs. Washburn. "Why don't he remonstrate?"

"You should bite off the twisted end, and then put it in your mouth," continued the husband, turning to the paper again.

Aided by these directions, the lady took another cigar, which she succeeded in lighting. The first taste of the tobacco smoke was horrible; but she had determined to be a martyr for her husband's sake; and taking her sewing, she continued to puff away as she plied her needle, till a certain nausea compelled her to abandon the experiment for that time. Casting the Bagdad into the grate, she began to wish she had not listened to Mrs. Volant.

"What is the matter, my dear? Wasn't it a good cigar? Try mine; they are Monte Christos of the first quality," and the imperturbable Mr. Washburn offered her a choice from his case.

"No, I thank you, my dear; I will not smoke.any more to-night."

"But what's the matter, Mary? You are as pale as a sheet!"

"I feel a little faint; I shall be better in a moment," and Mrs. Washburn was obliged to leave the room.

Poor woman! she was sick all the evening! But the next day, Mrs. Volant, who had called to learn the success of the experiment, advised her to try again, assuring her it would not make her sick the second time.

CHAPTER III.

Mr. Washburn had a couple of his intimate friends at his house to play a game of whist the next evening, and the devoted wife resolved to try the effect of a smoke in their presence.

When the party were seated, Mr. Washburn passed round his cigar case.

"Won't you smoke, my dear?" asked he, tendering the cigars to his wife.

"I will; but you know, Joseph, that I never smoke *your* cigars; they do not suit my taste."

Whew! that was cool!

Mrs. Washburn lit a Bagdad.

"Is it possible you smoke, Mrs. Washburn?" asked Mr. Barnes, astonished at the singular spectacle of a woman puffing away at a cigar, for all the world, like a loafer in a bar room.

"Occasionally, just to please my husband," replied Mrs.

18

Washburn, after she had blown out a long wreath of blue smoke.

"Yes, Barnes," interposed Mr. Washburn; "it is more sociable, you know, to have company when one smokes. We are generally alone in the evening, and she is so kind as to smoke with me. Ah, Barnes, teach *your* wife to smoke, it is so pleasant to smoke with one's wife."

The lady was thunderstruck. Was it possible that he had no more respect for the proprieties of life than that? She smoke? She had already acquired the reputation of being a smoker, without having produced any of the anticipated good results.

Mrs. Washburn threw the lighted Bagdad into the stove. She had almost cried with vexation.

"Not smoke, my dear?" said her husband.

"I think you can be sociable to-night, if I don't smoke."

"*Do* smoke, my dear; it gives me so much pleasure to see *you* enjoy a good cigar."

"That's too bad, Joseph."

Mr. Washburn laughed outright, and throwing down his cards, explained the event of the preceding evening.

"I will own up; I did it to break him of the habit. I give it up!"

When the gentlemen had taken their leave, Mrs. Washburn explained by whose advice she had adopted the plan.

"Mrs. Volant has the reputation of being a perfect shrew. Her husband is a laughing stock for all State Street. She is a bad adviser."

"How slick you have turned the joke upon me!" said Mrs. Washburn, laughing heartily.

"To tell the truth, I overheard some of your conversation when the plot was laid."

" O, ho! you did ?   No wonder it failed, then."

" I · did ; but, Mary, are you so very much against my smoking ?   I love the weed, but I love you more ; " and Mr. Washburn kissed her tenderly.

" Nay, I will say no more about it.   Perhaps I was selfish."

" Not selfish ; I will leave it off, my dear, for your sake."

" No, no ; I don't wan't you to do so.   If you are so very fond of smoking, I never will say another word about it."

And Mr. Washburn has smoked his cigar in peace ever since.

"OUT OF BUSINESS;"

OR,

THE HISTORY OF A SPLENDID "BUST UP."

CHAPTER I.

"Out of business, are you, Ned? Well, that is bad," said Mr. Joseph Murdock, a stock broker, to his nephew.

"Decidedly bad."

"But why did you leave Green & Smith? That is a good concern."

"Salary was too small."

"Better than you get *now*, at all events," replied the worthy old gentleman, with a look of displeasure.

"Couldn't pay my way on it."

"Not on five hundred dollars!" and 'uncle Joe,' as he was commonly called, held up both hands in astonishment.

"I am in debt at this moment," returned Ned, with a rueful glance at his uncle.

"And likely to be. Of course you don't expect to pay your debts by wandering about the streets."

"I expect to find business again."

"You do not expect to get five hundred dollars the first year, do you?"

"I intend to strike for a thousand."

" Strike! you won't hit it."

" Perhaps I shall."

" Ned, you are going to the deuse as fast as high living and dissipation in general will carry you."

" Why, uncle, I'm sure you don't know me."

" Sit down, Ned; let us talk it over. I want a young man in my office, and perhaps we can make a trade."

" Thousand dollars, uncle Joseph; " and Ned Murdock attempted to look sly.

" Not out of me, Ned."

" Can't live on less."

" Better die then. I want a young man to assist my book-keeper, run of errands —— "

" An errand boy, you mean; " and Ned felt hurt at the slight put upon his dignity.

" An errand boy, then. My clerk intends to go into business himself one of these days, and if you are attentive to business, here is an opportunity to advance yourself; " and uncle Joe looked seriously into the face of his nephew.

" What is the salary ? "

" Four hundred, for the present."

" I should starve on it."

" Live within your means. When I was of your age, I lived on two hundred."

" Times have changed since then."

" What do you pay for board, Ned ? "

" Six dollars a week. I board at a hotel."

" Six dollars a week! Ned, you are crazy; " and uncle Joe's eyes stuck out " like two tallow candles."

" Two of us room together in the attic, so that they board us low."

18 *

"Should think they did — low for them, but high for you. Costs you a hundred for clothes, I suppose, don't it?"

"About that," replied Ned, evasively.

"Do you go to the ' play ' often?"

"Not above once a week, except when there are ' stars ' on."

"Not *above* once a week! Ned, you are an extravagant dog; you will die in the poorhouse!"

"Pshaw! Uncle Joseph, *you* are old-fashioned!"

"If it is old-fashioned to live within one's means, to pay one's debts, and wear an honest face, then — thank God! — I *am* old-fashioned!" replied the worthy old gentleman, with considerable spirit.

"I mean to be honest, and practise all your old-fashioned virtues."

"You can't do it, Ned, on five hundred dollars a year with your habits."

"Can't be honest?"

"No; it is not honest to run up a bill at your tailor's which you have not the ability to pay; it is not honest to get in debt to support extravagant habits."

"You don't mean to say that I am *dis*honest, uncle Joseph?" asked the young man, with a blush on his cheek.

"Well, well, we won't talk about *that*, now. I want a young man, and if you have a mind to lay aside your extravagances, and go into my office determined to stick to your business, I will see to the rest."

"What salary shall I have, uncle Joseph?"

"Four hundred the first year," replied uncle Joseph, firmly.

"But I can't live on that."

" Yes, you can. Leave your hotel, and board in a private family. Quit the theatre and the opera, and pay as you go."

" But my debts ? "

" How much do you owe ? "

" About two hundred and fifty dollars."

Uncle Joe scratched his head, contracted his eyebrows, and looked decidedly stormy.

" Bad business, Ned," said he, after a few moment's consideration. " I could easily get you out of the scrape, provided I saw any hope of amendment on your part. You don't even say that you will reform."

" To be serious, uncle Joseph, I can't see how I can reform. I must *live*, you know."

" And you must live within your means."

At this moment the penny post deposited a letter on the table, by the side of the stock broker, the contents of which perfectly amazed him.

CHAPTER II.

THE letter was from the attorney of Miss Mary Marker, a maiden aunt of Ned Murdock, formerly residing at the west. It contained the intelligence of the spinster's death. The old lady, happening to have a fit of generosity when she made her will, had bequeathed to her graceless nephew the sum of ten thousand dollars.

Here was a godsend, and Ned leaped up six feet in the air with astonishment and delight.

But the worthy stock broker was troubled; for although he was a broker, he was a good Christian, and had the welfare of his dissolute nephew near his heart. There was something about the youth that he liked, notwithstanding he went to the play and boarded at a fashionable hotel.

His only object was the reformation of the young man, whose ruin and premature decay were foreshadowed in his daily habits. His proposition to employ him in his own office was merely a stratagem to obtain a hold upon him.

This legacy seemed to step between him and the accomplishment of his benevolent purpose.

"What are you going to do with this money, Ned?" asked he with a troubled countenance; "I am named as your guardian, you perceive."

"Bah, guardian! I am twenty-one next week, uncle Joseph," replied the young man, unable to conceal the elation the astounding intelligence had produced in his mind.

"True; but this legacy may be the ruin of you, Ned."

"You are absurd, uncle."

"I am sorry your aunt died so soon; I wish she could have been prevailed upon to live till you had come to the years of discretion."

"If I had known she intended to remember me in her will, I should certainly have expressed my desire that she might have lived forever, or some such hyperbole."

"What are you going to do, Ned? It is rather a serious question."

"Time enough to decide it when I get the money."

"Take my advice, Ned; settle yourself down in some quiet position; get another clerkship; don't go into business till you are more experienced in the ways of the world. You had better accept my offer, and take your first lesson in learning to live within your means."

" Be an errand boy on four hundred dollars a year, when I have ten thousand dollars in my possession ? Did they do so in old times?" and Ned bestowed a good-natured sneer upon his quiet old uncle.

" They learned to creep before they walked. If it will make any difference, I will give you the same salary you received at Green & Smith's."

" Couldn't think of it, uncle Joseph. A thousand would not procure my services *now*."

" The stock broker sighed. Ned was as good as lost, in his opinion. There was no hope for him, and much as it troubled him, he saw no method of preventing the catastrophe.

For an hour longer uncle Joe tried to prevail upon his wilful nephew to adopt a system of prudent living, and preserve his capital until a favorable opportunity occurred for investing it.

Ned was resolute. Visions of balls, operas, theatres, fast horses, and a rich wife flitted before his excited imagination. The sum of ten thousand dollars appeared to be inexhaustible. In vain uncle Joe reasoned that its possession was only equivalent to an income of six hundred dollars. Ned was sure of being worth twenty thousand in five years, and fifty in ten. It never occurred to him that fast horses and the opera could not be supported without encroaching upon the principal.

CHAPTER III.

WHILE they were debating the question, Tom Murdock, a cousin of Ned, entered the office.

"Ah, Tom," said Ned, " here we are; I had quite forgotten to inform our good uncle that you too were out of business."

"Is it possible!" exclaimed uncle Joseph. "Both out of business? I hope you have not been foolish, Tom."

"No, uncle, Tom is never foolish — one of your dignified boys — proper, and all that sort of thing," replied Ned.

"My services were no longer required. You know I only supplied the place of another," added Tom.

"You have been there three months."

"Yes."

"On thirty dollars a month!" added Ned, "and saved money at that. Tom will just fit your place, uncle."

"Do you want a-clerk, uncle Joseph?" asked Tom, meekly.

"I thought of having another; but it is very small pay," answered the stock broker, a little nettled; for he had created the want only to save the reputation of Ned.

"I should be very glad to enter your service, even at a small salary. Any thing is better than being out of business."

"Right, Tom, right!" exclaimed the old gentleman. "The salary is four hundred, and you shall have the place."

And Tom took the place, while Ned, instead of adopting his uncle's excellent advice, moved down two flights at the hotel, rode out to Porter's every day, and went to the opera every night.

In due time the legacy reached uncle Joseph, who placed Ned in full possession.

In another month a large gilt sign, bearing the "name and style" of a new firm, (E. Murdock & Co.,) astonished the mercantile world, and Ned was no longer out of business.

The dignity of the new firm — the "Co." was merely a flourish of the artist's pencil to give *éclat* to the thing — demanded that the senior partner should have a wife. Fortunately for the felicitous carrying out of Ned's idea on this subject, things had for several months been progressing towards this event.

Our young merchant had paid his addresses to the daughter of a mercantile man, reputed to be wealthy; and now that he "had come to his possessions," there was no obstacle to an immediate marriage.

A house in a fashionable street was procured; the cage being ready, the bird was caught, and Ned found himself in the full enjoyment of life. He was no niggard, and things went on swimmingly. Dinner parties, and tea parties, and evening parties followed each other in rapid succession.

Money flowed like water. Notes on three, six, and nine months were given, and Ned said the business was bound to prosper.

One half of his legacy only had been invested in his business at the commencement of the operation. Six, nine, and twelve months did the rest. But his housekeeping affairs absorbed the other half in less than six months. His wife was from a rich family, he reasoned, and must be supported in state.

At the end of those six months, when the first of the notes became due, Ned was not a little astonished to find that he had nothing to pay them with. He looked over his books to see where the ten thousand had gone to; it was only dust in the balance when weighed against his business and his family expenditures.

Bad debts and unfortunate speculations stared him in the

face from every page, and Ned began to be a little troubled. A dim consciousness that he had been going too fast crept into his mind. It was a disagreeable reflection, and when he went home to dinner that day, he dodged round a corner to avoid meeting uncle Joe.

In the mean time, Tom had acquitted himself to the entire satisfaction of his uncle. The head clerk had left, and he had been installed in his place. Living within his means, indulging in no fashionable dissipations, the future was bright with hope.

CHAPTER IV.

ONE morning, while Ned was pondering the unsatisfactory state of his affairs, a neighbor brought him the news of the failure of his wife's father.

Ned was horrified, for, it must be confessed, that in his present emergency, he had based some rather extravagant hopes on the fact of having a rich father-in-law.

It was a heavy stroke to his philosophy. The little financial theory based upon his rich wife, which he had matured to meet the approaching emergency, suddenly and violently exploded.

A five hundred dollar note came due that day, and he had been thinking of dropping into his father-in-law's counting room about one o'clock, to see if he had "any thing over."

The thought of applying to uncle Joe occurred to him; but the worthy old gentleman was too blunt by half, and would be likely to tell him some homely truths.

The day wore away with vain devisings of means to extricate himself from his embarrassments. The note was not paid — was protested.

The next day, people, who had long suspected that Ned was travelling too fast, began to see with a clear vision the true state of the case. Before two o'clock, Ned was in chancery!

"How's this, Ned?" asked uncle Joseph, entering the counting room.

"Don't mention it, uncle; don't mention it! Before you say a word, I will own that you were all right, and I was all wrong," replied Ned, groaning in spirit.

"I did not come to reproach you, Ned; far from it. I gave the best advice I was capable of giving; but as you did not deem it advisable to follow it, of course I shall not taunt you in your troubles."

This was kind of uncle Joseph, and it was spoken in a kindly manner, without the slightest appearance of that triumphant "I knew it would be so," which wise old men sometimes assume. It went to Ned's heart, for Ned had a heart, notwithstanding the little foibles of his character.

"Why did you not come to me for assistance, Ned? I always meant well by you."

"My case was a hopeless one; and to tell the truth, uncle Joseph, after what passed between us, I was ashamed to meet you."

"Fie, Ned!" and the old gentleman was highly flattered by his nephew's humility.

"I wish I had accepted your offer, even at a salary of four hundred dollars a year. I should have been a great deal better off now."

19

" Well, well, we will not mind that now. The place is still open."

" Is it ? " asked Ned, eagerly.

" Tom is my head clerk. Of course I could not displace him."

" No, certainly not."

" But as you have a wife, I will make the salary six hundred now."

" Thank you, uncle ; I will gladly accept the place."

Ned did accept it, and though it was a sad fall from his former position, he took his place at the desk in his uncle's office as the assistant of Tom, with the best grace in the world.

It is surprising how misfortunes will humble a man ; how they will make him accept with joy a position at which, in the days of his prosperity, he turned up his nose in disgust.

Mrs. Murdock was, in the main, a sensible person, and made the best of her altered circumstances. Three rooms in a retired street were obtained to supply the place of the fashionable residence in Tremont Street, and the young couple went to housekeeping on a reduced scale.

Ned kept within his means this time. The humiliation of his fall gradually wore away, and he was surprised to find himself and his wife much happier than when they had been surrounded by all the appliances of wealth and luxury.

Ned remained three years with uncle Joseph, who annually increased his salary, thus enabling him to add to the comforts of life, and still keep within his means.

At the end of this period, the old gentleman, finding himself old enough and rich enough to retire, gave up the business to his two nephews, who, we are happy to record, are now doing remarkably well.

MORAL. — When you are out of business, do not be over nice; and when you have a legacy left to you, do not be rash.

"SIX MONTHS AFTER DATE."

CHAPTER I.

"You are of course aware of the object of my repeated visits at your house, Mr. Miller?" stammered George Harrison to the father of his intended.

"O, yes, of course," replied the father, carelessly.

"And you must be favorably disposed towards the matter, or you would not have permitted it to continue as long as it has."

"Well, Mr. Harrison, those are affairs that I don't like to meddle with, though my opinion is, a great deal of judgment ought to be used in relation to them."

"Certainly, sir; they affect the parties for life," replied George, seriously.

"You do not intend to be married at present, do you?"

"Yes, sir; we have been thinking of it; that is, not under a month."

"A month! Pray, Mr. Harrison, what have you got to support a wife with?" asked the careful father, gazing with considerable astonishment into the face of the candidate for matrimony.

"Well, sir, I have not got much now, it is true; but I think I shall be able to pay my way."

"You *think* so, but you may be laboring under a mistake. Young men are apt to be rash."

"I am going into business, as you are aware, next week. I have hired a store, and have no doubt I shall do well."

"I suppose not. Have you the capital wherewith to stock your store?"

"My capital is small, but I have friends."

"Every body has friends. Who are they?"

"There is Mr. Redman, who offers to let me have half my stock on six months."

"And the other half?"

"I can obtain it on the same terms from other parties."

"And you propose to lay in all your stock on six months' credit?"

"Yes, sir."

"Rather a dangerous scheme, young man."

"I think not. I have no doubt that I shall be able to sell goods enough to pay most of the notes; if not, I can easily get them renewed."

"You are confident."

"Perhaps I am vain; but I trust a great deal to my ability as a salesman. Why, Smith, Jones, & Co. offered me a thousand dollars for the next year if I would stay with them."

"You had better accept the offer, young man."

"I think not; if I am worth a thousand dollars to them, I am worth it to myself. No, sir; I mean to have the benefit of my own talents."

"Bah!" exclaimed the prudent Mr. Miller.

"Perhaps I *am* vain."

"You are, Mr. Harrison. You will find that your ability

19 *

in a concern like that of Smith, Jones, & Co. is much more
available than it would be in your own hands."

"We differ in that matter," replied George Harrison, with
some display of wounded dignity. "If you please, we will
turn to the subject to which my present visit relates."

"To be sure, young man, if you wish. I have no desire
to force my advice upon you, though I cannot help thinking
you had better heed the counsel of those who are older and
more experienced than you are."

"I am very willing to hear any advice."

"More willing to hear it than to follow it."

"I wish to be reasonable. If a young man never attempts
to better his condition, it is plain that he never will get
ahead in the world."

"Very true; but let him labor as hard as he may, without
proper discretion, he never will succeed."

"You question my judgment, do you, sir?" asked George,
rather sharply.

"Excuse me, Mr. Harrison, but I do. The relation in
which you stand to my family prompts me to speak very
plain. No man in his senses would stock his store on six
months' credit, and expect to succeed. How can you pay
your notes, coming all together as they do?"

"With your leave, I will take care of that matter," replied George, with dignity.

"Very well," replied Mr. Miller, smiling at the young
man's warmth. "You propose to be married in about a
month?"

"We do."

"Have you got a house?"

"I have looked at one."

"Have you the means of furnishing it?"

"Rowe & Co. have offered to sell it to me on six months."

"Then in six months, Mr. Harrison, I will talk with you about marriage. In the mean time, I must decline all negotiation."

CHAPTER II.

GEORGE HARRISON was a "crack salesman," and save and excepting that he rather over-estimated his talents and business ability, he was a fine fellow.

He did not believe in looking on the dark side of things. His heart was full of hope, and he confidently expected that whatever he put his hand upon would be instantly turned into money.

George was a young man of spirit, and he did not relish the manner in which his prospective father-in-law had treated him.

"He used me like a boy," mumbled George, as he left the counting room of Mr. Miller; "just as though he knew every thing, and I didn't know any thing. But I'll teach him better than that."

Directing his steps to the house of Mr. Miller, he found Hannah, his lady love, arrayed for a walk.

"I have bad news, my dear," said he.

"Bad news! Why, what, George?"

"Let us walk to the Common, and I will tell you all about it."

Seated on one of the stone seats by the "Frog Pond," George narrated the substance of his interview with Mr. Miller.

"But he only postponed the matter for six months, George," said Hannah, relieved by his statement. "Perhaps it would be better to put it off."

"You know, dearest, we intended to be married next month."

"Still, we can wait."

"There is no need of waiting, Hannah."

"Perhaps there is not; but if my father thinks so, hadn't we better humor him?"

"I don't think so."

"Why, what would you do?"

"Be married;" and George told her how romantic it would be to run away to New York, and come home man and wife — how it would surprise their friends.

Hannah's "spirit" was fully equal to that of George; and the moment she began to feel that her "cruel father" was persecuting them, she was ready for any thing, even for an elopement.

The arrangement was made, and George hired the house he had looked at. Rowe & Co. furnished it, and took George's note on six months in payment, with a mortgage for security.

The new store was opened, and things went on "swimmingly." Business was good, and every body said George was making money "hand over fist."

At the appointed time the elopement took place. The newspapers duly chronicled the event, and, for a time, George was a lion. The ladies, eager to behold and converse with a gentleman who had the "spunk" to tear a persecuted daughter from the grasp of a cruel father, and elope with her flocked to his store. The elopement was a decided hit, and George's gains were largely augmented by it.

The happy couple took up their residence in the new house. It was beautifully furnished, and Hannah felt that she was a queen in paradise. To her the day was not long enough to hold all the happiness that crowded upon her.

And her father, too, instead of treating her harshly after the rash step she had taken, came to see her, was as kind to her as though nothing had happened, and never said a single word about the elopement. Her cup of joy was full.

George was a prince. He was coining money ; he snapped his fingers at the notes, and wondered what Mr. Miller said *now !*

Flushed with success, he returned home one night after an unusually good day's sale, and, after kissing his wife, — they were just married, — and playfully chucking her under the chin, he vented his exuberant satisfaction in a rhapsody on the joys of life.

" Happy as princes ! " exclaimed he. " The money pours in as fast as I care to handle it."

" How glad I am ! " responded Hannah, artlessly.

" We have nothing more to wish for, have we, Hannah ? "

" Well, I don't know."

" You don't know ! Why, I thought you were perfectly happy."

" So I am, dear George ; but I was thinking, the other day, how pleasant it would be to have a piano in the house," replied she, with some little diffidence.

" So it would, Hannah ; what a dolt I have been not to think of it ! I have felt all along as though there was something wanting."

" But I hope, George, you will not buy one if you cannot afford to do so."

" Afford to !   Certainly I can ; I shall be a rich man in one year.   You shall have one of Chickering's best to-morrow."

On the following day the piano came.   George paid cash for it from his surplus funds.   But no sooner had the piano come than Hannah began to feel that the rest of their furniture in the parlor did not correspond with it.   George agreed with the proposition, and their parlor furniture was sent to Leonard's forthwith.   A new and expensive set was furnished, and paid for in cash.

Thus things went on for several months.   It took all of George's profits to keep house and buy the new things which were every day discovered to be wanting.

The dull season had come on, and George suddenly found that there was no more business to be done.   He had not even money enough at the end of six months to pay his second quarter's rent, to say nothing of the notes which came due at that time.

CHAPTER III.

THE six months had fully expired, even down to the last day of grace.

Hannah sat at the piano, playing " Home, sweet home," anxiously waiting the return of George.   The hour at which he usually came home had gone by, and she occasionally cast an impatient glance at the clock.

She had observed that for several days he had worn a

troubled air, and had even been so cross as to repulse her when she offered her accustomed caress; but the thought that his business matters were in an embarrassed condition never occurred to her. He had often boasted of his success, and of course she had no reason to dread the calamity which her father had pointed out to her before her marriage.

A violent pull at the door bell started her from the piano. A rough-looking person was ushered into her presence.

"Very sorry, ma'am," said he, with an awkward bow; "but I've come to take possession."

"What do you mean, sir?" exclaimed Hannah, affrighted by the crowd of disagreeable thoughts that rushed to her brain.

"Why, simply, ma'am, that the notes haven't been paid, and Mr. Harrison's creditors have attached the property. This furniture now belongs to Messrs. Rowe & Co."

The deputy sheriff, having placed a keeper over the goods, politely bowed himself out, leaving Hannah a prey to a thousand anxious forebodings.

The arrival of George was an intense relief to her.

"Just as I supposed!" exclaimed he. "My creditors have had their heads together, and every thing has gone by the board at once."

"Pray, what does it all mean, George?" asked Hannah.

"I have failed; my creditors have driven me into an assignment. I am a beggar."

"Why, George, I thought you were doing remarkably well."

"I was; but, with all the business I have done, I doubt if I could ever have met these notes."

"But how much do you owe, George? Can't you sell the piano, and pay it?"

" It would be only a drop in the bucket. To come right to the fact, I suppose my creditors saw that I lived up to my income, and so it was no use for them to be gentle. I must find a situation now as a salesman, and we must give up this house, and board."

" You ought not to have bought that piano ; you know I didn't want you to if you couldn't afford it."

" And a thousand other things ought not to have been bought. If I had saved the money, my creditors would probably have given me an extension on my paying a part of their demands. But it is too late now ; I have been a fool. Your father was right, after all."

" I am afraid he was ; but here he comes."

" Six months after date," said Mr. Miller, entering the room.

" You were right, sir ; I have been a fool," replied George, with due humility.

" Well, the victory is half won when you see the error. But I have not come to reproach you for your folly, George. How much do you owe ? "

George stated the amount.

" Very well," continued Mr. Miller. " I have already seen your creditors, and with my name on your paper, they have agreed to give you an extension."

" Sir ! " exclaimed George, starting back in amazement.

" But you must let Messrs. Rowe & Co. take these useless traps ; your house is furnished well enough for a prince."

" George is fully sensible where the error lies, father ; we are ready to profit by the lesson."

" All right. Young folks *think* that old folks are fools,

and old folks *know* that young ones are.   Well, well; we must live and learn."

" I am *very* grateful to you, sir," began George.

" There, there! that will do.   All I desire is, your prosperity.   When I objected to your marriage, I foresaw the event which has now happened.   You have done remarkably well in your business; but the best business in the world wouldn't pay for a stock of goods in six months, to say nothing about a thousand dollars in furniture and knickknacks."

George went to work again on a better principle.   When he entered a note on his " Bills Payable," it was not until after he had made a close calculation upon the means of meeting it.   He was successful at last, though, like a majority of young men on the same street, he won his way to success through failure and disaster, over the rough road of bitter experience.

A smaller house was procured, and furnished in a neat and plain style, and Hannah is quite as happy as she was during the honeymoon in her more ample establishment, especially as George — who is now never embarrassed by money matters — is always cheerful, contented, and withal a loving and devoted husband; and the prospect now is, that he will be so " *Six Months after Date.*"

20

CHAPTER I.

"I AM so glad you have come, Thomas!" exclaimed Mrs. Butler, a pale, care-worn young wife, as her husband entered the room in which she had prepared the evening meal.

"Why, what is the matter *now*?" returned the husband, laying a wicked emphasis upon the word "now," as though he meant to imply that there always was something the matter.

"Nothing; only I wanted you to bring in a pail of water, for I am *so* tired, that I declare I can hardly keep upon my feet."

"Is that all? I did not know but what the baby had had a fit, or got scalded, or something of that sort."

"Nothing of the kind; I have trouble enough to get along with, without sickness in the family. I feel just as though I should die every night when I get my work done;" and Mrs. Butler sighed, as she placed the smoking tea upon the table, and threw herself into a chair, apparently so exhausted that she could not have stood another moment.

"You must have a girl, Mary; you know I don't want you to work so hard. I have often told you so before," said Mr. Butler.

"A girl, indeed! Can you afford to keep a girl, Thomas?"

(230)

" Certainly, I can. I am earning twelve dollars a week
now, and I am sure our expenses are not above eight. A
dollar and a half a week added to this sum would still leave
me a handsome surplus."

" Just like you, Thomas ; that is one of your calculations."

" Certainly, that is one of *my* calculations," replied Mr.
Butler, a little tartly.

" I suppose you wouldn't reckon any thing for the girl's
board," sneered the wife.

" A mere trifle."

" Every thing is a mere trifle with you."

Thomas stuffed half a hot biscuit into his mouth to help
him keep his temper.

" And then she would waste double her wages," continued
the lady.

" Pshaw ! that is an old woman's bugbear," replied Butler, impatiently.

" Yes ; that's just the way you always talk."

" It is correct talk, though."

" Girls don't waste, I suppose ? "

" I presume they do, many of them ; but you abominably
exaggerate the amount."

" No, I don't ; I say they waste double their wages."

" No such thing."

" Ask any one who has kept help."

" What articles do they waste to such an enormous extent ? "

" Every thing — provisions, groceries ; and they burn up
twice as much fuel as there is any kind of need of."

" Twice as much ? "

" Yes ; *twice* as much."

" Let me see ; " and Thomas pulled out a bit of paper and a pencil, and went to figuring with all his might. " We use three tons of coal in six months. Twice as much would be six tons, which would come to forty-two dollars, or twenty-one dollars waste. That is eighty cents a week."

" Clear waste ! " exclaimed Mrs. Butler, with palpable horror depicted on her countenance.

" Now, allow that she wastes one half the provisions and one half the groceries, which is absurd, and she would just double my bills. They were fifty-two dollars for the last six months, which makes a waste of two dollars per week. Why, Mary, we have only made the waste to be two dollars and eighty cents, even with these figures. Double her wages would be three dollars."

" She would waste enough, as you would find out to your sorrow, if you kept one," added Mrs. Butler, not pleased with the state of her side of the argument.

" You don't believe she *could* waste half the fuel and stores ? "

Mrs. Butler did not believe it, but she did not like to say so.

" Probably, my dear, under your excellent supervision, she could not possibly waste more than fifty cents a week."

" Well, that is twenty-six dollars a year."

" But I can afford to lose that, rather than that you should make a slave of yourself."

" I don't want a girl; it would be more work to look after her than it would be to do the work myself."

" As you please, my dear."

" I don't want your friends to think you have got an extravagant wife."

" Fudge on my friends ! "

" Yes, it is easy enough for *you* to say so."

" And for you, too, if you choose."

" I don't want to spend all we get."

" Nor I, my dear ; but, to be very plain with you, I had much rather do it, than hear you everlastingly complain how hard you have to work."

" Don't I work hard ? "

" I don't know but you do."

" Just think what I have to do."

" Well, I have to work hard, too ; but I am sure it does not make one feel any better to be continually grumbling about it."

" Who's grumbling? Can't a body speak without being accused of grumbling ? " said Mrs. Butler, rather pettishly.

" I only mean to say, that you work twice as hard with your imagination as you do with your hands ; your thoughts make the work hard."

" Yes, it is easy for you to say so," said the wife, wiping away the tears from her wan cheeks.

" When have I come into the house, Mary, for the last six months, and you have not told me a heap of troubles as big as a mountain ? I can't stand it."

" I never thought you *could* be so harsh to *me*. You did not use to speak to me in that way," sobbed Mary, feeling that she was the most cruelly used wife in the world.

" You irritate me with your troubles."

" I can't help my troubles ; I do the best I can to keep your house in order, and take good care of the baby."

" I never found any fault with your management. I am

20 *

abundantly pleased with all you do, save and except your croaking and grumbling."

" What can I do ? "

" Go about your work cheerfully, and with a disposition to make the best of every thing. By a cheerful and contented disposition, you will make even the hardest day of toil a day of satisfaction. You look darkly upon your lot, and that makes it black."

" I can't help my feelings."

" Yes, you can, Mary. At any rate, you ought not to imbitter my existence with your incessant complainings."

" I have tried to make you happy."

" If you have, you have signally failed ; for it has come to that, I almost hate to come into the house, so much do I dread to hear your tale of woe."

" I will try to do better."

" Do, Mary ; home will become a curse to me, instead of the brightest spot upon earth, as it ought to be, if you do not."

The baby cried at this point of the conversation, and Mrs. Butler wiped away her tears, and took the little cherub from the cradle where he had been sleeping, all unconscious of the matrimonial squall which had been blowing around him.

CHAPTER II.

WHEN Mrs. Butler was married, she was a bright, cheerful, and happy maiden. For more than a year she and her devoted husband had not known the meaning of matrimonial strife. It was a new state of existence to her, and while the novelty of the thing lasted, she was as happy as the day was long.

But in the course of events, she was deprived of the pleasure of going abroad much, and the pretty home in which she had spent a year of joy began to rust on her imagination. Not that her husband was less devoted; though he might not have been quite so dreamy and sentimental as he was in the days of their courtship, yet he was all that a reasonable wife could expect. He was indulgent, kind, and sympathized deeply with her in all those matters wherein a young wife needs tenderness and care.

Little Bobby was born; but the little stranger made such a heap of work for the fond mother, that she declared she should die under the infliction. She would not listen to her husband's suggestion to keep a girl. She had a kind of vanity in her composition, which led her to endure rather than subject her husband's purse to such an expenditure. She feared folks would say she was not as "smart" as she wished to be considered, or that Thomas's relations would deem her extravagant and lazy.

She continued to do her work, though each day was a day of misery. Before she got breakfast, dinner, or tea, she sat and moped over it, thinking what a terrible hard job it was for her to perform. She dreaded washing day from about Friday morning; and over the washtub she was as miserable as soapsuds and a rubbing-board could possibly make her.

The reader may imagine that she was lazy; but I do not think so. She lived in a "world of trouble;" she looked upon the dark side of every thing. Of course, there were many hardships she was called upon to endure — as who is not? She was obliged to keep occupied most of the time in the duties of the household and. the care of the baby. Her position was undoubtedly one of trial and vexation, as those who are experienced in these matters will readily understand.

But the principal difficulty was to be found in Mrs. Butler's unhappy disposition. She was not cheerful and contented with her lot. Her morbid imagination magnified the little trials of every-day life into monstrous woes, and she suffered intolerably in her mind, which was communicated to the body. She was the most miserable of women — the most unreasonably miserable.

Of course, her husband, who was of a directly opposite temperament, was rendered miserable also. Mrs. Butler seemed so wedded to her woe, that every effort on his part to alleviate it was promptly repulsed. He had grown disgusted. His wife was always complaining. He never came into the house without being assailed by a relation of her woes. He cursed his stars — blamed himself for ever becoming a husband.

But, then, poor fellow, what could he do? Mary was as gentle and pleasant a maiden before her marriage as one often finds. She had never been placed in a position to try her character. He might have heard her fret over a new dress that did not fit, or something of that sort; but he never dreamed that a tempest could ever blow out of such a little cloud. It was only when she felt the cold touch of life's realities that she showed out exactly what she was.

It was too late now; the mischief had been done. She was his wife; she was the mother of little Bobby. He loved her still, though his affections had been terribly shocked by her thoughtless grumbling.

Mary had promised to do better; but, alas for the vanity
of human promises, they were words written in sand.   The
habit had become deep rooted.   Thomas was in despair.
He had tried by threats and by persuasions to make her
reasonable, but all in vain.   His house was a hell to him.
If she had scolded him, been negligent of her household
duties, a gadder in the street, a gossip — any thing but a
grumbler, he felt that he could have endured it, loved her,
and continued to be happy.

But it was an ever-present leaf of woe her countenance
presented to him, and when home had ceased to be a pleasant place, he gradually absented himself, and the still loving
but incorrigible wife smelt the rum in his breath when he
returned from his evening amusements.   •

One night, about two months after the conversation we
have narrated, as the clock was striking the midnight hour,
he was brought home, helplessly drunk, in the arms of two
watchmen, who had picked him up in the street.

What a sight for a young and loving wife, to behold the
father of her child drunk!   They placed him in bed, and
she spent a sleepless night in weeping over his senseless,
imbruted form.   O, the agony of that bitter time!   Her
husband a drunkard!   she a drunkard's wife!   Earth has
its miseries, but none like those of the inebriate's wife.

Want, shame, the poorhouse, the court, and the prison
rose before her with terrible vividness.   A train of woes, —
real woes, — so long she could not see the end of it, marched
in solemn procession before her.   There was her child in
rags, her husband a homeless, idle, degraded sot.   There
was the gaunt form of Hunger, the glaring eyes of the

demons of crime — there was every thing there, from which the heart of woman would instinctively shrink.

Thomas rose the next morning, and ate his breakfast in silence — the silence which shame seemed to impose upon him. He was about to leave his house for his workshop, when Mary spoke.

"Thomas," said she, in the subdued tones of anguish, while a flood of tears rained down her wan cheek.

He looked at her, as though he had already divined what she meant to say.

"Thomas, you can't think how unhappy I was last night, when you were — when you came home."

"Well, what's the matter now?" answered Thomas, sullenly.

"O, Thomas, last night!"

"Well, what of it?"

Mary was amazed that no appearance of contrition mitigated his flagrant error.

"You don't come home in the evening now."

"No."

"But you will come to-night, Thomas?"

"Perhaps I will."

"Nay, you *will?*"

"What for?"

"Come for my sake, Thomas."

"Your sake! Well, that *is* a good one," replied he, coarsely.

Mary was shocked.

"Last night, you were — were ——" she could say no more.

"Yes, I *was.*"

" You were —— "

" Drunk! Out with it."

" O Thomas! "

" Well? "

" What misery is in store for us! "

" Can't help it."

" Nay, Thomas, promise that you will not —— "

" Get drunk," laughed Thomas.

" Do not again."   .

" Can't promise."

" O God! has it come to this? "

" Fact! "

Mary threw herself into a chair, and wept as though her heart would break. . The sight seemed to move the husband, who was not yet lost in transgression. A tear stole into his eye, and he bent over her and took her hand.

" Mary, I have sinned."

" You will not again? " said she, eagerly.

" But, Mary, is there no fault on your part? "

" My part? "

" My home is hateful to me. Even the presence of that sleeping, innocent child removes not the curse which seems to hang over it."

" Why, Thomas, what do you mean? "

" You know what I mean. Have I not often reasoned with you? "

" O God! " exclaimed Mary, burying her face between her hands, conscious that the misery which menaced her was of her own seeking.

" I never will complain of any thing again as long as I live! " she continued.

"Ah, Mary, I have often heard you say so before."

"Trust me this time, Thomas."

"I will, Mary."

"Come home to-night; you shall find me all that you could wish."

"Bless you, Mary. I trust for your sake, as well as my own, and for the sake of our own dear boy, that you may be true to your resolution."

"I will, Thomas," replied she, with a gathering smile, as her husband kissed her.

"And I promise never again to taste the fatal cup. You snall be the guardian of this my solemn pledge; for in no way can you more effectually secure the keeping of my promise than by observing your own — in short, by making home happy."

Again the husband kissed her, and then went to his work.

CHAPTER III.

A DRUNKARD's wife! This were a real woe. What were all her little vexations compared with it? Mary's resolution was a firm one, and in her earnestness to observe it, she knelt and prayed for strength from above to enable her to be equal to the duty before her.

Last night a terrible fate had menaced her. The lot of a drunkard's wife — the most appalling woe that can overtake a woman — had threatened to be her portion. The sombre cloud had risen, and her destiny was in her own hands.

She knew her husband well enough to be satisfied that his pledge would be held sacred — that, till she drove him from his home by her unamiable peculiarity, he would be true to the words he had spoken.

Grumbling is only a habit. It may even have a root in the natural temperament of the individual; but it is not an incurable disease. Mary felt that happiness here and hereafter depended upon her fidelity to the promise she had made — that a single complaining word would be like a match placed near the magazine — and another word would involve her in hopeless ruin.

But she had sense enough to know, and she strove to feel, that it were useless to avoid the word, while the disposition existed. It were useless to whitewash a sepulchre — it is still "full of dead men's bones." She determined to perform a radical cure. She resolved to *be* contented, and then the hasty word would not be spoken.

She went about her daily duties with the feeling that a mountain had been removed from her heart. She was cheerful — happy — happy to feel that it was in her power to avert the terrible catastrophe which had menaced her — that she could avoid the yawning abyss that was before her.

All her trials and vexations dwindled into trifles compared with the fate which last night had been so vividly presented to her imagination, and the comparison made her happy.

Punctual to his accustomed hour, Thomas came home. He had not drank any thing, and he appeared cheerful and happy. She met him with a smiling face, and never mentioned a word of the difficulties that had beset her. She had even been so far as to draw a pail of water herself, and bring up a hod of coal; but she said nothing about it.

They were happy again; but perhaps it was as much the

21

effect of the contrast as the actual change in the circumstances. Thomas fondled little Bobby on his knees, and
undressed and put him to bed himself. Mary was delighted,
and from her soul she prayed that her own weakness might
not dissolve the blissful picture of domestic happiness their
home at that moment presented.

A year passed by. Thomas was true to his vow, and Mary
to hers. Whenever things went wrong with her, and the
old spirit rose in her heart, her husband had only to say, —
"You absolve me from my oath, Mary?" and she became
gentle and cheerful in an instant.

Those words were a charm. That solemn promise broken,
and again the poorhouse, the penitentiary, the bloated father,
the ragged child, the long procession of woes rose in her
mind, and she was true to herself.

But she really improved her disposition. The habit was
radically cured. The home of Thomas Butler is no more a
"world of trouble;" it is "home, sweet home" — the
abode of the angel of contentment, the dwelling-place of
truth and love, and the most effectual preventive of the
curse of drunkenness.

Our story is not all a story — it is true to the letter. We
beg the complaining wife to ask herself if she is not making
for her husband a path to the drunkard's grave — for herself
and her children a bed of thorns.

"SEND FOR THE DOCTOR."

CHAPTER I.

My excellent old uncle Jesse — peace to his ashes! — used to tell me that every thing depended on the "bringing up;" and a little experience in this world of strange men and things — but a very good world, for all that — has convinced me that he was considerably more than half right.

Some people have learned to depend upon themselves in the hour of peril. The energy, firmness, and decision of their own characters are their sword, shield, and steed when

> " Giant danger threatening stands."

Their fortress is within themselves. They have been taught by their instructors or by their circumstances to rely upon their own strength.

Others are weak, nervous and vacillating in the presence of danger, throwing the burden of their salvation on the shoulders of the first "Good Samaritan" who approaches them. Their tower of strength is the doctor, the minister, the lawyer, or some sympathizing friend. They have never been taught, either by their instructors or their circumstances, to depend upon their own resources, moral, mental, and physical, for guidance and support.

If the house takes fire, one puts it out; but another runs to the church and rings the bell for his neighbors. If Tommy wheezes, papa, who has no confidence in himself, sends for the doctor; while mamma, who has been taught from childhood to think and act for herself, is in favor of giving the little fellow "an onion and a little goose oil."

But extremes are always silly or dangerous, as the case may be.   People laugh at papa, because he is so ridiculously timid; and mamma delays sending for the physician till Tommy is almost dead with the croup.   One lets his house burn down while he is summoning his friends to help him put it out; and another's is destroyed because he attempted to put it out alone when he actually needed the assistance of his neighbors.   After all, it requires considerable judgment to get along in the world.

We have no intention of writing a homily on the proper conduct of men and women in connection with the casualties of life.   Whether or not it be expedient to send for the doctor when the baby sneezes, we leave to the judgment of the parties immediately interested.   We have a story to tell which illustrates both sides of the question; and either disputant in the important controversy is at liberty to appropriate the moral to sustain his or her cherished theory.

Millbrook is a manufacturing village, and the most important person there, at the time of which we write, was Mr. Milton Barrington, who, to use the metaphorical language of the villagers, "run" the principal mill.   Though quite a young man, he had amassed a handsome fortune, and by his enterprise, public spirit, and general character as a person of integrity and fairness, had attained the most influential position in the village.   People looked to him for advice and assistance in their extremity, and no one ever thought of making a motion in town meeting to build a new school

house, lay out a road, or of making any important move-
ment, until he had been consulted. The people were mainly
on his side in politics, religion, and philosophy. Whatever
he did, he was pretty sure to have plenty of imitators.

Mr. Barrington had spent the flower of his manhood in
the pursuit of wealth; and the idea of getting married did
not occur to him till he had reached his thirtieth year. Probably he would not have thought of such a thing then, if a
pretty and otherwise eligible young lady had not at that
time crossed his path, reminding him of his duty in the
premises.

Three years after, we find him in the full enjoyment of all
the blessings of the connubial state, and the father of a pretty
little boy just eighteen months old. Mr. Barrington was
the happiest of fathers, and to use grandma's enthusiastic
expression, " he set his life by that boy."

It was a cold night in December. Mr. Barrington was
reading Mrs. Stowe's Sunny Memories to his wife, while
little Charley lay asleep in his crib beside them.

The clock struck ten, and as the father laid aside the book,
Charley coughed rather hoarsely, and waking up, began to
scream most lustily. Mrs. Barrington took him up and tried
to quiet him; but he obstinately refused to be quieted.

Mr. Barrington was alarmed. Charley was not accustomed
to have such freaks.

" What do you think ails him ? " asked he of his wife.

" He has got a little cold, probably."

" Don't you think I had better send for the doctor ? " continued Mr. Barrington, nervously.

" Not the least need of it."

" But the croup, my dear ? "

21 *

"That cough was nothing like the croup."

Mr. Barrington was comforted by this assurance, and in a little while, Charley got tired of crying, and went to sleep again.

The child was carried up stairs, and they retired. But Mr. Barrington was not wholly satisfied. The croup was so sudden and so fatal that the cough he had heard seemed to haunt his imagination. He could not go to sleep for thinking of it. He trembled at the thought of losing the darling little one. He had passed almost into a confirmed old bachelor before his marriage, and the diseases of children had never received much consideration from him. He had heard people tell how dreadful the croup was, and only a week before the only child of one of his overseers had died with it, after an illness of scarcely twelve hours.

The clock on the village church struck one, and he was still awake. His wife slept soundly. She was better acquainted with the nature of the dreadful disease, and had felt no alarm when the child coughed.

While he was thus thinking of what might possibly happen, Charley coughed again, and jumping up in the bed, began to scream as he had in the evening.

Mrs. Barrington took him in her arms.

"Did you hear him cough?" asked the trembling father.

"I did not. His screams awoke me."

"Don't he breathe hard? Are you sure he has not got the croup?"

"I do not think he has. He seems to breathe freely," replied Mrs. Barrington. "He is a little hoarse, but I do not think it is any thing serious."

"I am afraid it is. Don't you think I had better send for the doctor?"

"There is no occasion to do so."

"I am really alarmed about him."

"Do as you wish; though I think it is only a little cold."

Mr. Barrington was satisfied it was the croup, and the consent of his wife, thus doubtfully given, was all he required. The "man of all work" was called up and despatched for Dr. Broadbeam, with a request that the physician would come with all possible haste.

CHAPTER II.

Mrs. Barrington used all her maternal arts to quiet the little patient. He did not appear to suffer any pain, and his respiration was apparently as free as ever. In a short time, her efforts were successful, and Charley sunk away into a peaceful slumber.

It was half an hour before Dr. Broadbeam arrived. It was possible he had used all convenient despatch in waiting upon his influential patron; but being a man of two hundred pounds, his swiftest movements were necessarily slow.

Dr. Broadbeam had the reputation of being a very skilful physician; but unfortunately he had such a "grouty" way of dealing with his patients and patrons, that his popularity in Millbrook was on the decline. People did not like to be "snapped up" when they were sick; and the only circumstance that enabled Dr. Broadbeam to retain- even a moiety of the practice of the village was the fact that Mr. Barrington still employed him.

At the suggestion of a small portion of the population, who had the hardihood to break away from Mr. Barrington's lead, a young physician of good parts, and with an easy and pleasing address, had been induced to locate himself in the village. Dr. Broadbeam raved like a madman at the advent of the interloper, stigmatized him as a quack, and obstinately refused even to be civil to him. But when a year in the young doctor's professional experience had passed away without sensibly augmenting his practice, he condescended to laugh at him, and call him a fool. The crusty old leech felt that he could have every thing his own way; that his skill and experience were amply sufficient to offset his morose address and sour temper.

To get out of a warm bed in the middle of a cold December night is never agreeable to any body, unless perchance the house be on fire; and young gentlemen who aspire to the honors of the medical craft ought to think of this before they choose the profession.

To Dr. Broadbeam night duty was especially unpleasant. He was rather indolent and luxurious in his habits, and always made it a rule to believe that poor folks could wait till morning before they had the doctor. But when Mr. Barrington summoned him, why, it was quite another affair.

"What's the matter with the child?" growled Dr. Broadbeam, as he entered the apartment.

"I don't know, doctor, but I am very much afraid of the croup," replied Mr. Barrington, handing the physician a chair.

"Humph!"

"The croup prevails to some extent in the village, you are aware," added the nervous father.

"Always does at this season of the year," replied the doctor, bending over the child to listen to his respiration.

"Does he breathe naturally, doctor?" asked Mrs. Barrington, to whom her husband's alarm had to some extent communicated itself.

"Naturally?" sneered the physician. "Nothing under the sun ails the child."

"What made him cry so, doctor?" inquired Mrs. Barrington.

"Cry so, madam? cry so! You gave him too much supper, madam; and I am tumbled out of my bed to see a child that has the stomach ache!" growled the doctor, enraged when he thought of the comfortable bed which he had been so unceremoniously compelled to leave.

"But his cough, doctor?" said Mr. Barrington, controlling his indignation at the rudeness of the physician.

"Mr. Barrington, you are a fool!" exclaimed Dr. Broadbeam, as he violently jammed his hat upon his head. "Do you think I am to leave my bed on a cold night like this whenever your baby sneezes? Humph!"

"You are a physician, are you not?" asked Mr. Barrington.

He was angry; but keeping down his indignation, he put the question with tolerable calmness.

"A physician! Of course I am; but is that any reason why I should be turned out in the dead of the night for nothing at all?" replied the enraged leech.

"You chose your own profession."

"What if I did?"

"What is your charge for a night visit?"

"Five dollars, sir! Five dollars!" answered the doctor, maliciously.

"And you believe that I am able to pay it?"

" I do, or I would not have come."

" That is enough, sir; if I am content to pay five dollars for the assurance of a physician that nothing ails my child, I take it that I am at liberty to do so."

" Humph!"

" When I send for a physician, I consider it a business transaction. He gives me his advice for the money I pay him. If his conduct entitles him to be cherished as a friend — as an angel sent with healing balm for the soul as well as the body," — and Mr. Barrington looked sternly at the doctor, — " I cheerfully accord him his due."

" Well, sir!"

" If I send for my millwright, I do not leave it optional with him to determine whether I need him or not. If he does not choose to come, there are other millwrights in the state."

" Do you compare a physician to a millwright?" sneered the doctor.

" If I send for my millwright to come and tell me whether my water wheel needs repairs, he comes; he examines it; perhaps he decides that nothing is the matter with it, and that I ought to have known that it was perfectly sound. If he should reproach me for sending for him, I should call him no business man. I pay him for his time, though he lift not an axe."

" Humph!"

" It is a great satisfaction to me to know that nothing ails my child. I am able and willing to pay for that assurance."

" Pay! Do you take me for a hireling?" exclaimed the doctor, with a fresh outbreak of anger, as he abruptly turned on his heel and left the chamber.

CHAPTER III.

On the 1st of January, Dr. Broadbeam's bill for professional services, amounting to over two hundred dollars, was presented to Mr. Barrington, and was promptly paid. He was not one of that numerous and highly respectable class of people who make it a point to grumble at doctor's bills.

The manufacturer was a peaceful, prudent man, not disposed to stir up strife in the neighborhood; so he kept silent in regard to his unpleasant interview with the physician. .

About a month after, Mr. Barrington was roused from his slumbers at midnight by the sound of an ominous cough from Charley. But this time it did not awake the little fellow. The fond father was still fearful of the croup; yet the child slept so soundly that his fears subsided, and he was just dropping asleep again when the cough was repeated.

In a few minutes the child awoke, and his respiration began to grow difficult.

"What do you think?" asked he of his wife.

"He is a little croupy; but I do not think there is any occasion to be alarmed. I will give him the 'Hive Sirup,' which I doubt not will immediately relieve him."

Mr. Barrington got up and brought the sirup. A dose was given, and the parents waited with anxiety the effect.

An hour elapsed, and the child was no better.

"Don't you think I had better send for the doctor?" said Mr. Barrington.

"No, I can get along very well."

"But the croup; hasn't he got it?"

"He has a croupy cough, which may lead to croup, if it is not attended to," replied Mrs. Barrington, giving the little sufferer another spoonful of the sirup.

Two hours more passed away, and instead of getting better, the child grew worse every minute. But Mrs. Barrington did not like to send for the doctor. In the family of her father, a physician had rarely ever been called, and she had come to regard the faculty with something like contempt.

"He grows worse," said Mr. Barrington, beginning to lose confidence in the efficacy of his wife's treatment.

"The medicine has not had time to produce its effect yet," replied Mrs. Barrington. "He will begin to grow better soon."

"I think we had better send for the doctor," added the anxious father. "It may be too late in the morning."

"I do not want any more fuss with the doctor. The last time he came, he made me so nervous that it took me a week to get over it."

"We will not have Dr. Broadbeam, then."

"He will be better soon."

"Do not delay it too long."

Another hour elapsed, and still the little sufferer was no better. His breathing was extremely difficult, and the cough was more frequent and hard. The mother's remedy had apparently produced no effect whatever, and she began to be alarmed herself.

"Perhaps you had better send for the doctor," said she.

"Dr. Broadbeam?"

"I don't know."

"I determined, when I paid his last bill, never to employ him again."

"Dr. Slender has been very successful in croup," added Mrs. Barrington, "and I should feel just as much confidence in him as in Dr. Broadbeam."

"I will send for him."

In less than fifteen minutes after the messenger left the house, the young physician arrived. Of course he was not a little astonished to be roused from his bed by a summons from the "leading man of the village;" but he had chosen his profession, and considered it a duty to go whenever and wherever he was called.

Dr. Slender examined the child.

"You should have procured a physician before," said he, shaking his head ominously.

Mr. Barrington's heart rose to his throat. His frame trembled, and he was so nervous that he was forced to cling to the bedpost for support.

"Is he dangerous, doctor?" asked he.

"Three hours ago, it would not have been a bad case. I doubt if he can be saved now. But there is no time to be lost. Bring me some cold water and some linen cloths."

Dr. Slender gave the child a potion of medicine, and applied himself with so much energy to the means of effecting a cure, that the parents were inspired with hope, and felt entire confidence in his skill.

Morning dawned upon the little patient, and he was apparently in the last stages of the fell disease. Dr. Slender still remained by him, and was now adopting the last resort known to the physician. The agony of the parents can be conceived by those who have watched over the death bed of a cherished little one, but it cannot be described.

Providence smiled upon the young physician, and he had

22

the inexpressible satisfaction, before noon, of declaring that the child would recover. A pæan of praise rose from the grateful hearts of the devoted parents. In a few days little Charley was as well as ever, and the reputation of Dr. Slender was made.

The star of Dr. Broadbeam had set. The young physician in a few months secured the entire practice of the place. The potent influence of Mr. Barrington was all he needed to insure his success. He was polite and affable in his professional intercourse with his patients, and the contrast between him and his crusty rival was so striking that every body wondered how they had been able to endure the latter.

Dr. Broadbeam was compelled to "leave town." Whether or not he has learned that a decent deportment towards his patients is expedient, we are unable to say. But we infer that he has, from the fact that, unable to establish himself again in practice, he turned his attention to the manufacture and sale of patent medicine; and "Broadbeam's Celebrated Chinese Antibilious Pills" are as popular as advertising and false certificates can make them.

Mr. Barrington has decided that it is best to send for the doctor when the baby sneezes. Dr. Slender is always willing to come when he is sent for, and laughingly maintains that he is just as well satisfied to pocket his fee for saying nothing ails the baby, as for giving it an emetic.

"FOUR KINDS OF CAKE."

CHAPTER I.

"It is all folly, wife!" exclaimed Mr. Jotham Somes, a matter-of-fact, plain-spoken sort of man, to his better half. "There you have got no less than four kinds of cake, three kinds of pies, two kinds of preserves, to say nothing of knickknacks and gimcracks."

The fact was, that Mrs. Somes was having the minister and his wife and two grown-up daughters to take tea with her. She had been engaged for three days in the preparations, and such a display of nice things was calculated to astonish the minister and his family — to give them a twofold surprise — first, at the variety and extent of her culinary resources, and, secondly, at her folly in attempting to make a display far beyond her means.

The Someses were in comfortable circumstances. Mr. Somes was a farmer, and probably his income might have amounted to four hundred dollars per annum.

Mrs. Somes was a prudent, careful housewife, who wasted no more of her culinary skill upon her own family than was absolutely necessary; but she delighted in making a grand appearance when she had company. Mr. Somes and the boys were sometimes so ill natured as to growl at her careful catering when the house contained no company, and it cut them to the bone to see such extraordinary preparations for the neighbors. It was "kiss the cook" when they were alone; but the board groaned with plenty when there were guests present.

Mr. Jotham Somes had just come from the sitting room, where the table, with all its tempting array of viands, was spread. He did not like it a bit, and after passing the time of day with the parson and his family, he proceeded to the kitchen, where his wife was just taking the hot biscuit out of the oven.

"What do you mean by folly, I should like to know?" replied Mrs. Jotham Somes, somewhat tartly.

She was a second wife, and having been redeemed from one of the advance stages of maidenhood, her temper had grown a little sour before she became a wife.

"The folly of setting a table as you have yours," replied the husband. "I should think you were going to have the president and the royal family to take tea with you."

"I am going to have the Rev. Mr. Meeklie and his family."

"But I can't afford such extravagance as this. You will ruin me."

"I will take care of my business if you will of yours," returned the lady, slamming the oven door.

"Perhaps this is not my business."

"No, I'm sure it is not."

"Who pays for all them gewgaws and gimcracks?"

"You do, of course."

"But it is none of my business?"

"No; I never thought before you were so confounded mean," said the lady, her face reddening with anger.

" Mean! I'm not mean. But when you get victuals for your own family, you think almost any thing is good enough for them. We never see any pies, and cakes, and knick-knacks."

" Do you think I'm going to make pies and cakes for the men folks to eat every day? " retorted the indignant house-keeper.

" Then don't do it for company. What is good enough for me is as good as I can afford to give my visitors."

" I really believe, if you had your way, you would have me as mean with company as the Smiths."

" The Smiths are as good folks and as liberal as any in town; and I'll warrant Parson Meeklie thinks a heap more of them than he does of you, with all your four kinds of cake."

" You're a fool, Mr. Somes! "

" I am fool enough to know that folks are not judged by the quantity of sweet cake they put upon the table when they have company. I repeat it — there is no better folks in town than the Smiths."

" I s'pose not; but they had nothing but cold biscuit and molasses gingerbread when we took tea there."

" That's as good as they can afford; but it is no better than they have every day, and I admire their independence."

" They're contemptible, mean folks, there! "

" Why? Because they don't attempt to make folks be-lieve they live better than they do? For my part, I don't think it is any better than hypocrisy to make such a parade as you do, especially when it is hard work for me and the boys to get a decent meal of victuals."

" Did any body ever hear the like? " groaned the lady,

22 *

who had by this time arrived at that pitch of excitement when tears are more effective than words.

" Perhaps they never did ; but if ever I see any thing of this sort again, they will be pretty likely to hear of it," replied Mr. Somes, throwing off his blue frock, and commencing his preparations for taking tea with the minister.

CHAPTER II.

THE plate of hot biscuit was placed in the midst of the profusion of fancy eatables with which the table was crowded. The minister and his family were duly seated, and the ceremony was proceeding decently and in order.

Mrs. Somes had not wholly recovered from the excitement of the interview in the kitchen, and her hand trembled slightly as she handed Mrs. Mecklie her tea. Mr. Somes had donned his best blue coat, with brass buttons, which had done duty as a Sunday garment for the past fifteen years.

He seemed to be somewhat uneasy ; and though he and the minister had always been on the best of terms, his answers were too short and crusty for a courteous host.

" Won't you pass the biscuit to Mrs. Mecklie, husband ? " said Mrs. Somes, with her sweetest smile, albeit not very sweet at that.

Mr. Somes did pass the biscuit to Mrs. Mecklie, and she took one ; but when he passed them to Mr. Mecklie, he smilingly declined.

" No, I thank you, Mr. Somes ; I never eat hot bread. It does not agree with me," said he.

Mrs. Somes passed the cold bread, thinking all the time

now very uncivil it was in the parson to refuse the hot biscuit she had taken so much pains to prepare.

But Mr. Meeklie was very respectful to his stomach; for
he found, when insulted and imposed upon, that it was ty-
rannical and disagreeable; and he paid more deference to his
digestive organs than he did to the feelings of his vain parishioners.

" My biscuit are not very nice; I did not have as good
luck as I generally do," suggested Mrs. Somes, as Mrs.
Meeklie took a second cake.

" Better," interposed Mr. Somes.

The lady looked at him with very evident marks of displeasure.

" They are very nice," said the parson's wife.

" Take a little more of this quince preserve, Miss Meeklie.
I dare say it is not so nice as your mother makes; but the
truth is ——"

" It has stood too long," interrupted Mr. Somes. " The
jar has not been opened since you were here last fall."

Mrs. Somes looked daggers; but the parson very consid-
erately asked Mr. Somes whether he had done planting just
at that moment, and her anger evaporated without any unpleasant effects.

" Husband, won't you pass that cake to Mr. Meeklie? "

" Thank you, Mrs. Somes; I never eat cake. Your bread
is very good; I will thank you for some more."

" Really, Mr. Meeklie, you will take some of this cake?
It is not rich; there is very little butter in it."

" Not any, I thank you; I never eat cake, unless it be
something very simple, such as gingerbread or molasses
cake."

What a calamity! Four kinds of cake, and the parson wouldn't touch one of them!

" But you will take some of these jumbles; I made them on purpose for you."

" That's a fact, Mr. Meeklie," added Mr. Somes, maliciously.

He would further have added that his wife never made pies and cakes for her own family; but he was afraid of frightening the parson.

" You must excuse me. I doubt not they are very nice; but I have to be careful."

Mrs. Meeklie and her two grown-up daughters were more courteous, and each nibbled a small bit of the rich pound cake; but they seemed to do it against their consciences, and against their better judgment.

The truth was, they felt embarrassed by the extraordinary display Mrs. Somes had made. They did not feel at home. The whole affair was too set and artificial to be enjoyed, and at an early hour the whole party withdrew, mentally determining to make it a long time before they took tea with Mrs. Somes again.

CHAPTER III.

" Wife, where is the piece of meat I sent home for dinner?" asked Farmer Somes, as he and the boys came in for their noonday meal on the day following the tea party.

The farmer glanced inquiringly at the table which was spread before him. Involuntarily his nasal organ contracted longitudinally; it would not be polite to say he " turned up his nose," though such was the fact beyond the possibility of denial.

Farmer Somes was not, in any sense, an epicure. He liked a plain, substantial diet, that "which was good, and enough of it," as he forcibly expressed his ideas of table economy.

Lest the reader should suppose he was one of those grouty, ill-natured "feeders," who would grumble at the ambrosia and nectar of the gods, we deem it necessary to particularize the articles on the board of the lady who placed four kinds of cake before company.

Certainly there was variety enough to satisfy the most fickle taste. On a broken plate — the best dishes were religiously reserved to the use of company — was the half of one sausage and two thirds of another, making one sausage and one sixth, all told. They were partially embedded in a petrified sea of suspicious-looking fat, and, altogether, the aspect of the dish was singularly forbidding.

On a white plate, with a long black fracture extending quite across it, lay, in an aggregated mass, three dozen baked beans, and an infinitesimal fragment of a pork rind. This was an antiquity. Farmer Somes and the boys had a very distinct remembrance of having seen this dish every day during the previous fortnight, proving that Mrs. Somes was not only one of the most economical, but one of the most persevering dames in the world. The farmer and the boys had virtually said they would not eat those same beans, and Mrs. Somes virtually said they should.

On a worn-out blue plate, superannuated, and "nicked" in a thousand places, were four pork bones, looking as though they had been preyed upon by that army of mice which Whittington's cat destroyed. These bones had seen service during the last twelve days ; the joint, of which they were the disintegrated members, had graced the table just a fortnight before.

There were sundry other articles, antique, old-fashioned "titbits," which might have been set before Noah and his friends in the ark. Six long red potatoes, unpeeled, even unsprouted, completed the array of edibles, ornamental and substantial.

The farmer's nose contracted, as before related.

" Where is the meat I sent home ? "

" Hanging in the well."

" Hadn't we better eat it ? "

" I want it for company next Sunday."

" The —— ahem ! Company again ? "

" I expect my brother will dine with us then, and I want something fit to set before him."

Mr. Somes looked sulky.

" And you mean to starve me and the boys in the mean time ? "

" I should like to know if there is not enough for you?" said the dame, pointing at the table.

Farmer Somes turned up his nose.

" Did I ever refuse to buy victuals when you wanted it?" said he, rather sternly.

" Not that I know of; but I didn't suppose you wanted to buy fresh meat *every* day," returned the wife, sourly. " I am sure I try to be as economical as I can."

" Four kinds of cake, which nobody would touch, I suppose is prudent, ain't it ? "

" Ah, good morning, Mr. Somes ; I am glad to find you

at home," said Mr. Meeklie, walking into the room unannounced.

Good gracious! the minister, and with such a table as that spread before the family! What a commentary on four kinds of cake for company!

Mrs. Somes was all confusion. Though the parson intended to look right at the farmer, she could see that more than once his eyes wandered over the table.

" Glad to see you, parson; sit down and take some dinner with us," said Mr. Somes, shaking the minister's offered hand.

" Thank you; I don't care if I do," replied Mr. Meeklic. " I have a long walk to take before I return home."

Farmer Somes was pointing him to a chair, when the lady interposed.

" We have got a picked-up dinner to-day. Husband sent home a joint of veal; but it didn't get here till half after eleven; so I had no time to cook it."

" Got here by eight o'clock," said Farmer Somes; "no fibs to the parson."

" But if you will wait only a few moments, I will fry some of the veal."

" Sit down, parson; it is every day fare; but then, what is good enough for me is good enough for my friends."

" Right, Mr. Somes," replied the minister, drawing up his chair. " My business relates to the new bell for the meeting house. I am carrying round the subscription paper."

" I am with you, parson."

Farmer Somes was in most malicious good humor, and, with a broad laugh on his honest phiz, he opened the paper the minister gave him.

" Smith, twenty dollars."

" Twenty dollars ! " exclaimed Mrs. Somes; " I should not think he could afford it."

" He gives his friends nothing but gingerbread," said the farmer. " Put me down for thirty; we have four kinds of cake."

The parson consumed one " long red," and one of the vulgar fractions of a cold sausage. He preferred brown bread to white, and wouldn't touch any of the pies which the prudent housekeeper set before him.

Mrs. Somes was awfully mortified. Her reputation was sacrificed, and Farmer Somes never again had occasion to find fault with her for making a vain show of three kinds of pies, two kinds of preserves, and four kinds of cake.

EXTREMES MEET;

OR,

FACT AND FICTION.

CHAPTER I.

"WHAT are you reading, sis?"

" Hard Times."

" A novel!"

"Yes; why not? Dickens's last new novel, and a capital thing it is, too."

The two ladies, between whom this conversation passed, were sisters, and nieces of one of the better class of New England farmers, with whom they resided. 'Squire Fairbank, without being a very brilliant man, had acquired considerable distinction in the village where he lived, probably because, besides being "worth money," he was a straightforward, conservative, reliable man, and had frequently served the town in an acceptable manner, both in the legislature, and as moderator in town meeting. He was the most notable man in the village, and won the title of 'Squire, which was universally accorded to him, simply by being a very respectable person and a man of influence.

Susan and Mary Fairbank were orphans, inheriting from their father the very pretty little sum of five thousand dollars each. Both had attained their majority, and consequently

23

were in full possession of their portions, untrammelled even by the authority of as indulgent a guardian as 'Squire Fairbank had proved to be.

They had been well educated at a celebrated female seminary in the vicinity of Boston, and as a matter of course, had brought home to the quiet village of Poppleton many strange notions and remarkable peculiarities. But they were sensible girls in the main, and though their habits and education elevated them above the reigning *ton* of the place, it was generally conceded that they knew " what was what," and were not " a mite more stuck up " than would naturally have been expected.

Mary and Susan were essentially different in temperament and disposition. The former was exceedingly open and free hearted, while the latter was rather disposed to truckle to the formality of the world, or to the circumstances in which she happened to be placed. Mary never asked what the world would say or think, and while her notions of duty were very clearly defined, she chose to be independent and straightforward. People said she " took after " her father.

Susan, on the contrary, was nicely sensitive to the good opinion of others. She had not the energy to do any thing in opposition to popular sentiment. Indeed, she was very much like some of the distinguished public servants at Washington, who do every thing with an eye to a reelection or to government patronage.

A short time before our story opens, a young minister had been settled in Poppleton, and being a single man, 'Squire Fairbank had consented as a special favor to receive him into his house. The Rev. Mr. Carlisle was universally allowed to be a very promising young man. He was talented

had a graceful elocution, and, what pleased the young ladies
better still, was decidedly a handsome person. Those who
were not much influenced by talent, elocution, and personal
beauty, thought he was rather bigoted for one so young, and
hoped that time would wear off the rough corners of his
repulsive theology.

Susan Fairbank was deeply interested in the young clergyman, and as a natural consequence to one of her vacillating temperament, became deeply interested in spiritual
things. We do not believe she had any intention of playing
the hypocrite; but her devotion to the young minister involuntarily led her to assume an interest, which, if Mr. Carlisle had been old, ugly, or married, she would not have felt.

"A novel, sis! only think of it!" exclaimed Susan,
holding up both hands with pious horror.

"Pray, Susan, how long is it since you have possessed
this holy repugnance to novels? It was only last winter that
I saw you reading The Children of the Abbey," returned
Mary, laughing heartily.

"I have not read one since, and I never mean to again."

"Fudge!"

"What do you think Mr. Carlisle would say if he should
see you reading a novel?"

"I shouldn't care what he said."

"Why, Mary!"

"I shouldn't; if he does not like it, he may whistle for
all me."

"Don't talk so, Mary."

"Why will you make a fool of yourself, Susan? Mr.
Carlisle cares no more for you than he does for the fifth
wheel of a coach; I would not stand in such fear of him for
the world."

" Fear of him ! I do not fear him ; I only respect him as a very good man."

" You have set your cap for him ; but let me tell you to be more independent, or you never will catch him," said Mary, laughing.

" How absurd you talk ! "

" Do I ? "

Susan fell to biting her finger nail — a very vulgar habit, by the way — and to thinking of something which her sister had no difficulty in discerning.

" Do you really love him, Susan ? " asked Mary.

" Love him ! No ; I never thought of such a thing."

Perhaps she never did.

" What makes you go to all the prayer meetings, and mope round the house like a sick owl, then ? "

" I think I am under conviction," replied Susan, demurely.

" Conviction of what ? "

" Conviction of sin."

" Conviction that Mr. Carlisle is a very handsome fellow, more like."

" How absurd you are ! "

" And I have heard a report round town that you were going to join the church."

" I have spoken to Mr. Carlisle about it."

Mary looked serious for a moment.

" If you really feel so, I commend your conduct ; but I advise you not to be too hasty. Examine your heart attentively, and do not bring scandal upon the church by having side motives. But here comes Mr. Carlisle," said Mary, as she again turned her attention to the fascinating pages of Hard Times.

CHAPTER II.

The young minister entered the room. Susan had taken up Saints' Rest, which lay by her, and commenced reading where she had left off, when she saw Mr. Carlisle coming up the yard. As he came into the room she laid down the book, and looked, for all the world, as though she had not a friend in the world. The assuming of this appearance was involuntary on her part; it was in accordance with her nature.

Mr. Carlisle seated himself by her side, and commenced catechizing her in regard to the impression the contents of the book produced upon her mind — whether it afforded her consolation in her troubled mind — and finally whether she really thought she had a hope. To all these queries Susan replied in a satisfactory manner, assuring the handsome young shepherd that she had been much edified by her reading.

There was a smile of mischief playing upon the pretty and expressive face of Mary, as she peered over the top of Hard Times, to observe the ghostly interview. She could see that Mr. Carlisle engaged in the conversation with her sister merely as a matter of professional interest — sincerely, it is true, but with no unusual interest in the penitent. He regarded her as a wandering sheep, whom it was his duty to bring into the fold.

But she compassionated her sister, who had deluded herself into the belief that she could win the heart of the shepherd by becoming one of his sheep; and she was provoking

23 *

enough to tell her that instead of making a sheep, she had made a calf of herself.

When the minister had finished his professional counsel, he turned to Mary. As he did so, an involuntary smile came upon his lips. It was not the smile of a ghostly father, but of a young man who has flesh in his heart and blood in his veins.

Mary laid down her book as she noticed his intention to address her.

"What are you reading, Miss Fairbank?" asked he.

"Hard Times," promptly replied Mary.

"A novel?"

"Yes, sir."

The jaw of the young minister dropped down two inches.

"Do you like it?"

"O, very much, indeed!" replied Mary, with wicked enthusiasm; "I admire Dickens's of all the novels I ever read."

"Do you make a practice of reading novels?"

"I seldom read any thing else. I did read Reveries of a Bachelor and Dream Life."

The minister shook his head.

"I take the newspapers, and I always read them through — stories, poetry, sentiment, editorials, and all."

"Will you allow me to suggest some reading for you? and I shall take the greatest pleasure in lending you the books."

"Thank you."

"Baxter's Call to the Unconverted is an excellent book for —— "

"It is *so* stupid!"

Mr. Carlisle was horrified.

" I would not be hired to read it."

" Bunyan's Pilgrim's Progress, perhaps, would suit your ste better."

" I have read it; but don't you call that a novel ? "

" An allegory."

" If I mistake not, I saw you reading Uncle Tom's Cabin. I'm sure that is a novel, and no better novel either than any of Dickens's."

" It is a moral and philanthropic work."

" So. are Dickens's works. Indeed, I have never read a novel from which a great deal of good might not be obtained, though I know there are such."

" Mere fictions generally have a debasing tendency."

" I judge novels as I do any thing else — by their own merits. If I understand you, Mr. Carlisle, you object to works of fiction, as such, and not on account of any evil they may contain."

" Certainly."

" You insist that the book must be true in its narrative in order to be good."

" I do."

" Then you despise the teachings of Him you profess to serve. He spoke in parables — in fiction. I do not understand the Prodigal Son to be a narrative of facts."

" Perhaps not."

" Then why may not Scott, Dickens, Irving, Miss Bremer, and Miss Leslie teach us love and charity through the same medium ? "

" Such works vitiate the taste."

" O, it is the taste, and not the heart, that is damaged."

" Both; the latter through the former. Let me induce

you to read Baxter's Call, and you will then allow that you have obtained more real good from it than from all the novels you ever read in your life."

" It is too dull and insipid for me. I must draw my inspiration from more sparkling fountains."

" You misjudge the book."

" Perhaps I do. I am not a saint, I am willing to acknowledge ; therefore it does not suit me. And I fancy it is so with half the world, who, rejecting the counsels of the church, get their wisdom and their goodness from works of fiction. They are readable to those whose taste, like mine, has not become sanctified ; without them they would read nothing, and thus the world is the better for novels."

Mr. Carlisle could not but grant that there was some truth in what Mary had said ; and though he did not, in so many words, yield the point, an impression was produced upon his mind which could not fail to soften down the bigotry of his views.

But the merry, fearless, independent tones of the eloquent advocate of works of fiction went deeper down than the mind, and touched a weak spot in his theological heart. Her pretty, sparkling eye, roused and animated by her earnest thought, were irresistible ; and the Rev. Mr. Carlisle, maugre the carnal nature of the fair debater, actually fell in love with the contemner of Baxter's immortal works.

Mary was undoubtedly a great sinner, but she was a beautiful and spirited girl for all that. We will not trouble the reader with the ingenious plans which the enamoured minister laid that night to reclaim the erring beauty ; it is only necessary to say that, within a week, he popped the question to her ; and that she, out of consideration for her sister, refused to consider the proposal.

CHAPTER III.

Susan was a docile lamb, and her conversion progressed to the entire satisfaction of her spiritual adviser. It was rumored that she was to be "propounded" on the following Sabbath.

Mary had quite as strong a veneration for spiritual things as her sister; but she was too straightforward to assume what she did not possess, and too sensible to be led into imaginary raptures by any extraneous influence. She knew Susan too well to believe her holy aspirations were real; she knew that the poor girl had involuntarily deluded herself. She was not surprised to hear that she had concluded to join the church.

"Susan, you are deceiving yourself. You love the fold for the sake of the shepherd," said she.

"Nay, sister, you wrong me. Can you think me a hypocrite?"

"Not a hypocrite; you have misled yourself."

"I have carefully examined my heart, and I am confident that I am not deluded."

"What would you say if I should tell you that Mr. Carlisle can never love you?"

"I should say that you knew nothing about it," replied Susan, unthinkingly; but in an instant she corrected the mistake. "But that has nothing to do with it."

"I fear it has. Tell me honestly, Susan, do you not love Mr. Carlisle? I will not laugh at you."

Susan hesitated.

' Be candid, sister."

" I do not love him; but if he loved me, I feel that I could return his affection."

" He does not love you, Susan."

The ambitious "sheep" looked earnestly into the face of her sister.

" How do you know? "

" I *do* know."

Susan looked pensive and sad.

" What do you know? "

" That he has even offered his hand and heart to another."

" The hypocrite! " exclaimed Susan, with a flushed face.

" Why, sis! " and Mary was filled with astonishment, for it appeared from Susan's violent ebullition of feeling that the matter had passed much farther than she had suspected. " Why do you use that pointed word? Did he ever speak to you of love? "

" Never; but he has led me to believe by his constant attentions that he was interested in me."

" That was professional, sis; you have mistaken his zeal to bring you into the fold for love. I warned you of this."

" You did; I am a fool. But to whom has he offered himself."

" It is a secret."

" Tell *me!* "

" Will you be discreet? "

" I will."

" To me! "

" To you! You who despised Baxter's Call and Saints' Rest? "

" Even so. Extremes meet sometimes."

" I wish you joy, Mary."

" But I declined the offer."

" Why ? "

" For your sake. I knew that you loved him."

Susan was deeply affected at the generosity of her sister.

" I do not love him, sister. Do not let me be an obstacle in the way of your happiness."

" I have not said that I loved him."

" But you do ? "

" I have refused him."

" Nay, he is a noble and a good man, besides being handsome and talented. You need not be a fool because I have been. I assure you I am completely cured; I think he is a flirt."

Mary did not think so, and the young minister was too deeply enamoured of her, too devotedly admired her wit and beauty, no less than her innate goodness of heart, to be content with a refusal. When he renewed his suit, the spirited girl was more tractable, and in process of time they were married.

Whether Mr. Carlisle ever succeeded in removing those pernicious notions about novels from the mind of his wife, we are unable to say; but we do know that Scott, Dickens, and Irving have found a place on the shelves of his library, beside the tomes of theology and history; and we infer that a mutual influence has brought each to adopt more reasonable views both of Baxter and the novelists.

THE MERCANTILE ANGEL.

CHAPTER I.

"THE contemptible little jackanapes! he had the audacity to ask me to play whist with him!" exclaimed Sophia Danvers to her sister.

"And why should he not, sister?" answered Mary Danvers, calmly.

"Why should he not, indeed! Did he think I would demean myself by playing whist with a clerk — one of my father's servants?" and Sophia tossed her head in proud disdain.

"I can see no impropriety in your associating with him, Sophia. He is certainly a handsome, intelligent, and well-behaved young man."

"Behaves well enough, for aught I know; but only think of it — a clerk in our drawing room! For my part, I wonder how father could ever think of such a thing as admitting him into the family."

"I suppose it was because he liked the looks of him."

"What will Mr. Augustus Fitzherbert say when he finds us associating with poor clerks — the trash of counting rooms?"

"It matters little to me what he thinks; he is a conceited

(276)

puppy, and I wonder that you can endure his presence," replied Mary, smartly.

"But he is the leader of the *ton*, Mary," said Sophia, astonished at the plebeian notions of her sister.

"He is a perfect flat, for all that, and infinitely inferior, in all that constitutes a man, to Mr. Harlowe, whom you affect to despise."

The conversation was interrupted by the entrance of Mr. Danvers.

"How could you bring that horrible clerk into the house, papa?" said Sophia, as the merchant prince seated himself by the blazing grate.

"Horrible clerk! Pray, what is the matter with him?" asked Mr. Danvers, evincing some surprise at the plain speech of his daughter.

"Why, he is a clerk."

"But a respectable young man."

"Respectable enough, but not fashionable, papa."

"I was a clerk once, Sophia; I commenced by sweeping out a store, and carrying bundles about the city."

"How absurdly you talk, papa!"

"But Mr. Harlowe is a very estimable young man; I am confident you will find him agreeable company."

"I shall have nothing to say to him," replied Sophia, with a shrug of the shoulders.

"Beware, Sophia; there is an old proverb, you know, about entertaining angels unawares."

Sophia laughed heartily at the idea of a poor clerk being an angel.

"But what says Mary?" asked the merchant, turning to his gentle-hearted daughter.

24

" O, *I* like him very much ; we are already fast friends,'
replied Mary, and a slight blush seemed to emphasize the
remark.

" Just like her, papa ; I should not wonder if she got
head over heels in love with your mercantile angel."

" She must do as she pleases about that," replied Mr.
Danvers, smiling.

" Pooh, Sophy ! who said a word about falling in love ?
Can't a body be civil to a young gentleman without falling
in love with him ? "

The pretty Mary blushed as she spoke, in good earnest —
blushed so palpably that her father began to think the affair
was something more than a mere jest.

" But pray, papa, when does your new partner arrive ?"
asked Sophia.   " If all the accounts I have heard of his wit,
gallantry, and personal attractions are true, I shall certainly
set my cap for him."

" He will appear one of these days," replied Mr. Danvers.

" I hope you will not keep this stupid clerk in the house
after he comes."

" I certainly shall."

" But, papa, we shall ' lose caste ' if you do ; it is really
abominable."

" Small loss, my child.   If we are dependent upon the
apes and puppies of fashionable life for our position in society, the sooner we lose it the better for our own self-re-
spect," said Mr. Danvers, smiling good humoredly.

" You are absurd, papa."

" Now, Sophy, you have given me a lesson, let me give
you one.   The idol you worship is more senseless than those
of the Feegee Islands.   Fashionable society is as hollow as a

brass pan; place no reliance upon it. The fops and fools who follow in your train are as soulless as they are brainless."

"I wish Mr. Augustus Fitzherbert could hear you say so," added Sophia.

"Mr. Augustus Fitzherbert was a journeyman barber in New Orleans less than a year ago. I had the honor of being shaved by him last winter when I was there."

"O, horrid, papa! Why have you not exposed him?"

"Why should I, my child? He is as good a fellow, as sensible a person, and, according to your statement, as fashionable a man, as Mr. Finstock, whose great grandfather was the governor of the state."

"Is it possible that Mr. Fitzherbert was a barber?" exclaimed Sophia, horrified at the appalling statement.

"Nothing else, my child."

"An impostor?" added Mary.

"Just so. Probably he is trying to obtain a rich wife."

"It is abominable, I declare! One hardly knows, nowadays, who is respectable and who is not," said Sophia.

"Therefore, my child, we ought not to speak so disparagingly of persons in humble life as you have to-night."

"Pooh! a clerk!"

At this moment, Mr. Harlowe, the new clerk, entered the room, and, as Sophia would have expressed it, had the impudence to seat himself by the side of Mary Danvers, who appeared not at all averse to this close proximity with him.

Frederic Harlowe was, as Mary had said, a handsome, intelligent, and agreeable young man; and Sophia, if she could have forgiven him for being a clerk, would have appreciated his society quite as highly as did her sister.

With her father's permission, Mary accepted an invitation from Frederic to attend Alboni's last concert.

They had scarcely left the house before Mr. Augustus Fitzherbert was ushered into the sitting room. This gentleman was an exquisite of the "first water." In his personal appearance, he certainly was sufficiently well endowed to challenge the admiration of the fair sex; but, unfortunately, he was sadly lacking in that necessary element of a man of sense — brains.

Sophia could scarcely refrain from expressing the contempt she felt for the journeyman barber in disguise. The leader of the "ton," in her estimation, was a ruined man.

The dandy, as a matter of courtesy, inquired for Mary, and was informed that she had gone to the concert with Mr. Harlowe.

"With Mr. Harlowe — a clerk — aw?" said the ex-journeyman barber, with a sneer, as he twirled up the long "rat tail" of his mustache.

"A very worthy young man," replied Mr. Danvers.

"No doubt of it, saw; but a clerk — aw."

"Pray, were you never a clerk, Mr. Fitzherbert? *I* was."

"A clerk! No, saw — nevaw!"

"Did I not meet you in New Orleans last winter?"

The dandy started up like a parched pea from a hot pan.

"I have a faint recollection of having met you in a barber's shop there," continued the merchant, tormentingly.

"Aw, very likely, saw. I patronize the barbaws."

"And, now I think of it, you wore a little white apron, and, if I mistake not, I had the pleasure of being shaved by *you* in person."

"Quite a mistake, saw, I assuaw you."

Suddenly Mr. Augustus Fitzherbert, whose real name was John Smike, remembered an imperative engagement, and hastened to take his leave.

He was seen to enter the cars for New York on the following day, and nothing has been heard of him since.

CHAPTER II.

Of course the reader understands that Frederic Harlowe and Mary are deeply, irretrievably in love with each other by this time. The poor clerk had won his way to the heart of the fair girl, and she, poor thing, had been captivated by the manly attractions, the noble soul, of him who offered incense before her shrine.

As the world goes, it would be deemed a very wicked thing for a poor clerk to fall in love with the daughter of his aristocratic employer. Some people would say it was ungrateful in him thus to spirit away the affections of a confiding girl, when his position and prospects did not warrant his presuming to be her husband.

These questions are still open to the casuist. He may debate them to his entire satisfaction; but Mr. Danvers, either because he was more sensible than many of the aristocratic merchants of the day, or for some other equally potent reason, neglected to make any fuss about the matter, and suffered the clerk to wob and win his daughter, without even remonstrating against the wickedness of the act.

But Sophia was deeply grieved by her sister's folly, as she deemed it, and used all the arguments in the range of her

24 *

shallow sophistry to dissuade her from the folly and madness of wedding a clerk.

Mary was obstinate. The only excuse she offered in palliation of the flagrant misdemeanor was, that she loved him; and if she *loved* a scavanger, she would cling to him with the last breath she was permitted to draw.

" A ring!" exclaimed Sophia, one day, when matters appeared to have taken a very decided turn. " Well, well, I suppose you are engaged."

" We are, Sophia," replied Mary, with a face radiant with happiness.

" And you intend to be married ? "

" Certainly we do ; that is the end of an engagement."

" My conscience ! to think that the daughter of a merchant prince should become the wife of a poor, insignificant clerk ! "

" Nothing very alarming about it, Sophy ; it wouldn't be half so ridiculous as another daughter of a merchant prince becoming the wife of an ex-journeyman barber. I believe Mr. Augustus Fitzherbert was your beau ideal of what a fashionable husband ought to be."

" The impostor ! "

" I am at least sure that Frederic is not an impostor — a humbug ; one would not be likely to *assume* the character of a clerk."

" Perhaps not ; but pray, sister, when do you intend to become the wife of this counting room cherub ? "

" The day has not been fixed yet ; in the spring, probably."

" And may I ask what you intend to do with yourself? His salary is only a thousand dollars a year."

"We can get along very well on that sum."

"Yes, I suppose so, and live in some ten footer in a dark alley."

"We intend to live out of town, in a nice little cottage."

"Y-e-s! a nice little cottage!" drawled Sophia, in derision. "O sis, I will show you how to live when I am married. None of your nice little cottages for me. But I wonder when the new partner is coming."

"Papa told me this morning that he had deferred the arrangement till next spring, and that the gentleman would attend to his business at the south as heretofore."

"How provoking! I have been reserving my affections on purpose for him. I mean to make a conquest of him in just one month."

"How foolish you talk, Sophy! One would think you had entirely forgotten your maidenly delicacy."

"Pooh! I'm jesting; it's between *us*;" and Sophia relapsed into a revery, which, we are almost sure, related to the aforesaid new partner, who was not only a nice young man, but was to put thirty thousand dollars into the concern when he became a partner.

The winter passed away, and the spring came. Frederic and Mary were to be married in a few days. Mr. Danvers, to the infinite chagrin of Sophia, had readily consented to the match. The proud sister — though in the natural goodness of her heart she would not have had Mary's affections blasted — would fain have had a little opposition, to save appearances.

The bridal day came, and after the ceremony had been performed, the happy parties started for their new residence in the suburbs. Sophia, who had acted as bridesmaid, was to accompany them.

The carriage wound through an elm-shaded road, and suddenly brought to the view of the delighted party a splendid country residence.

"That is the cottage," exclaimed the bride.

"That a cottage! Why, Mary, it is a palace!" replied Sophia, in utter astonishment; for she had never taken interest enough in her sister's affairs to visit her proposed residence.

The carriage stopped before the door, which was half hidden behind a vine-laced portico, and the party alighted.

The place was a perfect paradise, and many were the encomiums lavished upon it by the bewildered Sophia.

"You cannot think how surprised I was when I first beheld it," said Mary, when she and Sophia were alone. "It seemed more like a dream of fairyland than a reality. But Frederic is so very odd about these things."

"I should think that he was! Why, sis, it will certainly ruin him, a poor clerk on a thousand dollars salary."

"Well, he knows best; he says the rent is nothing."

"Nothing, indeed; but it will eat up his poor pittance."

"Well, I gave him a lesson on extravagance; but he only laughed in my face, and said he knew what he was about."

"But here are Frederic and father; I am sure papa has been scolding him for his recklessness."

"He does not look as though the scolding had produced a very powerful effect," said Mary, as she saw her husband's smiling countenance.

"What a beautiful house!" exclaimed Sophia, as Frederic Harlowe joined the group.

" A fitting nest for my pretty bird," replied the husband, gayly, as he chucked his blushing wife under the chin.

" I should think your thousand dollars a year would have to suffer some," said Sophia, bluntly.

" O, your father has been so very good as to elevate me a peg, so that I can well afford to incur the expense."

" Yes, my child," interposed Mr. Danvers ; " you know I said something to you about entertaining angels unawares. Sophy, *Mr. Frederic Harlowe* is the new partner."

" What an abominable cheat, papa ! I'll warrant you told Mary of it in the beginning," said Sophia, with abundant good humor.

" Nay, she knew nothing of it till a few days before her marriage. This was all Mr. Harlowe's whim ; he must explain it for himself."

Mr. Harlowe did attempt to explain his motive in entering the family *incog.*, but it was a lame explanation. Probably the reader, who readily penetrates the secret thoughts of the hero of the story, has already divined his motive. He wanted a wife, and had the sense to seek for genuine goodness in preference to name and position in society. He won the daughter of a merchant prince as a simple clerk ; there was no doubt that she loved him.

Mary was very much surprised, and perhaps not a little chagrined, to find the romance of marrying a clerk so suddenly disappear ; but in the wealth of a mutual love they were richer than in the smiles of fickle fortune, which had blessed them with an abundance of the good things of this life.

CONFESSIONS OF A CONCEITED MAN;

BEING THE SUBSTANCE OF WHAT SOME YOUNG MEN THINK, BUT NEVER SAY.

CHAPTER I.

WHEN I was a boy, the schoolmaster succeeded in impressing upon my mind the truth of that common saying — "If a man thinks nothing of himself, no one will think any thing of him." The pedagogue believed it himself, and his daily deportment was based upon it. Whether I learned any thing else of him I cannot now say; but I am sure I learned to set a high value upon myself.

At the age of eighteen, I found myself in the service of an eminent merchant of Boston, in the capacity of assistant bookkeeper, on the paltry salary of four hundred dollars a year. I was worth more — I was sure of it. But perhaps my employer had not yet come to a knowledge of the treasure he possessed in me, and I wisely determined to wait till I had a better opportunity to distinguish myself.

Certainly I took a great deal of pride in discharging the duties of my position. I labored assiduously to please both the merchant and the head bookkeeper, and they seemed to regard me with satisfaction; but I resolved to make myself so necessary that the business could not be carried on without me.

Whether my imagination was more lively than my reason, or not, I do not know; but certainly, at the end of six months I made up my mind that Mr. Bancroft could not possibly continue in business a single month without me. As to my superior, he would be perfectly powerless if I should leave. In fact, I "conceited" that I was in reality *the* bookkeeper of the concern, though he received the salary and did all the dictating.

I was an ambitious young man. I built a great many ery pretty castles in the air; among them the idea of marrying my employer's beautiful daughter was not the least attractive. She was a splendid girl — people called her the belle of Boston — and what to me was just as insinuating she was an only child, and consequently the heiress of all Mr. Bancroft's reputed wealth.

I never was one of that sort who wistfully dream over fine things, without making an attempt to attain them. That stale old maxim to the effect that "faint heart ne'er won fair lady," was uppermost in my mind. I had come to the conclusion that Rosabel Bancroft should have the supreme felicity of becoming my household deity.

But the way was full of difficulties. I had never seen the peerless maiden, save on occasions when I had called at the house in the capacity of an errand boy — for the key of the safe, to get Mr. Bancroft to sign a check, or something of that sort. She was a proud beauty, and had never even taken the pains to look at me. "Ah, my fine lady," thought I, "when we are married, I will teach you what is what!"

Certainly I would! And as for marrying her, why, that was a settled fact in my mind — I had resolved to do the deed.

1 flattered myself that I was a decidedly good-looking fel-

low, and a great many young men cherish this idea in these progressive times. My looking glass had told me I was handsome, and there was no going behind its impressive declaration. But I was aware that my beauty needed a little cultivation, and accordingly I applied to Bogle for some of the "compounds," and in a few weeks, I had the satisfaction of contemplating the addition of a downy mustache upon my well-turned upper lip. I took a great deal of pains with this beautifier of my physiognomy, and felt perfectly sure that the charming Rosabel would be unable to resist my killing attractions.

There was to be a grand ball at Union Hall, and I heard that my divinity was to form one of the revellers. I will not trouble the reader with a relation of the difficulties that beset me in procuring a ticket — for the affair was intended solely for the " upper ten; " but I got one, though it cost me in the neighborhood of twenty-five dollars, to say nothing of twenty-five more expended in a fancy vest, cravat, and other little amiabilities.

When I was dressed for the occasion, the effect was perfectly stunning. Rosabel was certainly a goner!

My *entrée* into the drawing room seemed to create a profound sensation. All the gentlemen stared at me, and I felt assured of being the lion of the evening. It was plain that my " personal " had created a *furor* among the aristocratic dandies; but I tried to treat them all with respect and politeness. It is true I saw some of them turn up their noses at me ; and all evinced a disposition to avoid me. But I attributed all these unmannerly symptoms to the envy which my superior personal attractions had roused in their narrow minds. I did not resent their ill nature — I could afford to be magnanimous.

I walked like a king through the sumptuous apartments; indeed, I always prided myself on my gait. More than once, when I have been leisurely promenading Washington Street, I have felt sure that all the ladies had singled me out for especial admiration.

There was something magnificent about my style of walking, and I did not blame the dear creatures for sighing when I passed them. It was a great pity that, in the illiberality of our laws, only one lady could ever have the satisfaction of calling me her husband. I am naturally of a sympathetic temperament, and I assure the reader that it deeply grieved me to think of the number of fair, promising ladies who would be disappointed in winning my affections. I could not love them all, and from the bottom of my heart I pitied those who were doomed to be disappointed.

Rosabel Bancroft was destined to be my wife. I had deliberately made up my mind, and though I thought, in consideration of my condescension in choosing her from the thousands who would have rejoiced to win me, she ought to meet me half way. But I was not over nice, and in deference to the fashions of the times, I mentally consented to do all the courting myself.

I succeeded in getting an introduction to her, and she consented to dance with me. I was not much elated; I regarded my progress as a matter of course. During the quadrille, I did the agreeable to my own satisfaction, and though the impression was not as marked and decided as I had expected, I was assured that every thing was going on well.

" Procrastination is the thief of time," said somebody, I don't remember whether it was Plato or Diogenes. When the dance was ended, and I had conducted her to the drawing room, I made bold to express my admiration of her beauty and grace. She blushed, smiled, and looked confused. Poor thing! how could she help it?

Just then a dandy spoke a word to her, and then retreated. I was not to be balked, and with all the eloquence I possessed — and I would just hint that Demosthenes, Cicero, or Daniel Webster couldn't hold a candle to me in making a speech — I popped the question!

It was handsomely done, and Rosabel was taken all aback. I expected all this — I knew all about making love — Ovid couldn't tell me any thing about it. Girls, at this momentous crisis, do not always mean half they say; and I was prepared to hear her declare it was rather sudden, that she must ask papa about it, and all that sort of thing.

But my ardent confession seemed to throw her into a perspiration — if I may so unpoetically express the confusion which my declaration produced.

"You impudent puppy!" exclaimed she, her pretty cheek red with anger; "so you are one of my father's clerks, and have the presumption to ask me to dance with you, and then to offer me such an indignity! Leave my presence, sir, this instant, or I will ask my friends to kick you away!"

Whew! I did feel sheepish for a moment; but then, poor thing, she did not know her own mind. Some of those envious noodles had been exciting her prejudices against me. That dandy had told her I was her father's clerk, before I had had an opportunity to weave my spell upon her.

Comforting myself with the assurance that there were thousands of heiresses who were more discriminating than she, I whistled an air, and ambled away from her. If there is any person on the face of the earth whom I pity more than another, it is he or she who wilfully throws away a good opportunity.

Poor Rosabel! I pitied *her!* I believe I was unselfish enough to deplore her misfortune more acutely than I did my own. I had lost nothing that might not be regained; she had cast away one of the most brilliant opportunities that ever dawned upon the destiny of a maiden.

I have the credit, among those who know me best, of possessing firmness in a very remarkable degree; and it was melancholy to think she had cast me off forever, for, I am sure, if she had fallen upon her knees, and begged and pleaded, I should have been as firm as a rock. Those insulting, unlady-like words, had " fixed her flint" — to use a rather homely phrase, which I believe did not originate either with Addison or Macaulay.

I did not dance any more that evening. I found that I had fallen among fools, who could not appreciate me. And strange as it may seem to the unphilosophical reader, the fact did not in the least disturb my natural equanimity. Why should it? Did not Socrates experience the same coldness at the hands of the fickle Athenians, who put him to death by mixing poison with his " sherry cobbler " ? Why should I expect a better fate than others whose misfortune it is to be superior to the masses around them?

I left the hall regretting only that the eighth part of my year's salary had been wasted in the adventure.

When I went to the counting room next morning, Mr. Bancroft summoned me to his private office.

" You are a fool, young man!" said he, and his face was flushed with anger.

O the ingratitude of the world! This was a pretty return for the distinguished honor I had intended for his daughter, and which only her own wilfulness had prevented her from receiving at my hands.

"If you ever presume to speak to my daughter again, under any circumstances, I will immediately discharge you from my service," continued he, with the utmost coolness.

"Nonsense!" thought I — and I beg the reader will not suppose I uttered this unseemly expression — "you won't do any thing of the kind. You know your own interest too well."

Discharge me! I should have liked to see him do it. I believe I should actually have gone, if he had said the word, and left him to take care of his business as best he might! If he had got me mad, I should just as lief seen him fail as not — it is my temperament. To a friend, I am a friend; to a foe, a foe of the most determined sort.

But he knew better than to provoke me too far. Bancroft was a shrewd man. He knew just how far I would have permitted him to go, in deference to the dignity of his position, and he did not exceed that limit. It was a lucky thing for him that he did not. Disaster, mercantile ruin, would have been the inevitable consequence of such an imprudent act!

I regret that my space does not permit me to give the reader the details of my exploits in the arena of Cupid for the succeeding six months. They were rich and varied; but I am happy to console my friends and admirers with the assurance that I am at present engaged in writing out the history of the whole period, which in due time will appear, complete in seven volumes, with portraits and illustrations.

From the events of this campaign I deduce the melancholy conclusion that the fair sex are sadly wanting in good taste and nice discrimination. The fact that I am still a bachelor is a sad commentary on this truth. The ladies " are not what they are cracked up to be " — to use a rather inelegant expression, which I think was original with Hogg, the poet.

But disappointed of my matrimonial hopes, I determined to make commerce the study of my life. I had about made up my mind to offer my time and talents to Bancroft — in short, to offer to become his partner in business. I never was much in favor of these complications of mercantile affairs, and to become a partner of his might involve me in some future sacrifices, which it might not be pleasant to make.

I thought it best, on the whole, to retain my present situation. But the salary was too small. I must wait upon Bancroft, and consent to remain in his service, if he would add a hundred dollars to my pay. Of course he could not be so imprudent as to run the risk of failure and utter ruin for so trifling a matter as this.

"I beg your pardon, Mr. Bancroft," said I, in my blandest tones, — for even a highway robber is polite nowadays when he blows a man's brains out — "but I have taken the liberty to wait upon you for the purpose of asking you to advance my salary from four to five hundred dollars."

"Go to the devil!" said he, rudely.

It is astonishing how some folks will even kick an angel out of their presence. Poor Bancroft! he " stood in his own light," — to borrow from Carlyle or Mephistophiles, I forget which.

"You are dear help at two hundred a year; I don't want you any longer at any price," continued Bancroft.

25 *

" There's stupidity for you ! " thought I.

My blood was up, and I determined to leave him, let the consequences be what they might.

I did leave him, assured that the mercantile world would be startled to its centre by a crash, in a very short time. The concern has not broke down yet, but there is a moral certainty that it must soon " go by the board," — to quote from Captain Cook, or Sir John Franklin, it is not very material which.

I had not been out of business a week before I discovered that literature was the proper sphere for me. I intend to bring about a revolution in the world of letters, by introducing an entirely new style of composition, adapted both to prose and poetry. I have several works under way, including a complete History of the Musquito Kingdom, Annals of Hull, and a poem in two hundred and seventy-six cantos, on the Want of Appreciation and Correct Taste in the Female Sex, — all of which will appear as soon as written and published.

THE BACHELOR BEAU.

CHAPTER I.

"I CAN no longer struggle against the current of misfortune," exclaimed Mr. Whiting, a small merchant, who had by the pressure of hard times become somewhat involved; "I am ruined!"

"Nay, my husband, do not be distressed. Worse calamities than this might happen, and we will make the best of it."

"But, wife, I must fail; I cannot sustain myself another day."

"You have done all you can to avert the misfortune, and if it must come, let us not repine, but bear it like Christians."

"I will try to keep calm; but it seems hard, after weathering the worst of the storm, to be wrecked in sight of the land."

"Perhaps your creditors will give you more time," suggested Mrs. Whiting.

"I cannot hope it; the note which comes due to-morrow, and which I am utterly unable to pay, is in the hands of my bitterest enemy."

"He will not distress you."

"I know him well. He is a villain!"

"Whom do you mean?"

" Bacher."

" God help us, if *he* is your creditor ! "

" As near as I can learn, he bought the note on purpose to perplex me, and perhaps to obtain his revenge."

" Why is he so bitter against you ? "

" Because I exposed a swindling operation, in which he was engaged."

" How much is the note, father ? " asked a beautiful, hazel-eyed girl, who had not before spoken, but who had been listening with intense interest to the conversation between her father and mother.

" Three thousand dollars, Sarah," replied Mr. Whiting, fixing a glance of anxiety upon the fair girl.

" Can't you borrow it, father ? "

" Alas ! my child, my credit is very much impaired. My notes have been too thick in State Street for me to borrow without paying exorbitant interest ; and that, I think, would wrong my creditors in case any thing should happen."

" It is not so very dreadful to fail, is it, father ? "

" It would be ruinous to me, my child. If I could pay this note to-morrow, I could get along very well. I should not have been embarrassed, had it not been for the failure of Jones. But I suppose it must be, and we must content ourselves to live a little more closely than we have been accustomed to do."

Sarah asked no more questions, and though the conversation was continued by her father and mother, she seemed to pay no attention to it. She appeared to be musing deeply over something.

As the evening advanced, John Barnet, a clerk, who had for some months been attentive to Sarah, and who, report said, was a favored suitor, made his accustomed evening visit. Every body said that John Barnet was a nice young man, and every way worthy of so beautiful and amiable a wife as Sarah Whiting would undoubtedly make him.

If there is any thing in smiles and gentle words, the affection of the young clerk was warmly reciprocated by Sarah. They were not engaged, however, though he called at Mr. Whiting's house from four to seven evenings in a week.

Mr. Whiting and his wife retired at an early hour in the evening, leaving the lovers "to have it out."

As usual, John Barnet begged her to make him happy by promising to be his forever. To his utter surprise and consternation, she told him she could never be his wife, and entreated him to think no more about her. Of course, the lover pressed her for an explanation of this sudden and remarkable change in her manner towards him. But she could not even do this, and John took his leave, feeling that he had not another friend in the world.

CHAPTER II.

SARAH WHITING had another suitor in the person of a wealthy and eccentric old bachelor, who, after withstanding the assaults of thousands of bright eyes and bewitching smiles, had laid his heart at the feet of our beautiful heroine. We don't blame the old fellow for falling in love with her, any more than we blame Sarah for laughing at him when he threw himself at her feet and "popped the question."

Mr. Landyke Somerset was only about forty, so that, if Sarah had been less cruel, it would not have been exactly

" May and December," but about June and November. He loved her with all the fervor which the march of time had left in his heart, and was actually disconsolate when she told him " no."

Mr. Landyke Somerset was not an ill-looking man, though he was an old bachelor. True, his hair was not as black and glossy as it had been twenty years before; there was an occasional iron-gray hair, which looked a little suspicious; yet, when he began to make his court to the divinity of his dreams, even these suddenly disappeared, and people were malicious enough to say it was through the influence of a certain compound applied by the barber. True, also, there was now and then a wrinkle in his face, which some young ladies affect to dislike. But what of all these things? Old age is honorable, and the iron-gray hairs and the wrinkles did not in the least mar the kindly expression of his phiz.

He was a very clever fellow, and though the merry little Sarah Whiting could not help laughing when he " popped the question " to her, she would very willingly have had just such an uncle, or something of that sort. In short, she *liked* him, but she didn't *love* him.

Mr. Landyke Somerset was a firm believer in the ancient verity, that " faint heart ne'er won fair lady," and he determined not to faint or give up the chase till he had bagged the game, or had seen her the wife of another. Consequently he held out all the inducements in his power to engage her heart in his favor.

He was not what young ladies call an " old fool," for he had sense enough to feel that he should never be able to gain the victory on the strength of his physical attributes — his personal beauty. But he was an amiable man at heart, and trusted solely to the influence of his moral and mental qualities for success. They had thus far failed him, though he still persevered.

Mr. Whiting, readily understanding what these attentions meant, did all in his power to favor his suit; for he was an old-fashioned man, and placed more confidence in the power of a good heart and plenty of money to make his daughter happy, than he did in the more common attributes of youth and good looks, even though the possessor of the first-named commodities had passed the meridian of life.

But Sarah had a mind of her own in these matters, and though she appreciated her kind father's motives, she could not think of throwing herself away on a man of forty, even if he was an angel.

It was only the afternoon of the day preceding the conversation we have recorded, that Mr. Somerset had paid her a visit, and renewed his protestations of love to her. She had told him for the twentieth time, " no."

When she heard her father relate the particulars of his embarrassment, the image of Mr. Somerset had involuntarily presented itself to her mind. He was abundantly able to assist them in this emergency, and for the love he bore her perhaps he would.

But, then, if she applied to him, and he afforded the necessary aid, she would be under an obligation to him, which she might find it very inconvenient to discharge.

Ruin stared her father in the face. He had said it was *ruin*, and she was sure it was. What right had she to be selfish or over nice, when, perhaps, she had it in her power to avert the dreadful calamity? Her father was all in all to her; and though some girls are so sentimental as to sacrifice father, mother, home, friends, for a lover, she would sacrifice a dozen lovers for her father alone, to say nothing of her mother, who was at least worth two dozen more.

Let not the reader suppose the pretty Sarah did not love him upon whom she had smiled — she did ; but her bump of veneration was bigger than that other bump on the back of the head.

Her resolution was formed, and about eleven o'clock the next day, she put on her bonnet, and walked up to the Revere House, where Mr. Somerset boarded.

CHAPTER III.

MR. LANDYKE SOMERSET was a nabob, and retained a private parlor, to which the obsequious servant conducted Sarah Whiting.

Of course the bachelor was reasonably astonished at this visit.

" Indeed, Miss Whiting, I am delighted to see you," exclaimed he, with rapturous enthusiasm.

" I knew you would be, and that's the reason I came," laughed Sarah, and at the same time she blushed so sweetly that Mr. Landyke Somerset had almost dissolved in a rapture of delight.

" Ah, my dear Miss Whiting, you are not always so kind to me as you are to-day."

" But I always will be hereafter," and Sarah smiled though her heart beat like the boundings of a race horse."

" Ah, you are so good, and so pretty, too."

" I will save you the trouble of all these useless adulations by saying that I have come to accept your oft-repeated proposal."

"Indeed!" and the bachelor was taken "all aback;" he could hardly believe the evidence of his own senses.

"What, sir! Do you recede from your offer?" said Sarah, laughing with all her might — a very convenient cloak for young ladies sometimes.

"Capital joke, eh?" and the bachelor laughed too.

"No joke, sir; I am in earnest."

Sarah looked as sober as the matron of an orphan asylum.

"Nay, nay, my pretty Sarah, do not make sport of me."

"I will give you my promise in writing, with my signature, if you desire it."

"Is it possible that you mean so?" said the doubtful Mr. Somerset.

"Take my hand."

The bachelor took it, pressed it to his lips, and began to think himself the happiest fellow in the world.

"I am yours, Mr. Somerset."

"Bless you, Sarah!"

"On one condition."

"Name it."

Sarah recounted the story of her father's embarrassment.

"Fill me out a check for three thousand dollars, and I promise to become your wife within one year."

Mr. Landyke Somerset mused. He appeared to be in doubt. He was a high-souled man, and the idea of *buying* the hand of his wife was to the last degree repugnant to him.

"You hesitate, sir; I know you do not love me," said Sarah, with apparent pique.

26

" On my soul, I do ! I agree ; here is the check," replied Mr. Somerset, as he seated himself at the table and drew the check.

" Now enclose it in a note to my father, saying you learned his trouble from a mutual friend, and then beg the privilege of loaning him the amount of the check."

" And you sacrifice yourself to your father, my fair Sarah ! " said the bachelor, as he sealed the note.

" I do."

" You are an angel ! "

" Nay, I must go now."

The check did the business, and Mr. Whiting was as happy as ever he was in his life. Bacher could not sleep that night because he had been foiled in his revenge.

In the evening Mr. Somerset called at the house to see his future bride. She treated him kindly, and permitted him to sit by her side, hold her work basket, and pick up her thimble when she dropped it — which was glory enough for an evening, to one as moderate in his wishes as the bachelor beau of our heroine.

But about eight o'clock, to Sarah's utter consternation, John Barnet paid his usual visit. The poor clerk was sadly distressed, as well he might be, and had called to desire an explanation of the cool manner in which he had been dismissed.

The presence of Mr. Somerset was all the explanation he desired. He was uneasy ; he could not join in the conversation, and aware that he was making himself disagreeable to the party, he determined to take his leave ; but how could he leave her ?

He knew Mr. Somerset to be one of the best men in the

world, and he resolved to request an interview with him on the spot.

The worthy bachelor kindly condescended to walk down the street a short distance with him, and John Barnet told him the whole story; how he loved Sarah, and how he had every reason to believe that Sarah loved him. He was sure that some unfair advantage had been taken, and he wanted the matter explained.

"Come back to the house, young man, and I will give you all the satisfaction you desire."

John consented.

A few minutes sufficed to explain to Mr. Whiting and the discarded lover the nature of the sacrifice which the devoted Sarah had made for her father's sake.

"Bless you, my child!" exclaimed the merchant, his eyes filling with tears of love, as he tenderly embraced his noble-hearted daughter.

"You understand it now, don't you, Mr. Barnet?" said the bachelor, with a good-natured smile.

"I do, indeed," replied John, sorrowfully; "she is a noble girl, and I shall never cease to love her, though she can never be mine."

Sarah cast a sad glance at him, and her eyes filled with tears. She never knew till that moment how much she loved the poor clerk. But it was all over now — the bright dreams of love had passed away, and she could never be happy again.

"What, Sarah! do you recede from your promise?" asked Mr. Somerset.

"Nay, I do not. Farewell, John! farewell forever!" and the poor girl sobbed convulsively.

"Farewell, Sarah!" and the clerk seized his hat and rushed towards the door.

"Hallo! stop, young man!" exclaimed Mr. Somerset; "don't go off mad. Give me your hand."

The bachelor took the clerk's hand.

"You are a good fellow; I honor you. *Your* hand, Sarah," and Mr. Somerset took the little white hand of the weeping maiden, and placed it in that of John Barnet. "Be happy!"

"What do you mean, sir?" asked Sarah, bewildered at the actions of the bachelor.

"Mean? You love him, don't you?"

"With all my soul!"

"And you do not love me?"

Sarah began to understand.

"I *like* you."

"You are his; be happy! You did not for a moment suppose I could be so mean as to take advantage of such a noble act of self-sacrifice as you performed to-day? No! I love you, but I will not make you miserable."

Poor Sarah! How happy she was, and how she pitied poor Mr. Somerset, who loved her so much! She felt that, if she had never seen John Barnet, she would have been glad to become his wife, iron gray and wrinkles to the contrary notwithstanding — he was such a dear, good soul!

"Be happy! and that isn't all; when I die you shall have half my fortune."

The bachelor kept his word, and though he didn't die of a broken heart, he did not live many years; yet when he did die, the hand of woman — of as true and loving a woman as ever made home a paradise — smoothed his dying pillow, and closed his eyes in their last sleep; and there were sincere mourners over his bier.

Poor Mr. Landyke Somerset! though he found not a wife in Sarah Whiting, he found a true friend.

26 *

THE GRAND RECEPTION BALL.

CHAPTER I.

TIPTOP is somewhere in the State of Massachusetts; but, in consideration of the unpleasant nature of the details of my story, I do not feel at liberty to state its precise geographical position. Undoubtedly, too, there are within the limits of our ancient commonwealth a great many Tiptops, and, by assigning it a specific *locale*, many whom the coat fits will fail to put it on.

Tiptop was fully up with the times. The distinctions of caste were as precisely defined and protected as in New York or Philadelphia. It is true, a belle from one of the emporiums of fashion would not have felt at home there; but then the Tiptopites labored to-be as fashionable as the metropolitans, and if they did not succeed, it was not their fault.

There were balls, parties, and lyceums in Tiptop; but, unfortunately for the luminous propensities of the "upper ten," they were obliged to call in the aid of the *canaille* on these occasions, in order to make the expense fall as lightly as possible on the glorified few.

There was a great excitement in the place when it was understood that the Hon. Mr. Silas Lumpkin, M. C., from onē of the Western States, proposed to spend a few days with Squire Rogers, his "chum" in college.

The Hon. Mr. Lumpkin was a distinguished man in his day and generation. Though not thirty-five at the period of our story, he had made a mark on the country which time will not immediately obliterate.

But Mr. Lumpkin was a sensible man, notwithstanding the temptations of his position to be otherwise. We have referred to the Congressional Globe, but we do not find that he ever made a long speech, which, in our mind, fully establishes his reputation as a model Congressman.

The distinguished gentleman's visit to Tiptop promised to be an epoch in the history of the place. The notables were duly impressed with the honor which awaited them, and immediately put their heads together to devise a suitable plan for a public demonstration. They fully appreciated the great man's condescension, and it only remained to make a proper expression of it.

A voluntary committee of the most notable of the notables waited on Squire Rogers in this emergency. Unfortunately, the squire was a legal man, and did not feel competent to advise in an affair of this kind ; and the squire, too, was a sensible man, and had it not been for the fact that he was a candidate for the office of representative to the next General Court, would probably have expressed his disgust at the whole thing.

But while the voluntary committee were discussing a scheme for a public dinner in the town hall, the ladies decided that a grand reception ball should be given on the occasion of Mr. Lumpkin's arrival.

Of course the matter was settled, for Miss Araminta Pip-

kin and Annabellina Punkinton had said so.· Miss Dorothea
Pilkinton was opposed to it at first, on account of the short-
ness of the time; but Miss Pipkin was an Amazon in an
argument, and carried the day.

CHAPTER II.

It was after dark when the Hon. Mr. Lumpkin arrived at
Tiptop. The Lyceum Hall was already in a blaze of bril-
liancy, and the revellers were rapidly gathering to do honor
to the man who had distinguished himself by holding his
tongue.

Mr. Lumpkin, all unconscious of the honors that were in
store for him, cordially grasped the hand of Squire Rogers
and entered the house. He drank several cups of particularly strong tea, and found himself fully refreshed from the
fatigues of his journey.

"The hall was lighted as you passed, was it not?"
asked the squire, thinking it time to broach the subject
of the complimentary ball.

"The building on the hill?"

"Yes — next to the meeting house."

"It was."

"Something grand there to-night; we must go up."

"Political?"

"No, nothing of the kind; your friends in this place,
without distinction of party, propose to welcome you to
Tiptop in a grand reception ball."

"The deuse they do!"

"Fact!" and the squire grinned in sympathy with the
Hon. Mr. Lumpkin.

"But, Rogers, it's silly."

"Public men must humor the follies of their constituency."

"Not my constituents, thank my stars! I am not holden to them for my office; so I shall do them the honor to spend the evening with you, Rogers."

"But, my dear Lumpkin, the affair was got up wholly on your account."

"Infernally silly of them — decidedly flat."

"They will be disappointed;" and Squire Rogers looked sad, for he happened to think at that moment that he was a candidate for the legislature.

"No matter."

"But the aristocracy — bah! — will be mortally offended with me."

"The what?"

"The affair was got up by our fashionables."

"So much the better. If they wish to make fools of themselves, they shall not do it at my expense."

"But consider, my dear Lumpkin, what a terrible disappointment it will be to them. They are even now waiting your arrival. I have been appointed gentleman usher, to conduct you to the hall, and do the honors."

"Good, Rogers!" and Mr. Lumpkin, being a jolly, good-natured Congressman, laughed heartily, notwithstanding the consternation of his legal friend, who began to fear that his want of tact would insure the victory, at the approaching election, to his rival.

"But the ladies, Lumpkin."

This was a fortunate hit on the part of Squire Rogers. Mr. Lumpkin was a bachelor, and, like bachelors in general, he loved the ladies to distraction, while he kept them at a safe distance. The thought of being the centre of attraction, amid a galaxy of bright eyes and blushing cheeks, was rather inviting; but Mr. Lumpkin could not forgive the Tiptopites for making fools of themselves at his expense.

The honorable gentleman was a consistent man, and having before decided not to go, it was against his principles to change his mind. There was a villanous rumor in circulation that Mr. Lumpkin, having unhappily fallen asleep during the making of a certain motion, had suddenly woke up and voted "yea," in opposition to his colleagues, and against the instructions of his constituents.

Having always been considered sound on the question at issue, every body was surprised at his vote. He did not discover his mistake until the following day; but, being a consistent man, he defended his course, and made the longest speech he was ever known to make, on the folly of instructing public men who are sent to Congress for the good of their country. He would have lost his subsequent election, only that a majority, admiring his manly independence, saw fit to give him their suffrages.

Mr. Lumpkin had said no, and it was an exceedingly difficult thing for him to reverse his sentiments, and say yes. But the ladies, being — as he eloquently expressed it, in his speech on the necessity of reducing the duty on Cashmere shawls, and making it specific, instead of *ad valorem* — the bright, particular luminaries of a republican nation, seemed to beckon him to the ball — to be recreant to his principle of consistency.

But Mr. Lumpkin, in the true spirit of our glorious constitution, resolved to compromise the matter, and go. There was a codfish clique in Tiptop, and Mr. Lumpkin considered

it his duty to punish them.   After making some arrangements with his friend, whose urgent remonstrances were all
unheeded, he left the house.

CHAPTER III.

LYCEUM HALL blazed with beauty and tallow candles.
All the *élite* of Tiptop were on tiptoe with expectation.
After a long and rather stormy discussion, it was decided
hat Miss Pipkin should dance first with Mr. Lumpkin,

Eight o'clock came, and the distinguished gentleman did
not make his appearance.   The less pretentious portion of
the party began to grow impatient.   They cared nothing at
all about Mr. Lumpkin; they came to have a good time, and
were bound to enjoy themselves, whether Mr. Lumpkin and
his admirers did or not.

Joe Maple began to get a little mad.   He came with Lizzie Lee, had paid for his ticket, and — as he expressed it to
Mr. Adolphus Pipkin — he'd like to know why they couldn't
go ahead without Mr. Lumpkin.

" Hang me if I stay or pay for my ticket if they don't put
her through pootty soon," said he.

"What are they waiting for?" asked a stranger by
his side.

" For Mr. Stumpkins, or some sich name; but I ain't
a-going to wait any longer.   What do you say, boys — shall
we back out if they don't go ahead?"

" Sartin; go to the managers, Joe; we'll back you up in
any thing you say," replied several.

" They ought to go on," suggested the stranger.

" Tew be sure they had ; so here goes for the managers. They are so darn stuck up, they seem to think we ain't nobody ; we'll larn 'em better ; " and Joe Maple marched for the knot of gentlemen who had charge of the arrangements, and who were wondering why the distinguished guest of the evening did not appear.

At this moment Squire Rogers entered the hall. In reply to the managers' queries, he said Mr. Lumpkin had left his house half an hour before, promising to meet him at the festive scene.

Joe Maple said the " boys " meant to have a time, any how, and he insisted that the dance should be immediately commenced, or the " boys " would make tracks for " hum."

Joe Maple's party were in a very decided majority, and their appeal was irresistible. The band, who were prepared to play " Hail Columbia " for the " grand entrée " of Mr. Lumpkin, were directed to commence a cotillon.

· The sets were nearly formed, when the stranger who had before questioned him requested Joe Maple to introduce him to a partner.

" Sartin," said Joe, who was a good-natured, clever fellow ; " but I don't know ye. What's your name ? "

The stranger hesitated a moment, and then said it was Smith.

" You don't say so ! You ain't the Smith that's just moved on to the Pelatiah Hopkins place ? "

" Just so," replied Mr. Smith.

" Well, now, I am glad to see you ; " and Joe Maple cast about him for a suitable partner for the new proprietor.

Joe was always up to some mischief, and it seemed as though the very demon of mischief ruled. him when he glanced at Miss Araminta Pipkin, who was impatiently waiting the arrival of her distinguished partner.

Now, Mr. Smith was certainly not very prepossessing in his external appearance. He looked very much like a country shopkeeper dressed up in his Sunday clothes, and Joe Maple was perfectly satisfied that Miss Pipkin would never condescend to dance with him. But there was a prospect of some sport, and though he and the amiable leader of the Tiptop *ton* were not on speaking terms, he determined to present Mr. Smith.

"I want to introduce Mr. Smith to you," said Joe, mustering his most elegant expression. "He wants a pardner."

Miss Pipkin addressed a languid sneer, first to Joe Maple, and then to Mr. Smith.

"No, I thank ye," replied she, briefly, turning away her head from the suppliant at her feet.

"Hadn't ye better? This is Mr. Smith, that has bought the Pelatiah Hopkins place."

"You have my answer; I dance with Mr. Lumpkin;" and Miss Pipkin looked unutterably scornful at the thought of descending from a member of Congress even to the proprietor of the Hopkins place.

"That is very plain speech," suggested Mr. Smith.

"Short as piecrust; she's right down smart. But, Mr. Smith, as you have bought that place, you shall dance with the poottiest gal in the hall — that's Lizzie Lee. She engaged to dance with me —— "

"I could not think of disappointing you," interposed Mr. Smith.

"I don't stand on trifles. The fact is, Lizzie and I understand one another pootty well."

27

Mr. Smith was introduced to Lizzie, who was all the en-amoured Mr. Maple had said she was.

But the sets were all full save one, in which had been reserved a place for Mr. Lumpkin and the sighing Miss Pip-kin, who fondly hoped to make a conquest of the distin-guished bachelor's heart.

This set was at the head of the hall, and of course the three couples which now composed it were the cream of the aristocracy. Mr. Lumpkin had not come, and Joe, who was all attention to the new owner of the Hopkins place, directed Mr. Smith to lead his partner to this vacant position.

Mr. Smith did so. He was perfectly innocent of any in-tention to offend, and smilingly bowed to his pretty partner.

The three couples were aghast at the coolness and effront-ery of Mr. Smith. Mr. Adolphus Pipkin felt outraged, and stepped forward to remonstrate, suggesting to the new lord of the Hopkins place that the head of the hall had been reserved for Mr. Lumpkin and the accomplished Miss Pipkin.

"When *he* comes, *I* will go," replied Mr. Smith, quietly.

"How rude!" exclaimed Miss Punkinton.

"What horrible impoliteness!" added Miss Pilkington.

"Brought up in the woods," suggested Miss Smythson.

"I declare, he smells of the cow yard," sneered Miss Punkinton.

"Will you abandon your position?" asked Mr. Pipkin, fiercely.

"No, sir," replied Smith, calmly.

"On with the dance!" shouted Joe Maple.

And on it went, for the leader of the band, knowing who nis strongest friends were, started the music.

"Sir, you are no gentleman," continued Mr. Pipkin.

" First couple, lead up to the right!" shouted the caller.

Mr. Smith and Lizzie, being the first couple, *led* up to the right, and, in doing so, had nearly borne the enraged Mr. Pipkin under their feet.

"*Balancez !* "

" I demand satisfaction, sir."

" *Chassez* to the right! "

Mr. Smith danced furiously; but the rest of the set, horrified at the idea of dancing with such company as the owner of the Hopkins place and Lizzie Lee, abandoned their positions. Joe Maple instantly filled them again, and things went on as merrily as a marriage bell.

Squire Rogers was repeatedly importuned for information in regard to the Hon. Mr. Lumpkin, whose consistency seemed quite as prominent as it had ever been before. Tho squire assured them he would come — that it was only ten o'clock, and genteel folks never appeared till a late hour.

The Hon. Mr. Lumpkin *did* come at last.

CHAPTER IV.

But when he came, the proprietor of the Pelatiah Hopkins place incontinently *vamosed*.

" Rogers," said Mr. Smith, " *Lumpkin is come.*"

" High time," replied Rogers.

" Please announce the fact."

" There will be a tempest; hadn't we better have the smelling salts handy ? "

" Ay, cod-liver oil would do as well; there is a smell of codfish in this vicinity."

"Ladies and gentlemen," began Squire Rogers to the little knot of uppercrusts that occupied the head of the hall, "I have the honor of informing you that the Hon. Mr. Lumpkin has come."

This announcement produced a very decided sensation. Miss Araminta Pipkin heaved a deep sigh, and almost fainted in anticipation of the presentation.

"Where is he?" asked Mr. Adolphus Pipkin, glancing eagerly around the room.

"The illustrious gentleman is close at hand."

"Band, play the grand march."

The band struck up "Hail Columbia."

Mr. Smith, exhibiting a most wonderful command of himself, while every body else was excited by the event about to transpire, stood by the side of Lizzie Lee, engaged in a familiar conversation. Joe Maple, in view of the very marked attentions of Mr. Smith to his intended, had begun to grow a little jealous, and half regretted that he had been so polite to the owner of the Hopkins place.

"Mr. Lumpkin," said Rogers, breaking in upon the pleasant conference, "the company wait your presence."

"Hey, squire! this is Mr. Smith," said Maple.

"The Hon. Mr. Lumpkin," continued Rogers.

"You will pardon the little trick I have played upon you," said Mr. Smith; "my name is Lumpkin, M. C."

"You don't say so!" exclaimed Joe Maple.

"Just so."

"And I've been talking to you jest as though you was a common man."

"So I am"

"Ain't you one of them 'ere Congress fellers?"

"Certainly, but one of the people; and, between you and I and the barn, as we say out west, I am no friend of such folks as these over here;" and Mr. Lumpkin pointed significantly to the *élite* of Tiptop.

"You are a brick, squire!" and Joe hawhawed with right good will; "but I suppose we shan't see you again to-night if you are going over there?"

"Yes; Miss Lee, I claim your hand for the next dance, according to your promise."

"I shall be almost afraid to dance with you now," simpered Lizzie.

"Hush, Liz! talk up to him," whispered Joe; "a Congress chap ain't any better than any body else."

"Mr. Lumpkin, your admirers will become impatient," suggested Squire Rogers, with an ironical smile.

"Excuse me for a few moments, Miss Lee;" and Mr. Lumpkin, taking the arm of the squire, walked towards the head of the hall.

Joe Maple, whose keen relish for "some sport" did not permit him to remain in the background, followed in their wake.

"Miss Pipkin, the Hon. Mr. Lumpkin," said Squire Rogers.

The amiable lady raised her eyes, which had been fixed in maidenly coyness upon the floor, and beheld the abominable Mr. Smith, the abhorred owner of the Pelatiah Hopkins place!

"Why — I — yes — I declare — I have met — you before this evening," stammered the leader of the female *ton*.

"Should rather think you had!" roared Joe Maple, who has since declared that he thought "he should ha' died a larfin'."

27 *

"We have; I had the honor of being refused the pleasure of your hand at the first dance," said Mr. Lumpkin, with a full display of congressional dignity.

"Mr. Pipkin, the Hon. Mr. Lumpkin, M. C., from the west," continued Squire Rogers, who, notwithstanding he felt a little nervous on account of the seat in the legislature, was in very tolerable spirits, and heartily enjoyed the discomfiture of the "codfish" party.

"Happy to know you, Mr. Pipkin. You demanded satisfaction of me in the early part of the evening; should be happy to afford it."

"You will pardon me, sir; there was some mistake; I would not of course have spoken in that manner to a member of Congress."

Mr. Lumpkin, not being above the infirmities of human nature, sneered rather rudely at the Tiptop exquisite, as much as to say, "You ought to treat every body well, whether they are public or private individuals."

The master of ceremonies discharged the duties of his office with punctilious formality. It seemed to the sufferers that he was unnecessarily minute in his presentation ceremonial, permitting the distinguished gentleman to make a home thrust at each one of the persons who had been so rude to Mr. Smith.

The introductions were happily concluded, and a more chopfallen set than the *élite* of Tiptop never gathered together in the same hall.

Miss Pipkin was in an agony. She had actually turned up her nose to a member of Congress. Of course she could no longer hope to make a conquest of his heart; the vision of being a distinguished lady melted quite away.

But then "it is an ill wind that blows no one any good." If Miss Pipkin could not have a member of Congress, she at least had the consolation of saying that she had refused the hand of the Hon. Mr. Lumpkin, which, to a lady of her peculiar turn of mind, was an immense satisfaction.

Mr. Lumpkin returned to the side of Lizzie Lee, who, maugre her coyness, was tolerably sociable. Joe Maple, from the abundance of his good nature, vowed he might dance with her just as many times as he pleased.

About eleven o'clock, Miss Pipkin suggested to her brother that the delicate state of her health would not permit her to endure the excitement of the dance any longer, and when the leader of the *ton* left, the followers went after her.

But the common folks "staid it out," and Mr. Lumpkin confessed that he enjoyed the ball very much indeed; for, true to his duty as a public man, it had enabled him to administer a suitable reproof to the pretensions of the Tiptopites.

Joe Maple and Lizzie Lee — since Mrs. Maple — have not yet forgotten the part they acted, and perhaps they may be pardoned for a slight display of vanity as they relate the particulars of *The Grand Reception Ball.*

GETTING AN INDORSER.

CHAPTER I.

My friend, Frank Howard, was a dry goods dealer on Washington Street. When I made his acquaintance, he was one of the most active and successful salesmen in the trade, and being a prudent man, had saved a small sum of money, with which and the credit he might be able to obtain, he proposed to commence business on his own account.

Among his acquaintances he had the good fortune to include a wealthy merchant, whose judgment had led him to form a lofty estimate of the business capacity of my friend.

To him the young aspirant for mercantile honors stated his case, and the conference ended in a voluntary proposition on the part of the merchant to supply the goods necessary to stock his store, taking his notes, the first of which would fall due in one year, in payment.

The arrangement was completed, and in a few days Frank found himself installed in a convenient store, on the best part of the street, ready to strike for his fortune.

(320)

The notes had not been signed, and one evening, on some business connected with them, Frank called, by appointment, at the princely mansion of his worthy benefactor. He was ushered into the sitting room, where the merchant was reading the evening paper. By his side sat a beautiful young lady, to whom his patron politely introduced him.

My friend belonged to that anomalous class of beings styled "handsome men;" at least the ladies all said he was handsome, though for the life of me I never could tell wherein his beauty consisted. But as I have no particular fancy for masculine beauty, it may have escaped my notice, or the natural selfishness of mankind may have prejudiced my judgment.

My friend was acknowledged by all the ladies to be a remarkably handsome man; and, probably, this was the secret of his immense success as a salesman. Whether he reckoned his beauty as one of the items of his stock in trade, when he went into business, I am unable to say; but I have not the least doubt he based his hopes of success, to a great extent, upon the influence of his prepossessing personal appearance.

Frank fixed his eyes on the young lady, as the merchant, who had, when he entered, half read a money article in his paper, turned to finish it. Miss Allen — such was the name by which she had been presented to him — was busily engaged in crocheting a little silk purse, and as she bent over the work, Frank was perfectly satisfied that he had never seen so pretty a face in his life.

And then the neatest, most graceful little foot in the world protruded from beneath a light silk dress — a foot which completely turned Frank's head, so that he forgot all about the notes and the merchant.

Without the least regard to etiquette, politeness, good breeding, and all that sort of thing, he stared mercilessly at her, and never, for even the fraction of a moment, removed his gaze, not even allowing himself the luxury of winking, lest the time so employed should be lost.

Frank was perfectly sure that he had never before felt exactly as he did at that halcyon moment. It seemed as though all the divinities of paradise were concentrated in the fair form before him, as though he had been transplanted to an Elysium of love.

And the maiden was not altogether unmoved. The embryo merchant several times detected her in the act of stealing a glance at him through the long, fringing eyelashes that adorned her peerless brow. He plainly saw her blush; saw her bosom heave with a flutter as she caught his earnest gaze.

Frank Howard was a handsome man; and somehow or other, men and women who are favored in this respect always contrive to find it out. Frank knew that he was a handsome man, and never in his life did he more devoutly thank his stars, which had given him personal beauty, than at this particular moment.

The lady had already found out that he was handsome, and if the stupid fellow had not stared so furiously at her, she would no doubt have done the same thing he was doing.

Mr. Allen finished the money article, and laid down the paper. Frank has owned to me that he wished it had been twice, or even four times as long.

The details of the business were discussed, and the papers drawn. While it was in progress, Frank more than once detected the beautiful fairy in the act of looking at him;

several times detected her in the very act of blushing, when their eyes met.

The business was finished at last, much to the regret of my handsome friend, who, when he got into the street, went straightway into a fit of abstraction, and had walked half way across Charlestown bridge, on his way home, before he happened to think that he lived at the South End.

It was all up with poor Frank; he had fallen in love — was stark, staring mad in love — with whom he knew not, for it was well known that Mr. Allen had no daughter. She was a relative, however, for she bore his name.

But if Frank was in love, there was some consolation in the fact, that the fair creature who had stolen his heart was in the same predicament.

The next day, she came a shopping at his store, and the next, and the next; indeed, almost every day. No conversation had passed between them; and, though he had been introduced on the evening of his visit, he had been too much overwhelmed to use words.

My friend, however, did not lack that necessary attribute of a successful wooer, somewhat vulgarly termed "spunk." He had no further business with the merchant; but then his case was a desperate one, and he made an errand.

Miss Allen blushed as he entered, but she was social and agreeable to the last degree, so much so that Frank staid till the bells rung for nine o'clock before he knew it. The ice was broken, and my friend was in for it.

The lady was a niece of the merchant, twenty-one years of age, and an heiress. In the course of a few months, Frank's energy won the victory, and it was understood that they were engaged.

The merchant did not like it. Being somewhat exclusive in his ideas of social intercourse, the prospective marriage of his wealthy niece to a poor retailer was repugnant to the last degree, and he resolved to thwart the purpose of the loving couple.

At first, he appealed to the lady; but she only laughed at him; told him bluntly that she loved Mr. Howard, and *would* have him. Then he reasoned with Frank on his ingratitude to him, his benefactor. The young man was touched, and promised to consider it.

He did consider it, and his loving *inamorata* helped him consider it. After a hasty deliberation, it was unanimously agreed to lay the whole matter " on the table."

Mr. Allen was informed of the decision, and as old fogies always do when they cannot do any thing else, bit his lip and swallowed his words, fully resolved to do something dreadful, whenever an opportunity occurred.

CHAPTER II.

A YEAR after my friend went into business, as I passed his Store one morning, I was not a little surprised to find it closed. Before the window was that ominous white cloth, denoting that the occupant had failed.

I entered the store. Frank stood at his desk, glancing with a most woe-begone aspect at the pages of his leger.

"How's this, Frank?" I asked; and I never was more surprised in my life.

"Bu'st up! don't you see?" replied he, rather petulantly

"But what does it mean?"

"Mean! Why, that I had a note of a thousand dollars, due yesterday, which I could not pay; and this morning early, my amiable friend, Mr. Allen, put in a keeper — that's all."

"How does it happen? I thought you were doing a rushing business."

"So I was. I had the money to pay this note six weeks ago, and let Smith have it at two per cent. a month," replied he, with a ghastly smile.

"And Smith has failed?"

"Not exactly. He has stopped; but every body says he is good, if he has time to turn himself."

"And you must make a fail of it in the mean time?".

"If I could only stave off Mr. Allen a couple of months, I could get out of the scrape with flying colors."

"Won't he wait?"

Frank shook his head; he had mortally offended the proud merchant, and there was no prospect that he would be lenient in the slightest degree.

"Can't you raise the money?"

"No; times haven't been so hard for four years. Every body is failing, and the money men wont trust their own fathers."

At this moment Mr. Allen entered the store. He looked stern and severe, like one who has the power in his own hands, and is disposed to use it. I seated myself near the desk, as he approached.

The merchant politely saluted the unfortunate dealer, smiling as blandly as though nothing had happened; as though he had no niece, and Frank were a Stoic.

"Mr. Howard, this is unfortunate; but in the midst of

so much commercial disaster, you perceive that it was my only course," said the merchant, soothingly.

"I suppose it was; but you know the cause of my inability to pay the note," returned Frank, with a doleful expression.

"Ah, young man, you ought not to have lent the money to Smith; if you had asked my advice, I could have told you better."

"Smith was always supposed to be good."

The merchant shook his head.

"But, Mr. Allen, give me a short time, and I can pay the note. Smith assures me he shall recover himself."

"Mr. Howard, I certainly wish you well; I have done all I could to give you a fair start."

"So you have, sir, and I am very grateful to you."

"Are you?" and the merchant fixed a keen glance upon the young man.

"I assure you that I am."

"How have you manifested it?" continued the merchant, sternly. "But no matter; we meet now as business men."

"Well, what shall be done? You have stopped me; I can do no more."

"I don't wish to be hard. I would wait if prudence would justify it," said Mr. Allen, who was keenly sensitive in regard to his reputation for generosity and fairness.

In fact, he was a man of good feelings, and only that he meant to punish Frank for falling in love with his wealthy niece, would not have disturbed him.

"You will be just as secure two months hence as now," pleaded Frank.

"I have not that confidence in you, Mr. Howard, — I say

it frankly, — which I had once. You have lost a thousand dollars. I doubt if your stock, under the hammer, would pay my notes."

Frank looked savage, for though he was crestfallen, he was Frank Howard yet, and felt keenly the unjust imputation of the merchant.

" I wish to be fair, and even indulgent," continued Mr. Allen, before Frank had time to utter the ungracious sentiment that rose to his lips. " Here is the note ; give me one good indorser, and I will wait two months."

Frank looked up, and smiled in contempt at the miserable subterfuge of the merchant, who meant to crush him, and still preserve an appearance of fairness. He knew it would be impossible for the young man, with his stock encumbered, to procure the security.

"Will you take Smith ? " asked Frank, hurriedly.

"Of course not," replied Mr. Allen, with a bland smile.

" I will see what can be done; but I think the case is hopeless."

The merchant withdrew, assured in his own mind that his revenge was sure, and his reputation safe, at the same time.

Frank and myself canvassed the matter, but we could think of no person whose milk of human kindness was sufficiently abundant to prompt him to do such an insane act. While we were debating the matter, Frank was struck up by the entrance of Miss Allen.

" How gloomy you look here to-day, Frank," said she, laughing, and showing in the act the prettiest row of pearly teeth I ever saw.

" We are gloomy, indeed," replied Frank, mustering a sickly smile. " But you know the reason ? "

"Why, what reason?" asked she, her merry expression relapsing into a serious one.

"You see that man?"

"Yes."

"He is a keeper!" replied Frank, with tragic effect.

"A keeper! of what? Are you insane?" responded the lady, playfully; for it must be confessed she was not acquainted with the technicalities of business.

Frank laughed, and explained the disaster which had overtaken him.

"Poh!" exclaimed she, with an appearance of relief; and I really believe, if the keeper and myself had not been in the way, she would have thrown her arms around his neck, and kissed away his mortification.

I had before been introduced to the lady, and at this moment advanced to join in the conversation.

"And my uncle is the wretch?" continued she, merrily. "But what can you do? How can you get out of it?"

Frank explained the proposition to procure an indorser for the note. The light-hearted maiden appeared to have but little sympathy for the misfortunes of her lover, and asked all sorts of questions about indorsers, notes, and business forms.

"Where is the note you are to have indorsed?" asked she.

"Mr. Allen has it."

"How can you have it indorsed, then?"

"I can write another," replied Frank, smiling at the innocence of his betrothed.

"Then write one," said she, promptly.

Frank looked at her a moment, to ascertain what mischief

was lurking in her mind. She smiled, apparently without the power to prevent it.

The lover, impelled by curiosity as much as any other motive, wrote the note and signed it.

"Now how do you indorse it?" asked she.

"By writing the name across the back."

The lady approached the desk, and turning the note, wrote, with two dashes of the pen, "Isabel Allen," across it.

"It is indorsed," said she, with a smile, which told Frank all she meant.

"But, Isabel ——"

"Good morning, Frank," interrupted she, and hastened out of the store.

"Bravo, Frank!" exclaimed I.

He smiled doubtfully. His pride was a little touched.

"Would you use it?" said he, after a long pause.

"Use it? to be sure!" and he did use it.

In the afternoon Mr. Allen called, satisfied in his own mind that he should witness the complete humiliation of the young man, who had had the audacity to fall in love with an heiress. Knowing at what hour he would call, I was careful to be present.

"Well, Mr. Howard, how have you succeeded? I have really been in hopes you will be able to secure the paper," said the merchant; and I could plainly discern the malicious chuckle on his face as he spoke.

"I *have* succeeded, Mr. Allen; and I am infinitely obliged to you for your good will."

The merchant was completely staggered at the reply. It was wholly unexpected, and wholly unwelcome also.

"I trust you have procured a good one," said he, painfully.

28 *

"A wealthy one, but a name unknown on State Street."

"Can't take it, then," answered the merchant, promptly, and with renewed hope.

"But a name well known to you!" and Frank handed him the note.

Mr. Allen started back in surprise and anger, as he read the name of the fair indorser.

"Very well, sir; when a man of any delicacy can resort to such a trick as this, I have nothing more to do with him." And the crestfallen merchant, after throwing the old note on the counter, hastened indignantly from the store.

The keeper was withdrawn, and Frank heard no more from Mr. Allen. A week after Smith paid the money, and Frank took up his note.

Before another of the notes came due, Isabel Allen had become Mrs. Frank Howard. The stock and stand were sold out, the debts paid, and my handsome friend is as happy as a beautiful wife, with a heart full of love, can make him.

www.ingramcontent.com/pod-product-compliance
Lightning Source LLC
Chambersburg PA
CBHW020945030726
47496CB00005B/1364